Also by Jennifer L. Schiff

<u>Sanibel Island Mysteries</u>

A Shell of a Problem

Something Fishy

In the Market for Murder

Bye Bye Birdy

Shell Shocked

Trouble in Paradise

A Perilous Proposal

For Whom the Shell Tolls

The Crisis Before Christmas

Framed in Naples

<u>Novels</u>

Tinder Fella

Something's Cooking in Chianti

Finding Gemma Lovegood

A Mocktail for Murder

A Guin Jones Mystery

Jennifer Lonoff Schiff

A Mocktail for Murder: A Guin Jones Mystery
by Jennifer Lonoff Schiff

© 2024 by Jennifer Lonoff Schiff

Published by Shovel & Pail Press. All rights reserved. No portion of this book may be reproduced in any form without permission from the publisher, except as permitted by U.S. copyright law.

Cover design by Vesna Tisma

Formatting by Polgarus Studio

ISBN: 979-8-218-41155-8

Library of Congress Control Number: 2024914179

More information at https://ShovelAndPailPress.com

*If you need booze or drugs to enjoy your life to the fullest,
you're doing it wrong.*

—Robin Williams

CHAPTER 1

Guin stopped typing and looked over at her two cats. They were staring out her office window, chittering at a pigeon. Guin smiled. She was glad that Fauna, her sleek black feline, and Spot, her big white kitty who had a black spot on his head and another on his back, had adapted to life in New York City.

Manhattan was a far cry from Southwest Florida, where Guin and her husband Glen and the cats had lived until about six months ago. And while Guin missed Sanibel Island, especially its seashell-strewn beaches, she, like the cats, had quickly adapted to living in Manhattan, where she had been born and raised.

Guin watched the cats for another minute and then returned to her article. However, she was interrupted by a knock at the door.

"Yes?" she called.

"May I come in?"

It was Glen.

Guin sighed and told Glen to enter.

"What's up?" she said. Then she saw the look on Glen's face. "What's wrong? Is it your parents?"

Glen's parents lived in an assisted living community in Fort Myers, Florida, where Glen was from, and were not in the best of health.

"They're fine."

Well, that was good. So it must have something to do with work.

"Did another photographer bail on a job?"

Glen was the head of Photog US, a new photographer-on-demand business started in London by his friend Raj, which was having typical startup pains. It was also the primary reason they had moved to New York. That and Guin getting a job as a stringer for the *New York Times*, covering small business.

"Not that I'm aware of."

"But it has something to do with work, yes?"

"In a way."

"Go on, spit it out. What does Raj need you to do now? Is it about opening an office in LA?"

Guin knew that Glen's partner was eager to expand Photog in the US.

"No. It's about Margaux."

"Margaux? Margaux as in your ex-wife Margaux?"

That was the only Margaux Guin knew. Though she had never actually met Glen's ex.

"Yes."

"What does she want?"

"She wants to hire me."

"She wants to hire you? To do what?"

"She wants me to photograph her new line of mocktails and mixers."

"Margaux has a line of mocktails and mixers?"

"Apparently."

"Huh. But why hire you? There must be dozens of photographers in New York who specialize in food and beverage photography. That's not even your thing. Did she find you through Photog? I thought you had removed your profile."

"I've been a bit busy and didn't get around to it."

"Did you tell her you were back in New York?"

"No. We haven't spoken or communicated in years."

"So she just randomly found your profile on Photog?"

"I guess."

Guin looked dubious.

"And she's willing to pay your rate?" Glen's rate was among the highest on the site.

"Yes."

"You going to take the job?"

"That's why I'm here. I wanted to discuss it with you before I replied."

Guin looked thoughtful. Photog US had been doing well, but Glen had yet to land any big corporate accounts or do any commercial work. So far, their customers had been individuals looking for headshots or someone to photograph their wedding, event, or child's birthday party.

"Would it help the business? I know Raj's been pushing you to get some corporate clients and editorial and commercial work."

"Probably."

"You check out this mocktail business of hers, see if it was legit?"

Guin didn't consider herself the jealous type, but she didn't trust Margaux, who was model gorgeous—tall and thin with silky chestnut brown hair and high cheekbones— and had cheated on Glen when they were married. Was this a ploy to get Glen back?

"It seems to be," Glen replied. He saw the expression on Guin's face. "You think she has an ulterior motive?"

"It didn't cross your mind that maybe she wants you back?"

"You think that's why she wants to hire me?" Guin didn't say anything. "I seriously doubt that. Even if she did want to get back together, I'm not interested. You're the only woman for me."

"So, does this new business of hers have a name?"

"It does." Guin waited. "Château Margaux Mocktails."

"Seriously?"

"That's what it said on the form."

"Did she license the name?"

Though Guin doubted the famous maker of fine wines would have licensed its name to a startup mocktail beverage company.

"I have no idea."

"And your photographs would be used in their marketing materials?"

"That's the idea."

"Have you spoken with her?"

"With Margaux? Not yet."

Guin looked thoughtful.

"You should do it."

"Really?"

"You thought I would tell you not to? If it makes good business sense, you should do it."

"Okay then. I'll let her know."

"Just be sure to keep things professional."

"Always. Though, if you're concerned, you could always come to the shoot, be my assistant."

"Thanks, but I'll pass. I trust you. And Eric is a much better photography assistant than I am. So, when's the shoot?"

"Next Tuesday."

"Next Tuesday? That's less than a week away. Why did she wait so long to hire a photographer?"

"I have no idea. All I know is that Margaux, or her company, wants to hire me to shoot her and her mocktails."

"Hold up. What do you mean, shoot *her*? I thought this was a product shoot."

"It is. But part of the assignment is shooting people drinking the product."

"Margaux being one of them."

"Yes."

"Do you know who else will be there?"

"Other than me and Eric, assuming he's available? I've no idea."

Guin looked thoughtful again.

"And where's the shoot?"

"At a studio in Hudson Yards."

Well, at least it wasn't at Margaux's.

"Okay."

"So you're okay with me doing it?"

"I said I was. Now go accept the job and let me get back to work."

Glen went over to Guin and gave her a kiss.

"Have I told you how much I love you?"

Guin smiled up at him.

"You tell me all the time. And I love you too. Now let me get back to work. This article won't write itself."

"I'm going. Just remember, we're having dinner with Lance and Owen later."

Lance was Guin's brother, who owned a boutique advertising agency, and Owen was his husband, who ran a gallery in Chelsea.

"It's on my calendar. Now scoot."

"I'm going," said Glen.

"Château Margaux, eh?" said Lance as he took a sip of his drink. "Does she plan on putting a castle on the label?"

"I don't know," said Glen. "I suppose I'll find out Tuesday."

"Do you know if she's hired an advertising agency?"

"I don't."

"You're not seriously thinking of pitching her?" Guin said to her brother.

"Why not?" said Lance. "The market for mocktails is hot

right now. And we don't have any zero-proof beverage companies in our portfolio."

"But she cheated on Glen, left him for another man!"

"And if she hadn't," Lance calmly replied, "he wouldn't have moved back to Florida, gone to work for the *Sanibel-Captiva Sun-Times*, and met you."

Guin made a face. She hated to admit it, but Lance had a point.

"Fine. If you really want to pitch her…"

"We don't even know if she's looking to hire an advertising agency," said Glen.

"Well, if she happens to mention something…"

"Can we please change the subject?" said Guin.

"Fine," said Lance. "So, how are things going at the *Times*? Have they made an honest woman out of you yet or is there still a hiring freeze?"

"There's still a freeze, but I'm fine being a stringer. At least for now."

"Tell them about the piece you're working on for the *Magazine*," said Glen. "It's really interesting."

Lance and Owen looked at her.

"It's about the LEED building boom," said Guin.

"The LEED building boom?" said Lance.

"It stands for Leadership in Energy and Environmental Design. There's been a movement in the city to create more environmentally friendly office space, repurposing older buildings as well as building new, more energy efficient ones."

"Huh. Sounds interesting."

"It is. I've learned loads. The problem is, I have too much information. I could probably write a book about it."

"How long's the article supposed to be?"

"A couple thousand words."

"I'm sure you'll figure it out. And what about you, Glen? How's Photog doing? Any plans to expand beyond New York?"

"As a matter of fact, Raj wants me to open an office in LA."

"LA, eh? Will you have to move?"

"Hopefully not."

"What about Florida?" Owen asked.

When Glen and Guin agreed to move to New York for work, they had done so expecting to only stay in the city for around six months, then return to Southwest Florida. But now they weren't so sure when they'd return.

"We don't know," said Glen.

Lance looked over at his sister.

"So you're staying in New York?"

"For a little longer."

"Well, I, for one, am happy to hear it."

"Do you miss Sanibel?" Owen asked Guin.

"I do. But we can visit. I still have the house. But enough about us, what have you two been up to?"

Dinner had been delicious and fun. Guin always had a good time with her brother and Lance.

"So, when do you get back from San Francisco?" Guin asked her brother as they stood outside the restaurant.

"I'm not sure. It depends."

"You going to join him?" Guin asked Owen. Owen often accompanied his husband on business trips, looking for new artists while Lance met with clients.

"Not this time," said Owen. "I'm preparing for a new show. You should stop by and see it. I think you'd like some of the work."

"I'll do that. Let me know when it opens."

"I'll send you an invite."

"And let me know when you're back," Guin said to her brother.

"I will."

The couples then exchanged goodbyes and went their separate ways, Lance and Owen to Brooklyn, and Guin and Glen back to the Upper East Side.

CHAPTER 2

Guin looked at her phone. Where was Glen and why hadn't he replied to her texts? The photo shoot was supposed to have ended at six. But it was now eight o'clock, and Guin hadn't heard from her husband. She sent him another text, asking if everything was all right. Finally, around half an hour later, Glen texted her back, saying he was on his way home.

Guin wanted to ask him what was going on over there. Instead, she asked him if he had eaten.

"Margaux had food brought in," he wrote her back.

Guin frowned down at the phone. She had been waiting for Glen to eat and was hungry, which hadn't helped her mood. She tucked her phone in her back pocket and headed to the kitchen, Fauna and Spot following her.

She made herself a grilled cheese sandwich and gave the cats a few cat treats. When she was done, she went into the living area and turned on the TV. She was watching a travel show when she heard the front door. She looked down at her phone. It was just past nine-thirty.

"You're home," she said as Glen appeared. "Are you okay?" He looked exhausted.

He put down his camera bag and equipment.

"I could use a beer."

Guin followed him to the kitchen and watched as he took a beer out of the refrigerator, opened it, and took a long swallow.

"What happened with the shoot? You should have been home hours ago. I was getting worried."

"Sorry. I meant to text you, but things were pretty crazy."

"Crazy how? You were just shooting a bunch of mocktail bottles."

"Not exactly."

"Right. Margaux wanted you to take photos of her too."

"Not just her."

"She hired models?"

"Not exactly. She had her assistant, Ronnie; Ronnie's cousin, Jordan, who plays for the Knicks; and his friend Shaq, who also plays basketball; and the two stylists she hired serve as models—in addition to herself."

"Hold up. Margaux's assistant has a cousin who plays for the Knicks?"

Glen nodded as he took another sip of beer.

"Wow."

"Margaux thought getting a professional athlete to endorse her mocktails would be a good idea."

"It is. And he has a friend named Shaq who also plays basketball? Does Shaq play for the Knicks?"

"No, he plays in the EuroLeague."

"And you said there were two stylists? Why two?"

"One, Dionne, was the product stylist. The other, Fabio, was there to dress the people drinking the mocktails."

"Did Fabio have a mane of blond hair and a square jaw?"

"As a matter of fact, he did. How did you know?"

Guin laughed.

"What's so funny?"

"You don't remember Fabio, the famous romance novel cover model and actor?"

"No. Should I?"

"I guess you didn't read romance novels growing up."

"Can't say that I did."

"So why did the shoot take so long?"

"Margaux was being impossible. Nothing anyone did was right. I may have set a record in terms of the number of photos I took."

"Sounds like a nightmare."

"It was. I swear, I was ready to kill Margaux a couple of times."

"But you didn't."

"No. I controlled myself."

"Did you at least get some good photos?"

"I think so. But I'm not the client."

"How were the mocktails? Did you get to try any of them?"

"Margaux insisted everyone try them."

"And?"

"And they were good. She did a nice job with the bottles too."

"Well, I hope you charged her for overtime."

"I did. Or rather the app will charge her."

"Good. So she made everyone stay until eight-thirty?"

"Actually…"

"What?"

Glen sighed.

"Most of the people left a little after eight."

"Most of the people?"

"She asked me to stay."

"Why?"

"She wanted to see the photos."

"Uh-huh."

"Really, Guin."

Guin wanted to believe him.

"So did you show them to her? I thought you didn't like to show clients your photos until you'd edited them."

"I don't normally, but…"

"Was she happy with them?"

"I don't know. She got a call as I was showing them to

her, and I used that as my excuse to get the heck out of there."

"Well, you're home now, and I know just the thing to make you feel better."

"Oh? What's that?"

Guin took Glen's beer and placed it on the counter.

"Come with me," she said. Then she took Glen's hand and led him to the bedroom.

Guin woke up the next morning to find Glen not in the bed. She looked over at the alarm clock. It was a little after seven. She got up and went to the bathroom and then headed to the kitchen. There was a fresh pot of coffee on the counter. She poured herself a mugful and took a sip. It was strong, just the way she liked it.

She took the mug and headed to Glen's office. The door was ajar. She knocked and then poked her head in. Glen was at his desk. On the screen was a picture of Margaux, smiling seductively while holding a cocktail glass filled with one of her mocktails.

Margaux really was stunning, Guin thought.

"How long have you been up?" she asked him.

"A while."

"You going through the photos from the shoot?"

"Uh-huh."

"That's a good one of Margaux. Did you edit it?"

"Not yet."

"I'd love to see the rest."

"There are a lot."

"I don't mind."

"I'd rather show them to you after I've culled and edited them."

"Fine." She could tell that Glen was in the zone. He

often got that way when editing photos. "Just remember to eat."

"Mm," he said, continuing to stare at the screen.

Guin watched him for a few more seconds and then left.

Guin was working on an article when she heard the doorbell. She was still in her nightshirt, an old concert tee, so she hoped Glen would get it.

The doorbell sounded again. Had Glen not heard it? Or was he too busy editing photos? Probably the latter.

Guin wondered who was calling on them so early. Though when she looked at the clock on her monitor, she saw it was a little after nine. Not that early.

She went to the front door and peered through the peephole. There were two men on the other side, one of whom was wearing a police uniform. She frowned. What could they want? Had one of their neighbors complained about them? It wasn't as though they made a lot of noise. They didn't fight or play loud music, and she doubted they could hear the two cats. Not that the cats made that much noise.

She opened the door a crack.

"May I help you?" she asked them.

"We're looking for Mr. Anderson," said the man in plain clothes. "Is he available?"

"And you are?"

"Detective Spinosa of the NYPD." He held out an ID. It looked legit.

"I'm afraid he's busy, Detective Spinosa. Is there something I can help you with?"

"Is Mr. Anderson at home?"

"He is, but as I said, he's busy."

"Would you mind letting us in?"

Guin did mind, but she reluctantly opened the door. The

detective and the uniformed officer stepped inside. She saw Detective Spinosa looking at her and wished she had thrown on a robe or a sweatshirt.

"I'll go get Glen," she told them and hurried to Glen's office.

She knocked on the door and then entered, shutting the door behind her. Glen turned around.

"Is everything all right?"

"No. There's a detective and a policeman here, and they want to speak with you."

"Did they say why?"

"No."

"I guess I should go talk to them. Where are they?"

"I left them in the living room."

He looked at her.

"You let them in looking like that?"

Guin made a face.

"Just go see what they want while I go change."

Glen made his way to the living room where the detective and his colleague were being sniffed by the cats.

"I hope you're not allergic," said Glen.

"Mr. Anderson?" said the detective.

"That's me. How can I help you?"

"I'm Detective Spinosa with the NYPD." He offered Glen his ID, which Glen glanced at. "And this is Officer Spinelli."

"Gentlemen," said Glen. "So, what brings you to my door?"

"I understand you were hired by a Ms. Margaux Boucher," which he pronounced *BOO-cher*, "to take some photos. Is that correct?"

"It's *boo-SHAY*," said Glen. "And that is correct. Margaux hired me to take photos of her new line of mocktails. Why?"

"So you were at the Studios at Hudson Yards yesterday evening?"

"I was. What's this about, detective? Did something happen to Margaux?"

"You might say that. Ms. Boucher was found dead there this morning. And I understand you were the last person to have seen her."

CHAPTER 3

Guin stepped into the living room, now properly dressed, just in time to hear the detective's pronouncement.

"Margaux's dead?" she said. "How? When? What happened?"

"That's what we're trying to find out," said Detective Spinosa, still looking at Glen. "If you wouldn't mind coming with us down to the precinct, Mr. Anderson, so we can get an official statement?"

"I'm in the middle of editing photographs."

"The photos can wait."

Glen opened his mouth to contradict the detective. But one look at the detective's face told him the detective didn't care.

"May I have a minute to save my work?"

The detective nodded, and Glen headed to his office.

"You don't really think Glen had anything to do with Margaux's death, do you?" Guin asked the detective.

The detective didn't say anything, and a painful silence—at least to Guin—ensued as they waited for Glen to return. Finally, he reappeared.

"Okay, I'm ready."

"I'm coming with you," said Guin.

"I'll be fine," he told her. "I'm just going to the local precinct to give an official statement to the police. I'll be home before you know it."

Guin wasn't so sure about that.

"You should phone Tom, have him meet you there. Or I can call him."

"I'll be fine," Glen repeated. He turned to Detective Spinosa. "I don't need a lawyer, do I?"

"Like you said, we just want an official statement."

Guin wanted to believe the detective, but she couldn't help feeling anxious.

"Okay, but if you're not back in a few hours, I'm phoning Tom."

"Let's go," said the detective.

They had reached the door when Guin stopped them.

"Which precinct are you taking him to?" she asked the detective.

"The nineteenth," he replied. Then he escorted Glen out the door.

Guin stared at the door for several seconds. Then she pulled out her phone and looked for Tom Goodwin's number in her contacts. Tom was Photog US's legal counsel. But for some reason, she didn't have his number. However, she had his wife Judith's information. Guin entered Judith's number and waited.

"This is Judith."

"Judith, it's Guin Jones. I need to get in touch with Tom, but I don't have his number."

"Doesn't Glen have it? The two of them talk almost daily."

"Glen's not here. He was just taken by the police."

"By the police? Whatever for?"

"His ex, Margaux, was found dead over in Hudson Yards this morning. Glen had been with her the night before."

"What was Glen doing with his ex-wife in Hudson Yards?"

"It's not what you think. Margaux hired Glen to take photos of her new line of mocktails. The shoot was at a studio over in Hudson Yards."

"Ah. Did the police say how she died?"

"No, just that she was dead. But I have a bad feeling."

"Did they arrest Glen?"

"No. The detective who was here—his name is Spinosa—claimed they just wanted Glen to give a statement but, as I said, I have a bad feeling about this. Would you call Tom, tell him what's up?"

"Did they say which police station they were taking him to?"

"The one in the nineteenth precinct."

"Okay. I'll ring Tom right away. And Guin?"

"Yes?"

"Try not to worry."

Easier said than done.

Glen arrived home before lunchtime, much to Guin's relief. As soon as he walked through the door, she and the cats hurried over to him.

"I'm so glad they let you go," Guin said, embracing him.

Glen smiled and lifted her chin.

"Did you really think they were going to arrest me? I told you, Margaux was fine when I left."

"Yes, but I don't trust that detective. Did he tell you what happened? I have a feeling Margaux didn't die of natural causes."

"Detective Spinosa didn't say. He just asked me about the photo shoot."

"What did you tell him? Did you tell him that Margaux was being difficult? You didn't tell him you wanted to kill her, did you?"

Glen gave her a look, one that said, *What do you take me for, an idiot?*

"I told him that Margaux had seemed agitated throughout the shoot, making us do multiple reshoots, but that she seemed calmer by the time I left. Well, until she got that call."

"Any idea who called her?"

"No. I didn't stick around to listen. I just got the heck out of there."

"And did Detective Spinosa know that you and Margaux had been married?"

"He did."

"Did he ask you about your relationship?"

"He did."

"What did you tell him? Did you tell him that Margaux cheated on you and left you for another man?"

"I did not."

"What did you tell him?"

"I told him that our marriage had run its course and that I hadn't spoken or communicated with Margaux since the divorce."

"Did he ask you why Margaux hired you if you two hadn't spoken in years?"

"He did."

"And?"

"I told him I didn't know why, which is the truth."

"Did he ask you anything else?"

"He wanted to know if Margaux got into it with anyone."

"Hm."

"What?"

"That makes me think that he thinks she was murdered."

"You don't know that."

"Then why would he ask you if Margaux fought with anyone?"

Glen opened his mouth and then closed it.

"What did you tell him?"

"That I was too busy trying to take photos to pay attention to who Margaux was arguing with."

"Who did she argue with?"

Glen sighed.

"Who didn't she? She got into it with everyone. I told you, nothing anyone did was right, and tempers began to fray."

"Did anyone threaten Margaux?"

"Threaten her?"

"Yes."

"Not that I overheard. Look, we don't even know what killed her. She could have had a heart attack or a stroke. As I said, she was pretty worked up."

"Hm. She was pretty young, wasn't she?"

"She was forty-two."

"Did she have a heart condition?"

"Not that I knew of. Maybe she tripped on something and hit her head. There are any number of things that could have happened to her."

"Including someone killing her."

Glen looked exasperated.

"I know you covered crime back on Sanibel, but not every suspicious death is the result of murder."

"I know that. But you just said her death was suspicious."

Glen ran a hand through his hair.

"She wasn't murdered, Guin."

"How do you know that?"

"Can we please stop talking about Margaux? It's giving me a headache."

"You need food. Let me make you some lunch."

"I need to get to work."

"Have you eaten anything today?"

"No, but..."

"Let me make you an omelet and some toast. Then you can go work."

"Fine."

Guin smiled and went to take out eggs and bread.

Guin stared at her monitor. She had been trying to work, but she had been unable to concentrate. She kept picturing Margaux, lying on the floor of the photo studio, dead.

She saved the article she was working on and opened her web browser. When Guin first started dating Glen, she had looked up his ex. But she hadn't googled her again. Until now.

Guin typed *Margaux Boucher* into the search box and waited for the screen to populate. She didn't see anything about Margaux's death, but that wasn't surprising. She did, however, find dozens of articles about Margaux's former business, Alex + Margaux, the athleisure company Margaux founded with her former paramour, tennis instructor Alex Morgan.

The business had received lots of publicity, initially for its immediate success—several big-name tennis players and celebrities having endorsed the brand—and then for its dramatic demise, the two partners suing each other just two years later. Though they had eventually settled.

Guin wondered what would happen to Margaux's new business.

She did a search for *Château Margaux Mocktails*. There wasn't much online, mainly posts on Margaux's social media profiles.

Guin wondered if Margaux had registered the business. She went to the State of New York's Corporation and Business Entity Database and typed in *Château Margaux Mocktails*. She waited as the database searched. A minute later, it returned a hit. Per the search result, Château Margaux Mocktails was owned by an LLC by the name of

Mockingbird Beverages, with Margaux and someone named Aleksei Smirnov listed as the directors.

Aleksei Smirnov. The name sounded familiar, but Guin didn't know why. Though she knew there was a popular vodka with a similar name. Guin opened a new tab and typed *Aleksei Smirnov* into the search box.

Well, she wasn't expecting that. According to the search results, Aleksei Smirnov was a successful DJ who went by the handle DJ Smirnoff. Guin clicked on the link for DJ Smirnoff's Instagram account. He had an impressive number of followers. She watched a short clip from one of the parties he DJed at. It had garnered over a hundred thousand likes. Then she checked out his TikTok.

Huh. Guin wondered again how Margaux knew him. Were they old friends or had she met Smirnov at some party? She would ask Glen about him.

Over dinner that evening, Guin asked Glen if Margaux had ever mentioned someone named Aleksei Smirnov or a DJ Smirnoff. Glen said the name didn't sound familiar. Why did Guin want to know?

"According to the State of New York's business database, Aleksei Smirnov, who goes by DJ Smirnoff professionally, was Margaux's partner in Mockingbird Beverages, the parent company of Château Margaux Mocktails."

"Huh. Well, I don't recall her mentioning either an Aleksei Smirnov or a DJ Smirnoff at the shoot."

"He didn't stop by?"

"If he did, I didn't see him."

"So you have no idea how Margaux knew him?"

"None at all."

"We should ask Margaux's assistant."

"Why?"

"Well, he was her partner, and now that she's dead, I assume he's in charge of the business."

"So?"

"So, don't you want to know if they still want your photos and if you'll be paid?"

"A woman's dead, Guin."

Guin felt chastised.

"You're right. I'm sorry. But don't you want to know if they still want your photos? Have you been editing them?"

"I haven't had much time."

"You should reach out to Margaux's assistant." Glen gave her a look. "To give her your condolences. Have you heard from her?"

"I have not. I'm sure she's overwhelmed."

"You should send her a note."

"I'll do that."

Guin cleared the plates, giving them a quick rinse before putting them in the dishwasher.

"How would you feel about going out for ice cream?"

"Is that a trick question?"

Guin knew Glen loved ice cream.

"There's that new gelato place that just opened on seventy-seventh street, and I thought we could check it out."

"Let's go!"

Guin smiled.

"Let me just grab a sweater."

CHAPTER 4

Guin had been so busy working that she had nearly forgotten about Margaux. But that changed two days later. The doorbell had rung at nine a.m., and Glen had gone to answer it. A few minutes later, she heard him calling her name.

"I'm busy!" she yelled back.

"I really need you to come here," Glen replied.

Guin sighed.

"Can it wait a minute?"

"I don't think the detective wants to."

Guin immediately stopped what she was doing and ran to the front door. There was Detective Spinosa along with Officer Spinelli—and Glen in handcuffs.

"What's going on?" she asked the two policemen.

"We're arresting your husband for the murder of Margaux Boucher," said the detective, pronouncing Margaux's last name correctly this time.

"What?! That's ridiculous. Glen didn't kill anyone."

"He can tell that to the judge. Mr. Anderson?"

The detective turned.

"Wait!" said Guin, stopping him. "Where are you taking him, to the nineteenth?"

The detective nodded and Officer Spinelli led Glen out the door.

"I'll phone Tom!" she called to Glen.

As soon as they left, Guin phoned Glen's lawyer.

"Tom Goodwin."

"Tom. Thank goodness. It's Guin Jones. The police just arrested Glen. They think he killed his ex-wife."

"Do you know where they took him?"

"Back to the nineteenth, at least for now. Can you get over there?"

"I'm on my way."

It was quite late when Tom brought Glen home. Guin ran to the door and embraced him, kissing his face in relief.

"Thank you for freeing my husband," she said to Tom.

Tom nodded.

"I should go."

"Wait," said Guin. He paused. "Did they drop the charges?"

"No. He's free on bail. Glen can fill you in." He turned to Glen. "I'll follow up with you Monday." Glen thanked him, and Tom left.

Guin looked at her husband.

"Tell me everything."

"Can it wait until morning? I'm exhausted."

Guin bit her lip. She doubted she'd be able to sleep not knowing what had transpired at the police station, but she saw how tired Glen was.

"Of course. Can I make you some herbal tea?"

"You don't have to do that."

"It's no trouble. And it'll help you sleep."

He followed her to the kitchen and took a seat.

"Here," she said, handing him a mug a few minutes later. "Can I get you something to eat?"

"I'm not hungry."

"Have you eaten anything?"

"Not really." Guin frowned. "It's okay. The only thing I want right now is to crawl into bed and get some sleep."

Glen finished his tea and told Guin he was going to bed. Guin followed him to their bedroom and watched as he changed, brushed his teeth, and got into bed.

"You want to join me?" he asked her.

"I just need to change and brush my teeth."

A few minutes later, she got into bed and nestled next to Glen. He put his arms around her and held her close.

"I love you," he whispered.

"I love you too," she replied.

A few minutes later, Guin heard Glen gently snoring.

Guin woke up the next morning to find the space next to her empty again. She headed to the kitchen after going to the bathroom and helped herself to coffee, Glen having already made a pot. Then she took her mug to his office, knowing that was where he would be. He was looking at photos from the photo shoot.

"Trying to find Margaux's killer—the real one?"

Glen jumped.

"Sorry, I didn't mean to startle you."

Guin looked at the image on his monitor. She recognized Margaux but not any of the other people.

"I assume the two tall men are the basketball players."

"Correct. That's Jordan," said Glen, pointing to the man with longer hair, "and that's Shaq," he said, pointing to the other tall man.

"And the others? Though that must be Fabio," she said, pointing to the good-looking man with nearly shoulder-length blond hair.

"Correct. That's Ronnie, Margaux's assistant," Glen said, pointing to an attractive Indian woman who looked to be in her twenties. "And that's Dionne Davies, the product stylist," he said, pointing to a tall, attractive Black woman, whose age was hard to guess.

Guin studied the photo.

"You and Fabio look a bit alike."

"You think so?"

Guin looked at her husband and then at the photo again.

"You could be cousins."

"I'll take that as a compliment."

"You should. So, how does Margaux know him? Is she…"

"Is she what?"

"You know."

"You mean sleeping with him?"

Guin nodded.

"I don't think Margaux is his type."

"Ah. Though he's clearly hers. So, how does she know him?"

"He's her personal stylist."

"She has a personal stylist?"

"Apparently. I think they've been working together for a while."

"Can you send me the photo?"

"Why do you want the photo? Wait. Let me guess. You think one of them killed Margaux."

"Well, you certainly didn't."

"But they all left before I did."

"Do you know that for sure? The killer could have hung out somewhere, waited until you left, and then returned to the studio."

"I don't know, Guin."

"How did she die? Did the detective say?"

Glen went to take a sip of coffee, but his mug was empty.

"I need more coffee."

He got up and Guin followed him to the kitchen.

"So?" she said when he had refilled his mug and taken a sip. "What was the cause of death?"

"One of her mocktail bottles."

"She was poisoned? Is everyone else okay?"

"She wasn't poisoned. Someone hit her over the head with it."

"Someone hit her over the head with a mocktail bottle?"

Glen nodded.

"And they think you did it? Why?"

"They found a bottle lying next to Margaux's body with my fingerprints on it."

"Did you handle any of the bottles?"

"I did. Though not all of them."

"But you weren't the only one to touch the bottles, right?"

"Correct."

"Were anyone else's prints found on the bottle next to Margaux?"

"The detective didn't say."

Guin frowned.

"And are they sure that was the bottle that killed Margaux?"

"That's what the police believe."

Guin continued to frown.

"I still don't understand why they arrested you. The evidence is circumstantial at best."

"Well, I was the last one there."

"Supposedly," interjected Guin. "And your motive?"

"Unresolved anger towards my ex-wife."

"Is that what the detective said?"

Glen nodded.

"That's ridiculous."

"Witnesses also saw us arguing."

"You said Margaux argued with everyone. Did you tell the detective that?"

"I did."

"Yet he's convinced you were the one who killed her."

"He is."

"This is insane! You wouldn't hurt a fly! Did you ever hit Margaux when you were married to her?"

"Never."

"Did you tell Detective Spinosa that?"

"I did, but I don't think he believed me."

"I should speak to him."

"What? Why?"

"To tell him you'd never hit a woman—and that you didn't kill Margaux!"

"I appreciate you sticking up for me, but I doubt he'd take your word."

"Well then, we'll just have to find the real killer."

"*We?* I don't think…"

Guin cut him off.

"I'm not letting you go to jail for a crime you didn't commit."

"I appreciate you wanting to help, Guin, but I don't think you going in search of the real killer is a good idea."

"Why not?"

"You know why."

"No, I don't. Tell me."

Glen ran a hand over his face. He knew it was futile reasoning with his wife when she got like this. But he felt he had to try.

"What about your work for the *Times*?"

"What about it?"

"Don't you have a bunch of articles you need to work on?"

"Nothing's more important than helping you stay out of jail."

"My lawyer will do that."

"Did you hire Tom?"

"No, he's not a defense attorney, but he knows people who are."

"Still, you can't expect me to just sit on the sideline. Let me help you. Please."

Glen saw the look on his wife's face and sighed.

"Is there nothing I can say that will keep you from investigating?"

"Probably not."

"Just promise me you'll be careful."

"Always."

Though Glen knew that wasn't true.

"So, tell me about the shoot."

"What do you want to know?"

"Everything that happened that day. You said Margaux argued with everyone. Was there anyone in particular she was particularly hard on, anyone she could have pushed over the edge?"

"She was pretty tough on Ronnie."

"Her assistant."

"Yes. Though Ronnie seemed used to Margaux's moods."

"She wasn't upset when Margaux picked on her?"

"I could tell she wasn't happy, but she didn't throw a fit or cry if that's what you mean."

"What about the other people who were there? How did they react to Margaux's behavior?"

"I was doing my best to tune Margaux out."

"But you must have heard or seen something."

"I did see her yelling at Fabio. You couldn't not hear her."

"And?"

"He walked out."

"He left the shoot?"

"He did. But he came back."

"Anyone else she pissed off?"

"She said something to Jordan that caused him to walk out too."

"He's the one who plays for the Knicks, yes?"

Glen nodded.

"Though Ronnie got him to come back."

"Anyone else leave?"

"No. At least not that I was aware of. As I said, I tried to ignore or tune out Margaux's tirades."

"Do you think Fabio or Jordan could have killed her?"

"Not really. And both of them left before I did."

"Though they could have returned to the studio after you'd gone."

"I suppose."

"You didn't see anyone lurking about when you left the studio?"

"You mean from the shoot?" Guin nodded. "I didn't see anyone as I was leaving. Though there was a party going on up on the roof, some band shooting music videos. And there were lots of people going in and out of the studio building. I suppose I could have missed someone. I wasn't really paying attention."

"Did you tell the detective all of that?"

"I did."

"And he's still convinced *you* killed her?"

"I'm the one he arrested."

"But it could have been someone who was at the party."

"I suppose."

"I should talk to everyone who was at the shoot."

"Guin…"

"What?"

"I don't think that's a good idea."

"Why?"

"I don't think they'll talk to you."

"Why not?"

"You're my wife."

"They don't have to know that. It's not like we have the same last name. Did you tell them about me?"

"You know I don't discuss my personal life with clients."

"Though Margaux knew you'd remarried."

"Yes, but she wasn't interested in you."

Guin was going to say something, but she let it go.

"I'll just tell them I'm a reporter for the *New York Times* and make up a story."

"I don't know."

"Just give me Ronnie's contact info. I'll start with her. She knew Margaux best and probably arranged the shoot."

Glen hesitated.

"I'm sure I could find it some other way, but it would be easier if you just sent it to me."

Glen sighed.

"Fine. I'll send it to you when I go back to my office."

"And I want to see the photos you took."

"Why?"

"Just send me a link."

CHAPTER 5

Guin clicked through Glen's photos as soon as she received them. She wasn't sure what she was looking for. Maybe a shot of someone looking daggers at Margaux. But she didn't find anything incriminating. And she had paid work to do. Around half past noon, she messaged Glen.

"You want to have lunch?"

"Can't," he replied. "I'm troubleshooting."

"You need to eat."

"Would you make me a protein shake?" he asked, adding a prayer emoji.

"Fine," Guin wrote back.

She headed to the kitchen, the two cats, who had supposedly been asleep in their cat condo, racing ahead of her. She gave them some cat treats and proceeded to make Glen a protein shake.

Glen's door was ajar, but Guin knocked before entering.

"Come in," he called.

Guin entered and deposited the protein shake on Glen's desk. He was staring at his monitor, which was filled with computer code.

"What's the problem? Is there another bug in the scheduling software?"

Glen nodded.

"I've been working with the developer on it but…"

"Raj needs to hire a CTO."

"I know. And he said he's interviewing someone. But I'm pretty sure I can fix this particular problem."

Guin wasn't so sure, but she didn't say anything.

"Have some protein shake."

He looked down at the glass, picked it up, and took a sip. Then his eyes went back to his monitor.

Guin sighed.

"Just remember to get up and stretch once in a while. And we should go for a walk later."

Glen didn't say anything.

"Did you hear me?"

"Remember to get up and stretch and go for a walk later."

Guin shook her head. Then she leaned down and gave him a kiss on the cheek.

"I'll see you later," she said and then left.

The next day they were scheduled to have brunch with Guin's mother and stepfather. Guin had told Glen they could cancel if he wasn't feeling up to it. But he said they should go. He knew Guin's mother would be annoyed if they canceled, especially last minute.

"Just don't mention that you were arrested for killing your ex-wife," said Guin.

Glen looked at her.

"You seriously think I would bring that up over brunch?"

"You never know. It could just slip out."

"Trust me. My getting arrested is the last thing I want to discuss with your parents—or anyone."

"So, what are you going to say if she asks what you've been up to?"

"I'll just tell her I've been busy working on Photog."

"And?"

"And what?"

"What if she wants specifics?"

"I'll tell her I've been trying to debug the scheduling software."

"Well, that should get her to change the subject. Though… what if she's heard something?"

"Heard something?"

"About Margaux—and you."

"If she had, don't you think we would have heard from her?"

"Good point."

"Now stop worrying about your mother. Everything will be fine."

Guin mentally crossed her fingers.

They met Guin's parents at a restaurant near their apartment on the Upper East Side. Her mother and stepfather were already seated with drinks in front of them when Glen and Guin arrived.

"There you are!" said Carol. "We were starting to wonder what happened to you."

Guin dug her fingernails into her palm. They were only five minutes late.

"It's my fault," said Glen. "I was working and lost track of the time."

"You were working on a Sunday?" Carol seemed appalled.

"Glen works pretty much every day these days," said Guin. "That's what happens when you run a business. And I was working too."

Carol shook her head.

"You young people. I'm so glad Philip is retired. Though he never worked on a Sunday when he did work."

"Times are different now," Philip said in his posh British

accent. "And if I was running a startup like Glen here, I'd probably be working weekends too."

Guin's mother frowned.

"Well, thank goodness you're not!"

Just then the server came over and asked Guin and Glen if they'd like something to drink.

"I'll have a mimosa," said Guin.

"And I'll have a Bloody Mary," said Glen.

"So, how is Photog doing?" Philip asked him.

"Good. New York's doing so well, my partner Raj is looking to expand."

"He wants to open an office in LA next," said Guin.

"LA, eh?"

"Yes."

"Would you two move?"

Guin and Glen exchanged a look.

"I suggested he hire someone out there," said Glen, "someone who knows that market."

"Sounds sensible," said Philip. "And what have you been up to, Guinivere? Any new articles?"

"A few."

"Can you tell us about them or do we have to wait until they're published?"

"I guess I can tell you."

She then told them about some of the things she was working on.

"Sounds fascinating," said Philip.

Guin didn't know about *fascinating*, but she enjoyed writing about small business.

"And aren't you two about to head off on another cruise?" said Glen.

"We are," said Carol. "To Switzerland and the Rhine this time."

"Sounds great."

"We're looking forward to it."

The server reappeared with Glen and Guin's drinks and

asked them if they were ready to order. Glen said they needed a few minutes, and the server said she'd check back in a few.

Brunch had gone smoothly, much to Guin's relief. Of course, the two mimosas Guin had downed had helped. Indeed, she had been feeling so relaxed by the end of the meal that she had promised her mother she'd have lunch with her before she left on her cruise.

"See, you had nothing to worry about," Glen said as they walked home.

"Mm," said Guin. "Though Mom's bound to hear about Margaux at some point. And then she'll be furious we didn't say something."

"We'll cross that bridge when we come to it."

"Speaking of bridges, fancy a walk through Central Park? We could go to the lake and take a stroll over Bow Bridge."

"I should do some work."

"But it's Sunday."

"You sound like your mother."

Guin frowned.

"Please, don't ever say that."

"Sorry, but you know what I mean."

"Come on. Another hour won't kill you. And it's a beautiful day."

"Fine. I suppose a walk wouldn't kill me."

"Just the opposite." She then took Glen's hand and led him west towards the park.

Guin phoned Margaux's assistant, Ronnie Banerjee, Monday morning and was preparing to leave a voicemail message when Ronnie picked up.

"This is Ronnie."

"Hi, Ronnie. My name's Guin Jones. I'm a business reporter, working on a piece about hot new startups here in New York, and I'd love to include Château Margaux Mocktails in the mix."

There was a pause.

"Ronnie, are you there?"

"Sorry, it's a bit crazy here. Who did you say you were with?"

"The *New York Times*. I'm a stringer, mainly covering small business."

"And you want to include Château Margaux Mocktails in a story you're working on?"

"That's right. Are you interested?"

"I am, but I should let you know, we're in the process of rebranding."

"Oh? How come?" Though Guin had a pretty good idea why.

"We felt the old name might be confusing."

Guin didn't disagree.

"What's the new name?"

"Mockingbird Mocktails."

"I like it."

"We do too."

"So your founder, Margaux Boucher, approved the name change?"

There was another pause.

"I guess you haven't heard. Ms. Boucher is no longer with us."

"She left the company?"

Guin hated to play dumb, but she was curious to know how Ronnie would explain Margaux's death.

"In a sense. She died."

"Oh, I'm sorry to hear that. She was quite young, wasn't she?"

"She was."

"Was it cancer?"

"I'm afraid I'm not at liberty to discuss it. But I'd be happy to speak with you about the business. When were you thinking?"

"Do you have time tomorrow?"

"I'm a bit busy tomorrow. Though… I could chat with you at four. You want to call me then?"

"Actually, I'd prefer to speak in person if that's all right. I'd love to see what you've been working on."

"That's fine. I'll shoot you the address. We're in Chelsea."

"Great."

Guin spent the rest of the morning finishing an article for the *Times*. They had been throwing her a lot of work recently, a mix of short and longer pieces, which was keeping her busy.

When she was done with her article, she went to get something to eat. Then she took another look at Glen's photos from the shoot. Was one of these people a killer? Guin would research everyone who was there, starting with Ronnie.

She found Ronnie's LinkedIn profile and clicked on it. According to her bio, Ronnie had gone to Fordham University in the Bronx undergrad, where she majored in Business Administration, specializing in Marketing. After graduation, she went to work for Diageo, the big liquor company, in Marketing, moving up the corporate ladder. Then she had jumped ship to Mockingbird Beverages.

Guin wondered why Ronnie had left Diageo for the startup. Had Margaux offered her more money? Also, Glen had referred to Ronnie as Margaux's assistant. Yet on LinkedIn, Ronnie had listed her title as Manager of Marketing and PR. Had Glen gotten it wrong? Or had Ronnie inflated her title? Guin would ask her about that. Though with Margaux no longer around, Guin only had Ronnie's word for it. Of course, she could always ask Aleksei Smirnov, Margaux's mysterious partner.

Guin scanned Ronnie's connections, saw Smirnov's name, and clicked on it.

Interesting. Smirnov had been an investment banker before becoming a DJ. Actually, it appeared that he had done both jobs before becoming a DJ full-time. Guin wondered if DJing paid well. Or maybe Smirnov had saved enough money from his days as an investment banker to allow him to follow his passion. Had he funded Mockingbird Beverages? And how did he know Margaux?

Guin sent him a request to connect, along with a note. If he didn't get back to her, she would ask Ronnie for his contact information.

Guin decided to look up Fabio next. She had forgotten to ask Glen Fabio's last name. But how difficult could it be to find him? She typed *Fabio personal stylist* into the search box and waited. But she didn't have to wait long.

There were lots of mentions of the other Fabio, but Guin found her man, who, as it happened, had also been a model. Guin couldn't help looking at some of Fabio's modeling photos. He had modeled for several high-end men's clothing companies, including Giorgio Armani and Hugo Boss. That must have been where he had gotten his sense of style.

She then found an article from a few years back about personal stylists that mentioned him and clicked on it. Fabio worked mainly with busy women—businesswomen and celebrities—who didn't have time to go clothes shopping. Though he also had some male clients.

Guin had hoped for some names, but Fabio had told the journalist who interviewed him that who he worked with was private.

She found another article about the stylist, a piece about former models, what they were doing now. But it didn't provide any additional information about Fabio. So Guin went to see what she could find out about the other stylist, Dionne.

Dionne had an impressive resume. She had worked for all of the big culinary magazines: *Gourmet*, *Bon Appetit*, *Food & Wine*, as well as for the Food Network and several food and beverage companies, including Diageo. Guin wondered if she knew Ronnie.

She scanned Dionne's LinkedIn profile and saw that Ronnie had recommended her. So they had worked together.

That left the two basketball players. Though Guin couldn't imagine either of them killing Margaux. What motive did they have? However, both of them were certainly big and strong enough to have caused serious harm with a bottle. And Glen did say that Margaux had got into it with Jordan and that he had walked out.

Guin searched for Jordan first. He was easy to find. He had gone to UConn and been drafted by the Chicago Bulls his senior year and then traded to the Knicks a couple of years later. A respected point guard in his college days, Jordan hadn't seen a lot of playing time with either the Bulls or the Knicks. She wondered why.

Guin scrolled down and saw a piece about Jordan being suspended and clicked on it. Interesting. According to the article, Jordan had attacked a teammate during a game in Chicago and had been ordered to attend anger management classes. So was he a hothead?

Guin looked to see if there was anything more about Jordan getting into it with teammates or anyone else and found an article about Jordan arguing with an assistant coach. There was even a picture of him jabbing his finger into the assistant coach's chest. So, Jordan had anger management issues. Could he have been so angry at

Margaux that he had picked up a mocktail bottle and hit her with it?

And what about Jordan's friend, Shaq? Did he also have anger management issues? It took a bit of searching, weeding out all of the references to other athletes named Shaq, but Guin found him. He had gone to UConn with Jordan but hadn't been drafted by an NBA team, so he had gone to play ball in Europe and had done well there.

She looked to see if there was anything about Shaq getting into it with teammates or coaches. However, unlike his friend, Shaq appeared to be a model player, beloved by his teammates and his coaches in the EuroLeague.

Guin looked at the photos Glen had taken of Shaq and Jordan. Shaq was a good-looking kid with a ready smile. And while Jordan seemed to rarely smile, he was also quite attractive. Margaux had been smart to recruit them.

Could one of them have killed her? Guin found it hard to believe, especially of Shaq. Yet as she had learned from covering several homicide cases on Sanibel—and from reading too many mysteries and watching too many Hallmark Mysteries—the killer was often the last person you suspected.

CHAPTER 6

Guin arrived at the address Ronnie had given her in Chelsea right at four. The building housed dozens of small businesses. Mockingbird Beverages was on the twelfth floor.

Guin rode the elevator up and went in search of Mockingbird's office. It was around the corner from the elevator bank. It had a glass door, which was unlocked. Guin let herself in and immediately spied Ronnie. She was on her phone. Guin waited for Ronnie to notice her.

Finally, Ronnie ended her call and turned around.

"Guin?"

Guin smiled at her.

"That's me. Thank you for seeing me on such short notice."

Ronnie's phone was ringing. She looked down at it and frowned.

"Do you need to get that?" asked Guin.

"Probably." But Ronnie didn't answer. "Please, have a seat," she told Guin.

Guin sat.

"Before we begin, I'm curious to know who else you'll be profiling."

Guin had anticipated Ronnie asking that and mentioned three other startups, including one she had included in her LEED piece.

"All great companies," said Ronnie, "who are farther along than we are. Why do you want to include Mockingbird?"

"Zero-proof cocktails are hot right now. And I read somewhere that Margaux Boucher was the new Bethenny Frankel, and that Château Margaux Mocktails could be the new Skinnygirl."

"You must have read that on Margaux's Instagram account." Guin didn't deny it. "And while I wouldn't have called Margaux the next Bethenny, we expect our mocktails to have as big an impact on the industry as Skinnygirl did."

"I see," said Guin.

She took out her phone and opened her recording app.

"Is it okay to record the interview? It's just for my playback."

Ronnie told her to go ahead, and Guin started by asking her how Mockingbird Beverages came to be.

"Mockingbird was born out of a need," Ronnie began. "Almost everyone enjoys a cocktail, but not everyone wants or can have alcohol."

"And which one was Ms. Boucher?"

"The latter."

"Ms. Boucher had a problem with alcohol?" Glen hadn't said anything.

"It wasn't exactly a secret, but Margaux struggled with addiction."

"She was an alcoholic?"

"A recovering alcoholic. Margaux was very social. And drinking has always been a big part of socializing. When Margaux was younger, a few drinks weren't a problem. But as she got older and came under more pressure…"

"She couldn't handle alcohol as well."

"Exactly."

"It's not uncommon," said Guin. "You said that Margaux was a recovering alcoholic. Was she in a program?"

"She was. That's actually where Margaux and her partner Aleksei Smirnov came up with the idea to create a line of mocktails."

"She met Mr. Smirnov at AA?"

"She did."

"So what led them to come up with the idea?"

"They were at an AA meeting, and everyone was talking about how hard it was to go to parties or clubs where everyone was drinking. Aleksei said he would just order club soda with lime and pretend it was vodka. And someone else said they just stopped going to clubs because it was too hard.

"And then Margaux said that she would just ask the bartender to make her something yummy without the alcohol. And someone joked that there should be clubs that only offered mocktails. And that was when Aleksei and Margaux got the idea to develop a line of mocktails and pitch it to clubs."

"It was a great idea," said Guin. "When was this?"

"Going on a year now."

"And the Château Margaux name, was that Margaux's idea?"

"It was. She thought it sounded classy."

"She wasn't concerned that the Château Margaux Estate in France might sue?"

"She thought they wouldn't care. Though Aleksei was concerned. He tried to talk her out of it, but Margaux wouldn't budge, and Aleksei gave in."

"Did he often give in to her?"

"I wouldn't say that. It was just that he had his own business to run—he's a DJ—and didn't have the energy to constantly go rounds with Margaux. It was just easier to let her have her way. At least about some things."

"But now that she's dead, you decided to change the name. Who's idea was that?"

"Aleksei's. Though, to be fair, we both thought a name change was a good idea. We didn't want a lawsuit, and Mockingbird Mocktails has a nice ring to it."

"It does," said Guin. "So you're still planning on going ahead with the product launch?"

"Of course. Margaux would have wanted us to." Ronnie seemed to choke up.

"You okay?"

Ronnie indicated she needed a moment.

"I'm fine. It's just… I still can't believe she's gone. This business was everything to her."

"If you don't mind me asking, how did she die?"

Ronnie looked right at Guin, her expression no longer sorrowful.

"She was murdered."

"Murdered?" said Guin, pretending to be shocked.

"I know. It was quite a shock to all of us. It happened right after our big photo shoot."

"Did she get mugged on her way home?"

"No. It happened at the photo studio after everyone had left. Well, nearly everyone."

"What happened?"

"I'm not entirely sure. All I know is that they found Margaux there, dead, the next morning."

"That's awful. And you say she was murdered?"

Ronnie nodded.

"Do the police have a suspect?"

"I heard they arrested Margaux's ex."

"Her ex?"

"Her ex-husband. Margaux insisted we hire him to do the photo shoot. He's a photographer."

"Why did she insist on hiring her ex?"

"I think it was part of her twelve-step program, apologizing to the people you've harmed and making up for the harm you've caused them."

"What did she do to her ex?"

"She cheated on him."

"So she hired him as a way to make up for that?" It didn't make sense to Guin, but she had no idea how Margaux's mind worked.

"I think that's what she thought. She said he was a really good photographer who had wanted to pursue photography professionally, but she didn't think he could make a living doing it. Maybe this was her way of saying she believed in him."

"And you think he could have killed her?"

"He seemed like a nice guy, but I think Margaux got to him. At one point she told him she couldn't believe he got paid to take photos. Maybe he snapped. Not that I blame him. Margaux could be tough to deal with and she was pretty brutal that evening."

"You say she was brutal that evening. Did she say not nice things to anyone else besides the photographer?"

"Oh yeah. She pretty much picked on everyone. Nothing anyone did was right or up to her standards. She kept making us redo things and yelling at everyone."

"Everyone being…?"

"Me, Glen—that's Margaux's ex—Dionne and Fabio, the two stylists, and Jordan and Shaq. Jordan's my cousin who plays for the Knicks, and Shaq is his friend. He plays in the EuroLeague."

"What were they doing there?"

"Margaux was too cheap to hire real models. So she insisted I get Jordan and Shaq to help out—and made them and the rest of us pose with drinks."

"Your cousin and his friend modeled for free?" Guin knew athletes usually got a lot of money for promoting products.

"Margaux said she'd give them a piece of the business if they agreed to become brand ambassadors."

"How big a piece?"

"We were still working out the details."

"So they agreed to do it?"

"They did."

"What about now, with Margaux being dead?"

"Nothing's changed. We just need to hammer out a few things."

"And what about Aleksei Smirnov, Margaux's partner? Was he at the photo shoot?"

"He couldn't make it."

"How come? I would think he'd want to be there."

"He was DJing."

Guin thought it odd that he was DJing during the day but didn't say anything.

"I'd love to speak with him."

"He's rather busy, but I'll let him know. You said you were doing the article for the *Times*?"

"That's right. So with Ms. Boucher out of the picture, who's running the business?"

"I am."

"You are?"

"Don't look so surprised. I've been pretty much running things since Margaux and Aleksei hired me. Margaux was a great idea person but not a very good businesswoman. As you may know, her last business went bust after just a couple of years."

"I see. So Mr. Smirnov's not involved with the business?"

"I wouldn't say that. He's just more focused on his DJ business right now. And frankly, I know more about the beverage industry than he does. I majored in Business Administration at Fordham and spent years working in Marketing at Diageo, helping to launch or expand their brands."

"You mentioned that Ms. Boucher's previous business went bust. Didn't that concern Mr. Smirnov?"

"No. Margaux explained what happened, how her partner had embezzled money from the business and hid it from her."

Ronnie's phone was ringing again. She looked down at it and frowned.

"I need to get this," she told Guin, picking up her phone. "Can I call you back in a minute?" she said to the caller. "I'm doing an interview. Okay," she said a few seconds later and put down the phone. But as soon as she did, it started ringing again.

"I'm sorry," Ronnie said to Guin. "It's been crazy here since Margaux…"

"I understand," said Guin.

The phone continued to ring. Exasperated, Ronnie picked it up and answered.

"I can't talk to you right now, Fabio. I'm with someone." Guin couldn't help trying to hear what Fabio was saying to Ronnie, but it was impossible. "I understand, Fabio, but I can't talk right now. I'll call you back later."

Ronnie ended the call and put the phone face down on the table.

"Was that the stylist who was at the photo shoot?"

"It was."

"Is everything all right?"

Ronnie's phone was ringing again.

"I'm sorry," she said, trying to ignore her phone. "I should probably put it on silent but…"

"I understand," said Guin. "Maybe we could continue this conversation another time, when you're not so busy?"

"Sure. Or maybe send me the rest of your questions? It might be easier."

"What's your email?"

Ronnie gave it to her.

"I'd also love to speak to your cousin and his friend."

"Why?"

"You said they were to be brand ambassadors."

"They haven't actually signed a contract yet. So I'd prefer you waited to speak with them."

"I hear you, but I'd be interested in getting their take on the whole mocktail thing, even if they don't become brand ambassadors. Could you give me their contact information?"

"I'm afraid I can't do that."

Guin reached into her bag and took out her card case.

"Here's my card. Could you give them my information and ask them to phone me or shoot me a text? I have a little time until my story is due."

Ronnie glanced at her card. Then her phone began to ring again.

"Some days I want to throw it in the Hudson River."

"I know how you feel," said Guin. "I'll let you go and will send you the rest of my questions."

As soon as Guin got up and moved away, Ronnie picked up her phone.

"What now?" said Ronnie.

Guin stood by the door, wondering who Ronnie was speaking to.

"I told you. I've got it handled," Ronnie continued. Sensing she was being watched, Ronnie turned around, but Guin had already left.

CHAPTER 7

That evening over dinner, Guin asked Glen if Margaux had a drinking problem. Glen said that Margaux would typically have a glass of wine or two with dinner and would order a cocktail when they were out—and that she could get combative after a few drinks—but he didn't think she had a drinking problem. Why was Guin asking?

Guin told him about her conversation with Ronnie Banerjee and wondered if Margaux could have been drinking during the shoot.

"The only thing I saw Margaux drink were her mocktails and water. At least I assumed that was water in her water bottle."

Guin made a note to ask Ronnie if Margaux could have been drinking. That could explain her behavior. Of course, the autopsy report would also reveal if Margaux had been drinking that afternoon, but good luck getting a hold of that anytime soon.

"Was there anything else that could have set Margaux off?" Guin asked him.

Glen looked thoughtful.

"As I told you, I did my best to tune Margaux out."

"I know, but there could have been something—or someone—who upset her, that caused her to act the way she did."

"Hm."

Guin waited as Glen seemed to be mulling that over.

"Margaux received a phone call maybe a couple of hours into the shoot that seemed to upset her."

"Any idea who called her?"

"I don't know, but she yelled at whoever it was and told him to back off."

"You think it was a man?"

"I don't know."

The phone call reminded Guin of something.

"You said Margaux received a phone call that evening as you were showing her your pictures. Any idea who called her?"

"No, but now that you mention it, I think it could have been the same person who phoned her earlier."

"What makes you say that?"

"Something about the way she spoke to him, what she said."

"What did she say to him?" Though they didn't know for sure it was a him.

"I think she said, 'I told you before.' But I really wasn't paying attention. I just wanted to get out of there."

"If only we knew who called. Then we could prove Margaux was alive when you left. You told that detective about the call, right?"

"I did."

"Hm. We should find out if the police have her phone."

The next morning, Guin woke up to an empty bed again. Even though Glen seemed his usual calm self, she could sense that the case was bothering him. She wished she could make it go away, but the best she could do was to prove Glen didn't do it.

She went to get some coffee and then stopped by Glen's office.

"You okay?" she asked him.

"Just busy."

Guin went over and put her arms around his neck and gave him a kiss.

"We're going to get through this," she told him.

Glen leaned against her, closing his eyes.

"I know we will. I just can't…" His phone was ringing, and Guin saw Raj's name flash up. "I need to get this," he told her.

Guin gave him another kiss and then went to her office. She took out her phone and listened back to her interview with Ronnie. Except for the brief moment when Ronnie seemed to choke up, she didn't seem too shaken up about the death of her boss. Then again, people experienced or dealt with grief in different ways. And Ronnie did have a business to run.

Guin wondered how Aleksei Smirnov felt about Margaux's death. He hadn't responded to her LinkedIn request. So she went to his Instagram account and sent him a DM, saying that she was working on an article for the *New York Times* about Mockingbird Beverages and wanted to speak with him. If he didn't get back to her by tomorrow, she'd ask Ronnie for his contact info.

In the meantime, she'd reach out to Jordan and Shaq. She had discovered that they both had Instagram accounts. So she sent each of them a message, saying she was a journalist and wanted to interview them.

While she was on Instagram, she looked to see if Fabio had an account. He did. And there was a link to his website in his bio. She clicked on the link and then clicked on the Contact link. There was only a form, which she filled out, saying she was a journalist and wanted to interview him. For good measure, she also sent him a DM on Instagram.

He replied to her Instagram message that afternoon, saying he'd be happy to chat with her. And they arranged to meet that Friday at a coffee shop near Bloomingdale's.

Dionne Davies, the other stylist, wasn't on Instagram, but she did have a website with an email address. Guin sent her an email, requesting an interview, and Dionne wrote her back that she could meet with Guin after work that Friday.

Last on Guin's list of people to talk to was Glen's assistant, Eric. She had Eric's cell phone number, but before she reached out to him, she wanted to let Glen know she planned on interviewing him.

She was about to message her husband but decided to visit him instead. She hadn't heard him all morning and wanted to make sure he had eaten.

His door was closed, so she knocked. No answer. She knocked again and tried to ascertain if he was on the phone, but she didn't hear anything. She opened the door a crack and saw that Glen was on a Zoom call and silently closed the door. She would message him instead.

She had just sat down in front of her computer when her phone chimed with a notification. She had an appointment to go visit a doggy daycare place in an hour. It was for her new assignment. Guin had forgotten all about it. Good thing she had put it on her calendar with a reminder.

She quickly typed Glen a message, asking if he was okay if she reached out to Eric, then she took a quick shower, got dressed, and headed to her appointment.

Guin stood in front of the building housing Doggone Awesome in Midtown West. The place didn't look like much from the outside, but Guin knew better than to judge a building by its exterior.

She stepped inside and headed to Doggone Awesome. The daycare facility looked like a high-end salon, which it was, just for dogs. Guin introduced herself to the receptionist, a young woman who looked to be in her twenties, telling her she had an appointment with Gretchen Wolfson, one of the owners. The receptionist let Gretchen know and told Guin she'd be right out.

Gretchen appeared a few minutes later.

"You must be Guin."

Guin smiled at the woman, who she thought looked a bit like an Afghan hound with her long face and sleek blonde hair.

"I am."

"Well, welcome to Doggone Awesome! Would you like a tour before we chat?"

"I'd love one," said Guin.

The place was big with several playrooms where dogs could play and mingle: one for small dogs, one for medium-sized ones, and one for large dogs. Each playroom contained plenty of toys as well as hurdles and slides, just like you saw in canine agility contests. Several dogs were playing in each room, and all of the dogs Guin saw looked healthy and happy.

"We also have a space on the roof for the dogs to run around, and, of course, we take them for walks."

Guin asked how often people left their dogs there.

"It depends," said Gretchen. "We have some clients who drop off their dogs every morning and others who just leave them here when they travel."

Next, Gretchen showed Guin the grooming salon, which looked similar to a high-end hair salon. Guin was tempted to ask if the woman currently trimming the hair of a standard poodle could trim her hair, which wasn't that dissimilar to the poodle's.

"We use only organic, dog-safe products," Gretchen explained as they watched the groomers work. "And all of our groomers are trained in the latest canine grooming techniques."

Guin followed Gretchen down the hall.

"And this is where we board dogs," said Gretchen.

The room was filled with large, comfortable-looking crates that looked like doghouses. Several looked to be occupied.

"I don't have a dog," said Guin. "But if I did, I'd totally take him here." And she meant it. Heck, the place looked nicer than some hotels and spas she'd gone to.

Gretchen smiled.

"Would you like to see the rooftop dog run?"

"Sure," said Guin.

Gretchen led Guin to a service elevator that looked as though it could fit half a dozen dogs and pressed a button. A minute later, they got out.

"It's just through here," said Gretchen, opening a heavy-looking metal door.

They stepped out onto the roof, which was surrounded by fencing. Guin had wondered about having dogs up on a roof, worried about one jumping off.

"We got permission from the landlord to put up fencing on this side," said Gretchen, as though reading Guin's mind. "Couldn't have one of our fur babies having an accident."

The dog run was covered in artificial turf that looked like grass. It was currently empty, but Guin could picture a half-dozen dogs happily running around. They headed back to the service elevator and descended back down to Doggone Awesome. Gretchen led Guin to her office, which wasn't nearly as nice as the areas the dogs occupied, and told her to have a seat.

Guin took out her phone to record the interview and proceeded to ask Gretchen how she and her husband had come to own Doggone Awesome and about the business. Gretchen was more than happy to tell her story, and Guin was glad she was recording the interview as Gretchen barely drew breath.

When Gretchen had finished answering the last of Guin's questions, Guin thanked her for her time and left. As soon as Guin stepped outside, she checked her phone for messages. But there was nothing from Aleksei Smirnov, or the basketball players, or Glen.

Guin went to Glen's office as soon as she got home and got his permission to reach out to Eric. Then she sent Eric a text.

The next morning, after still not receiving a reply from Smirnov or the basketball players, Guin sent a text to Ronnie, asking for her help. She also sent another text to Eric, who she hadn't heard back from. Could she have the wrong number? She sent a message to Glen, asking him for Eric's number. Then she was off to another doggy daycare place. This one was on the Upper East Side, not far from where she and Glen were living.

Central Park Dogs was similar to Doggone Awesome but had the advantage of being just a few blocks from Central Park. And after interviewing the owner, who gave Guin a tour of the facility, the owner asked Guin if she'd like to go to the park with one of their dog walkers. As it was a beautiful day and she had some time, Guin said yes.

As Guin accompanied the dog walker through the park, they came across several other people walking dogs, some no doubt professionals. They also passed people roller-skating, biking, running, and just hanging out. It was one of the things Guin loved about Manhattan, that you had this enormous park in the center of it where people could walk their dogs, musicians could play, artists could paint, and mothers could take their children to play—all for free.

Looking around, Guin realized she had missed Central Park. Not that she hadn't loved living ten minutes from the Gulf of Mexico. But she had grown up near Central Park and had spent many happy hours there, biking, lounging on the banks of the Model Boat Pond reading a book, and hanging out with her high school friends in Sheep Meadow.

As she was reminiscing, she thought she heard someone calling her name.

"Guin?"

Guin turned to see an attractive brunette around her age coming towards her. She looked like she had just come from a yoga class and was walking a friendly-looking, apricot-colored labradoodle.

"Sophie?"

"It is you!" said Sophie, a big smile on her pretty face. "What are you doing here? Are you visiting your family?"

Guin suddenly felt guilty. Sophie was an old high school friend who still lived in New York. But Guin had lost touch with her—and many of her other New York friends—after getting divorced, laid off from her job, and moving to Sanibel.

"I'm actually living here. We just moved back."

"We?"

"My husband Glen and I."

"You remarried?" *And you didn't tell me?!* Guin heard her friend thinking.

"This spring."

Sophie's dog barked.

"I'm taking Ginger for her walk. Care to join us?"

The dog walker told Guin she had to go, and Guin thought about telling Sophie she had to go too. Instead, she told Sophie she'd be happy to accompany them.

"So, what have you been up to?" Guin asked her friend. "How are the kids and Warren?"

Warren was Sophie's husband.

"Warren just got a big promotion, and the kids are fine."

"How old are they now?"

"Noah just turned ten, and Izzy's going to be eight next month."

"Wow. It seems like just yesterday they were babies."

Sophie smiled.

"That's because you haven't seen them since they were little."

That was probably the main reason Guin and Sophie had drifted apart. Their lives had taken different paths after Sophie had her kids. Sophie had quit her job to be a full-time mom, and Guin had thrown herself into work after not being able to conceive.

"You should come over, have dinner one night, or we could meet up for brunch. I'm dying to meet Glen. What's he like?"

"Very mellow. Totally the opposite of Art. Or he was until he started running his company."

"How'd you meet him?"

"He worked for the same paper I did on Sanibel. He's a photographer."

"A photographer! And you say he has his own company?"

"It's called Photog. Have you heard of it?"

"I have! It's supposedly *the* place to hire photographers. My friend Joy just hired one of their photographers to photograph her daughter's bat mitzvah."

Guin smiled.

"So, what are you two up to this weekend?" Sophie asked her. "You want to meet up for brunch on Sunday? Where are you living?"

"We rented a place on the Upper East Side, and I'll need to check with Glen. We're both a bit busy."

"Come on. It's the weekend. You can't work all the time. I know: We could meet at BethAnn's Kitchen, like we used to."

"Is BethAnn's still open?"

"Oh yeah. It's a neighborhood institution."

BethAnn's was a cozy neighborhood spot near their high school that was known for its weekend brunch.

"Please say you'll come. The kids are spending the weekend with Warren's parents in Connecticut and won't be home until Sunday afternoon."

"I'll talk to Glen. Look, I should go. I need to work on an article."

"You're still writing?"

"I am. I'm a stringer for the *New York Times*."

"Wow! You always wanted to work there. That's amazing."

"It's not full-time, but it keeps me busy."

"So, what are you working on? Anything exciting?"

"I don't know about exciting, but I'm currently working on a piece about doggy daycare places."

"Fun! Speaking of doggies…" Ginger was barking. "Shush, Ginger! She's always barking at something," said Sophie. "So, you'll get back to me about Sunday?"

"I will," said Guin.

Sophie leaned over and gave Guin a hug.

"I'm so glad I ran into you!"

CHAPTER 8

Guin thought about her encounter with Sophie on her walk home. Sophie had seemed genuinely happy to see her. Sophie had also been one of the people who had written to Guin after hearing about her divorce and the layoff, saying she was there for her. However, Guin had blown her off.

Now things were different. Guin had a job she liked and a husband she loved, who loved her back. And she had enjoyed her walk with Sophie and Ginger. She should take Sophie up on brunch.

Guin arrived home to find Glen having a late lunch in the kitchen.

"Taking a break?"

He nodded and swallowed.

"You have lunch?"

"I grabbed a hot dog on my way home from Central Park." Another thing Guin liked about being back in Manhattan: all the great street food. "And you'll never guess who I ran into there."

"Who?"

"My old high school friend, Sophie."

"Sophie?"

"I must have told you about Sophie. She was one of my best friends."

"I don't think so."

"Huh." Guin felt a pang of guilt. Had she really not

mentioned Sophie to Glen? "Well, as I said, she was one of my best friends from high school, but we lost touch."

"What happened?"

"The usual stuff. Sophie got married, had kids, and left her job at *Vogue* to be a full-time mom. And I became a workaholic, then got laid off from my job and divorced, and moved to Sanibel."

"It happens. How old are her kids?"

"Ten and about to be eight."

"When was the last time you saw her?"

Guin thought.

"I honestly don't remember. Anyway, Sophie suggested we meet up with her and Warren for brunch this weekend. Are you free?"

"Which day?"

"Sunday."

"I think I can take time out for brunch on Sunday. What does her husband do?"

"Warren's an architect."

Glen finished his sandwich.

"Well, I look forward to meeting them."

"Great! I'll tell Sophie it's a date. She suggested we meet at one of our old haunts, BethAnn's Kitchen. It's not far from here. They have the best pancakes and waffles."

"Sounds great." Glen got up. "I need to get back to work. See you for dinner later?"

"Wait. Before you go, did you hire a lawyer?"

Tom had sent Glen a list of defense attorneys earlier that week.

"Not yet."

"Have you even called any of the people on Tom's list?"

"I've been a bit busy."

Guin looked at him.

"You need to start calling people."

"I know. It's just…"

Guin cut him off.

"No excuses. Nothing is more important than staying out of jail."

"The trial isn't for months."

"I know that. But if we can discover who really killed Margaux, maybe there won't need to be a trial."

"Guin…"

"Just promise me you'll start calling the lawyers on Tom's list."

"I promise."

"When?"

"Soon."

Guin gave him a look.

"I have a call. But I promise I'll consult Tom's list right after." Then he gave his wife a kiss and headed to his office.

Guin couldn't decide what to wear to her interview with Fabio that Friday and took so much time deciding that she worried she'd be late. But she was right on time. However, there was no sign of the stylist when she got to the coffee shop.

Guin hadn't had breakfast, so she ordered a cappuccino and a scone and took a seat with a view of the door. Ten minutes went by and there was still no sign of Fabio. She was about to send him a text when she saw him and waved.

"Guin?"

"And you must be Fabio."

"Sorry I'm late. One of my clients was having a minor crisis and insisted we Facetime so I could help her pick out an outfit for her board meeting."

"That's all right. You're here now. You want to get yourself a coffee and something to eat?"

He returned a minute later with a large coffee drink and took a seat opposite Guin.

"So, how can I help you?"

"As I wrote, I'm doing a piece on personal stylists, and I understand you're one of the best here in the city."

He smiled at that, and Guin could see why women hired him. And it wasn't just because of his style sense.

"I don't know about the best. But I do feel that I'm good at what I do."

"And what is that?"

"I help women develop their own personal style."

To make it seem like a real interview, Guin asked Fabio if she could record their conversation, which he gave her permission to do. Then she asked him a bunch of softball questions: why he became a stylist, what he thought of his chosen profession, and who his clients were.

Fabio was happy to talk about himself and told her that he had worked with dozens of successful businesswomen and celebrities. However, he couldn't share the names of his clients without their permission. Guin said that she understood and tried to think of a way to ask him about Margaux.

"I know you can't name names, but I heard that you worked with Margaux Boucher, the founder of Château Margaux Mocktails. Is that correct?"

"It is," he said. "Though I guess you hadn't heard. She died recently."

"Oh no!" said Guin, feigning shock. "She was quite young, wasn't she?"

"In her early forties."

"Was it cancer?"

"She was murdered."

He said it so matter-of-factly, as though people were murdered every day. Though in New York City, maybe they were.

"Murdered?" Guin said dramatically. She knew she was laying it on a bit thick, but she had never been a good actress.

"By her ex-husband."

"That's dreadful. What happened?"

"I don't know for sure."

"Was it recently?"

He nodded.

"It happened just after the photo shoot we did for her new line of mocktails. Her ex-husband was the photographer."

"Wow."

"I know."

"So how did you meet Margaux? Had you been working with her for a while?"

"We met through a mutual friend."

"And Margaux hired you to help with her wardrobe?"

"She did. Though she rarely took my advice."

"Oh?"

"Margaux was a bit of a diva. She had her own ideas about everything."

"And when did you two start working together?"

"Around four years ago?"

"Did you help Margaux with her athleisure line?"

"I was a consultant."

"Though I read that the athleisure business went bankrupt."

"Thanks to that partner of hers," Fabio said with a scowl.

"And then she hired you to dress everyone at the Château Margaux Mocktails shoot?"

"She did. Though she threw a fit when she saw what I had brought."

"She threw a fit?"

"Threw the clothes back at me and said she'd rather everyone be naked."

"Wow. That must have made you angry."

"I admit, I was annoyed. I'd been trying to discuss the wardrobe for the shoot with Margaux for days, but she kept blowing me off. Though I knew she was busy and under a lot of pressure."

"So you weren't mad at her for throwing clothes at you?"

"I was used to Margaux's little tirades and just brushed it off."

"I see."

"Why all the questions about Margaux?"

"Sorry. It's just… she sounds so interesting. And she was very beautiful."

"She was that. And she could be quite fun," he said with a smile, as though remembering something. "But the whole Château Margaux thing was stressing her out. You could tell at the photo shoot. She was yelling at everyone, telling them how to do their jobs. That's probably why the photographer killed her. He'd probably had enough of her sniping at him."

"You really think he killed her?"

"If she had treated me like that, I'd have thought about killing her too."

"Though you said she threw a fit when she saw what you brought. You didn't think about killing her after she humiliated you in front of everyone?"

Fabio took a sip of his coffee.

"The thought may have briefly crossed my mind, but I make it a policy to never talk back to my clients or lose my temper with them."

Guin studied the stylist, trying to decide if he was telling the truth.

"What about the other people at the photo shoot? You said Margaux yelled at everyone. Did anyone yell back at her?"

"No, though I think Dionne wanted to smack her."

"Dionne?" said Guin, playing dumb.

"Dionne Davies. She was the product stylist Margaux's assistant hired for the shoot."

"And what did Margaux say or do to Dionne?"

"Margaux kept having her rearrange the bottles and redo the mocktails—and then insinuated that the only reason

Dionne got where she was was because of affirmative action."

"Affirmative action?"

"Because she was a Black woman."

"Oh dear. And what did Dionne do when Margaux insulted her?"

"Nothing. Dionne's a professional. Though you could tell it rankled her."

"I see. Anyone else who Margaux offended who may have wanted to kill her?"

"I told you, they arrested her ex-husband."

Guin saw that Fabio's smartwatch was flashing.

"I'm afraid I must go," he announced. "I have another appointment."

"I had a few more questions."

"Would you mind emailing them to me?" He got up and eyeballed Guin. "And let me know if you'd like to make an appointment."

"An appointment?"

"To go shopping."

"To go shopping?"

"For some clothes."

"You don't like what I'm wearing?" Guin had agonized over what to wear to the interview.

"It's all wrong for your coloring. Is that your natural hair color?"

Guin touched her hair, which was strawberry-blonde and fell in curls around her face.

"It is."

"Hm." His smartwatch was flashing again. "I must be off. Let me know when your article will run!"

Guin watched him go, suddenly feeling insecure.

CHAPTER 9

When Guin got home, she went to her bedroom and looked at herself in the full-length mirror. She didn't think her outfit looked that bad. Sure, she could have dressed up a bit more. But she was meeting Fabio at a coffee shop, not the Plaza Hotel. Though she wondered what clothes he would have picked out for her to wear.

She went to her office and pulled up his website on her computer. According to the website, the first consultation was free. So she really had nothing to lose. And all of the women in the gallery looked so stylish. She wondered if they were actual clients or stock photos.

She opened a new tab and typed *Fabio Bertolini clients* into the search box. Most of the pictures she found were of Fabio from his modeling days. She was looking at an old photo of him when Glen came in.

"What are you doing?" he said.

"Research."

"On Fabio?"

"I wanted to know more about him."

"Like his inseam?"

Guin gave her husband a look.

"I was actually looking to see who some of his clients were, but I got his old modeling photos instead."

"Uh-huh."

"You don't believe me?"

"Why are you interested in his clients?"

"I'm curious to know what they have to say about him. He told me that he never lost his temper, at least with his clients, but I find that hard to believe."

"When did he tell you that?"

"This morning."

"This morning?"

"I thought I told you. I met him at a coffee shop near Bloomingdale's."

"You didn't tell me you were meeting him."

"I didn't?" Guin said innocently.

"No, you did not. Why were you meeting with him?"

"I told you, I wanted to meet with everyone who was at the shoot. And he had just as good a reason to kill Margaux as you did."

Glen ran a hand over his face.

"Please tell me you didn't accuse him of killing Margaux."

"Of course I didn't. I told him I was working on an article about personal stylists."

"And he believed you?"

"Why wouldn't he? I am a journalist."

"So, did you learn anything?"

"Not really. I asked him about the shoot, and he said pretty much the same thing you did, that Margaux was acting like a diva, yelling at everyone."

"Didn't he wonder why you were asking him about Margaux?"

"I told him that I had heard Margaux was a client. And he told me she'd been murdered. And I naturally asked him about that."

"He told you she'd been murdered?"

"He did. And then I asked him about the photo shoot."

"And he told you Margaux yelled at everyone."

"He did. And that she insulted Dionne. I was going to ask him more questions, but he said he had to get to another appointment. Though not before he dismissed what I was wearing and told me to make an appointment with him to go clothes shopping."

"Rather nervy of him."

Guin shrugged.

"That's his job."

"Insulting potential clients?"

"I admit, I was a bit miffed. I thought I looked nice. But my wardrobe could use a refresh."

"So, are you going to make an appointment?"

"I'm thinking about it. I have more questions for him."

"Can't you just email them?"

Guin gave her husband another look.

"I'd rather ask them in person. See how he reacts. I don't buy the fact that he never loses his temper."

"So, what? You're going to try to make him lose his temper? I don't know if that's such a good idea."

"I'm not planning on making him angry. I just want to see how he reacts to some questions."

"Just be careful, Guin."

"So why did you come see me?"

"I forget."

"Well, I need to do some work. So if you wouldn't mind?"

"I'm going."

He started to leave, but Guin stopped him.

"Aren't you forgetting something?"

"What?"

Guin tapped her cheek. Glen smiled and went over to her, kissing her on the mouth instead of her cheek.

"Mm," she said. "You better go or I won't get any work done."

"Would that be so bad?"

Guin shooed him out. Though as soon as he had gone, Guin realized she had never heard back from Eric. Had something happened to him? Glen hadn't said anything. Should she ask him if Eric was okay?

Guin sent Eric another text, asking if he was all right. He immediately wrote her back, apologizing for not getting back to her. He'd been insanely busy and had damaged his phone and had to get a new one. However, he had a few minutes now if she was free. Guin immediately called him.

"So, how can I help?" he said.

"Tell me about the shoot."

"What do you want to know?"

"How did Margaux seem to you?"

"Pretty on edge."

"On edge how?"

"You know, like, uptight about everything. Nothing anyone did was right. She was constantly rearranging things and getting into it with the stylists about how things should look."

"Did the stylists argue with her?"

"Not really. Margaux was the boss. But I don't think they were happy about being bossed around, especially Dionne. She was the product stylist. Margaux said some pretty racist things to her."

"Such as?"

"I heard her tell Dionne that she probably got where she was because of affirmative action, being a Black woman."

That was what Fabio had said.

"And how did Dionne respond to that? Did she tell Margaux off?"

"No. She didn't say anything, but she looked annoyed."

"I'd be annoyed too if someone said something like that to me. What about the other stylist, Fabio? Glen said Margaux laid into him and that he walked out at one point."

"Yeah. Margaux was pretty rough on him. She didn't like the clothes he'd brought and threw a dress at him, saying she'd rather be naked than wear it."

"Ouch."

"Yeah. I felt bad for the guy. But he didn't seem that fazed by Margaux's behavior."

"He didn't yell at her?"

"No, he kept his cool."

"Though Glen said he left the shoot."

"He probably just needed some space. He came back a few minutes later."

"Did Margaux yell at anyone else?"

"Her assistant, Ronnie. Margaux was pretty hard on her too. And she wasn't happy with Glen. Or with the basketball players. She said something to Jordan at one point that caused him to leave the studio."

"Jordan as in Ronnie's cousin, who plays for the Knicks."

"Yeah, him."

"Do you know what she said to him?"

"No. I wasn't close enough to hear. But I saw the look on his face. He did not look happy."

"So he walked out of the shoot?"

"Yeah, but he came back. No doubt because of Ronnie. She was really cool. I don't understand how someone like that could work for someone like Margaux. She kept trying to calm Margaux down, but that only seemed to rile Margaux. I felt bad for her."

Guin wondered if Eric might have a little crush on Margaux's attractive assistant, but she didn't say anything.

"And you said Margaux yelled at Glen."

"Oh yeah. Big time."

"Do you recall what she said to him?"

"I don't remember everything she said, but at one point she said she couldn't believe he was a professional photographer and that they had made a mistake hiring him."

Ouch.

"How did Glen react?"

"He was pretty cool considering. He told Margaux that

if she was unhappy with his work, he'd be happy to leave and she could hire someone else. But that made her furious. She said if he left, she'd sue Photog."

"She said that?"

"She did."

"And what did Glen say?"

"He didn't say anything."

"But he didn't hit her."

There was a long pause.

"Eric? You still there?"

"Yeah."

"Did Glen hit Margaux?"

"Not exactly."

"What happened? Did he hit Margaux after she threatened to sue Photog or not?"

"So, after Margaux yelled at him, Ronnie went to talk to Margaux. But whatever she said seemed to make Margaux angrier. Glen went over to them, I guess to tell Margaux to lay off Ronnie, and Margaux slapped him."

"She slapped him?" Glen hadn't mentioned that.

"Yeah. We were all pretty shocked."

"Did he hit her back?"

"No. But when she went to hit him again, he grabbed her wrists, and she started screaming at him to let her go. And he said he'd let her go as soon as she calmed down."

"Then what happened?"

"It was kind of weird. They stared at each other for several seconds, and then it was like Margaux deflated. One minute she was furious. The next she was calm, like all the fight had gone out of her, and she apologized."

"She apologized to Glen?"

"Yeah. Said she'd been under a lot of pressure and hadn't been sleeping. She actually apologized to all of us. It was a total one-eighty."

"Huh. When was this?"

"Near the end of the shoot."

"And were there any more outbursts after that?"

"No. It was pretty late at that point, and you could tell everyone was tired. And Glen said he had enough footage. So Margaux said everyone could go. Though she asked Glen if he would stay and show her the pictures."

"And he agreed."

"Yeah."

"Wasn't that unusual? Glen doesn't usually show clients raw files."

"I think he was worried about Margaux throwing a fit if he refused."

"So everyone left?"

"Yeah."

"Including you."

"I offered to stay and help with the equipment, but Glen told me to go."

"So you left."

"I did."

"And did everyone leave at the same time?"

"Pretty much."

"So you left the building together?"

"No. I stopped to use the bathroom."

"Where was the bathroom?"

"Down the hall from the studio."

"Did anyone else stop to use the bathroom?"

"Just Fabio."

"Did you see him leave?"

"No. I was done before him."

"So you didn't see anyone who was at the photo shoot actually leave the building?"

"No."

So Fabio or someone else from the shoot could have hidden out somewhere and then returned to the studio after Glen had left.

Then something else occurred to Guin.

"Did you see anyone else hanging out around the studio or on the third floor? I understand there was a party up on the roof, some musicians making music videos."

"Yeah, they were pretty loud. I saw some people in the stairwell, but I didn't see anyone hanging out outside the studio. Hey, sorry to not have gotten back to you sooner, but I need to go."

"That's okay. I just have one last question." Eric waited. "Do you think Glen killed Margaux?"

"No way! I haven't known Glen for that long, but I can't see him doing something like that. Glen's the most chill guy I know."

Guin smiled.

"Thank you, Eric."

CHAPTER 10

It was time for Guin to head downtown to meet with Dionne Davies. Dionne had texted Guin earlier to let her know her shoot, which was in SoHo, was running late and if Guin wanted to meet her there or reschedule. Guin wrote her back saying she'd meet Dionne at her shoot and asked for the address.

The shoot was in a loft on Mercer Street. Guin got there at five-thirty, just as things looked to be wrapping up. She saw Dionne speaking with two women, one of whom was holding a camera—no doubt the photographer—and the other Guin guessed was the client. While Guin waited for Dionne, she looked over at the set. It looked like someone's dining room, with the table set for a dinner party. Guin wondered who the client was.

Dionne finished up with the two women and came over to Guin.

"You Guin?"

"I am."

"Thanks for being flexible. I just need to grab my things and we can go."

"You don't need to help break down the set?"

"Not my job."

Dionne went to get her bag, which was large enough to fit a small child, and then ushered Guin out of the loft.

"You okay getting a drink? I don't know about you, but I could use one."

Guin hesitated. She didn't like to drink when she was working. Then again, this wasn't an official job, so she said sure.

Dionne led them to a French brasserie a couple of blocks away. Guin knew the place, though she hadn't been there in years. It was a popular watering hole, serving some of the best cocktails and fries—or *pommes frites*—in the city.

The place was busy, but there were two empty seats at the end of the bar. Dionne took one and immediately signaled to the bartender, asking him for an Aperol spritz. The bartender looked at Guin. Guin thought about ordering a club soda with lime but told him she'd have the same as Dionne.

"So," said Dionne, turning to Guin. "What do you want to know?"

"Why don't you start by telling me a bit about yourself, how you came to be a product stylist, and who you've worked with."

The bartender brought over their drinks and the women thanked him.

Dionne took a sip of hers.

"Best Aperol spritz this side of Italy."

"You've been to Italy?"

"Oh yeah. Florence, Rome, Milan, Venice. I love Italy. I keep telling my wife we should get a fixer-upper in Tuscany or someplace and retire there."

"Sounds nice," said Guin.

"Yeah," said Dionne. "But you wanted to know about my past, not my future." She took another sip of her drink and then told Guin her story, how she had worked at several magazines, making next to nothing as an assistant, before going to work for a product stylist and eventually going out on her own.

"And what made you decide to specialize in food and beverages?"

"I didn't have a lot of money when I started out, and I liked getting free food and booze. But I style other stuff too, not just food and beverages. Just not people. Or animals."

"Why not people or animals?"

"I prefer working with things that don't talk back or yap at you."

"Though your clients are people."

"True," said Dionne, taking another sip of her Aperol spritz.

"And I imagine some of them are difficult."

"I try not to work with the difficult ones."

"But how do you know if they're difficult if you haven't worked with them?"

"You hear things. Anyway, these days, I can pretty much pick and choose who I work with."

"That must be nice."

"It is. Though it took me a while to get there."

"Speaking of difficult clients, I understand you were hired to help with the Château Margaux Mocktails photo shoot."

"How do you know about that?"

"I interviewed Ronnie Banerjee for another article I'm working on and she mentioned you."

"Ronnie's all right."

"You know her from Diageo?"

"Yeah. We worked on a bunch of campaigns together. Still don't know why she left. Especially to go work for someone like Margaux Boucher."

"You didn't like Margaux?"

"I didn't like how she treated Ronnie."

"I heard she was a bit of a diva."

"More than a bit."

"I also heard she said some rather unkind things to you."

Dionne didn't say anything.

"Did that upset you?"

The stylist looked at Guin.

"Did what she say upset me? Sure. Had I heard that BS before? You bet. But I've learned to ignore it."

"I also heard she said some unkind things to the other people there."

"That woman had nothing nice to say to anyone. Like I said, I don't know why Ronnie put up with her. Why are you so interested in Margaux Boucher anyway?"

"I heard what happened to her."

"You mean someone killing her?"

"Yeah. How did you find out?"

"Ronnie phoned me. She was pretty freaked out."

Dionne drained her spritz and signaled to the bartender for another one.

"You want another?" she asked Guin.

"I'm good," she said. "Just a water," she told the bartender.

"And what did you think when Ronnie told you about Margaux?"

"Honestly?" Guin nodded. "That she had it coming."

Guin did her best not to look shocked.

"What makes you say that?"

"The way she was yelling at everyone, picking fights with people. Someone was bound to let her have it."

The bartender brought over their drinks, and Dionne immediately took a sip of hers.

"Do you think the photographer killed her?"

"I wouldn't have suspected him. He seemed pretty chill. Didn't seem that fazed by Margaux's constant nitpicking. And I give him props for defending Ronnie. But when I heard he and Margaux used to be married, it made sense. I would have bashed her skull in too if I had lived with her."

Again, Guin did her best to hide her surprise.

"Is that how she died, someone bashed her skull in?"

"Poetic license. I don't know how she died."

"So you think Margaux's ex killed her? It couldn't have

been someone else at the shoot or someone who wandered into the studio? I heard there was a big party up on the roof."

Dionne took a sip of her drink and looked thoughtful.

"If they hadn't arrested Glen, I would have thought Fabio or that kid had killed her."

"Why Fabio?"

"There was something going on with him and Margaux. I don't know what it was, but he had that look in his eyes when she yelled at him like one day he was going to let her have it."

"And when you say *kid*, who are you referring to?"

"Jordan, the kid who plays for the Knicks. He's Ronnie's cousin, and Ronnie told me he had anger management issues. Though he'd supposedly taken one of those anger management courses. Still, I saw the way he looked at Margaux when she yelled at him."

"And you think he could have killed her?"

Dionne shrugged.

"But the police arrested the photographer. Case closed."

Dionne took another sip of her drink and then turned to face Guin.

"Why are you so interested in who killed Margaux?"

"I covered crime at the newspaper I used to work at. I guess old habits die hard."

"You cover any murders?"

"A few. I even helped solve some."

"Huh. I've never solved one, but I like listening to those true crime podcasts and trying to figure out whodunit. You ever listen to them?"

"Not really."

Guin heard a phone ringing. It was Dionne's. She answered it and told whoever it was—her wife?—that she'd be home soon.

"I need to go," she told Guin after she'd put her phone back in her bag.

"Thanks for your time."

"No problem. You got this?" Dionne asked her, eyeing their drinks.

"Sure."

"Thanks. And let me know when your article will run."

"I will. Say, before you go, what's the best way to reach you in case I have more questions?"

"Shoot me a text. Though I'm pretty busy next week."

Dionne then picked up her bag and made her way out of the restaurant, leaving Guin to pay the bill.

Guin spent most of Saturday working, as did Glen. Then on Sunday they took the day off to have brunch with Sophie and her husband Warren at BethAnn's Kitchen.

They arrived to find Sophie and Warren already there, seated at a table sipping drinks.

"Are we late?" said Guin. She looked down at her watch. They were right on time.

"Not at all," said Sophie. "Warren and I just decided to take advantage of the kids being away and came a bit early to have a drink before you arrived. I hope you don't mind."

"Not at all," said Guin. She saw them looking at Glen and made introductions.

Sophie smiled up at Glen.

"So nice to meet you, Glen. Please, won't you two have a seat?"

Glen and Guin sat, and a minute later the server came over, asking if she could get them something to drink. Glen ordered a Bloody Mary, and Guin asked for a mimosa.

"So," said Sophie, addressing Glen. "Guin tells me you're responsible for Photog. Several of my friends have used the service and raved about it.

"I don't know if Guin told you," she continued, "but I used

to work at *Vogue*. And I'm curious, do you think Photog will change the way people hire photographers?"

"It already is," Glen replied.

They then proceeded to have a lively discussion about photography while Guin and Warren listened politely.

"But enough about photography," Sophie said several minutes later. "Guin, you must tell me what you've been up to. What was living on Sanibel like? I've never been."

Guin then told Sophie about her job as the general assignment reporter at the *Sanibel-Captiva Sun-Times*, the things she covered, and about looking for shells and the people she'd met on Sanibel.

"Sounds like paradise!" said Sophie. "You must miss it."

"I do. But I'm enjoying being back in the city and working for the *Times*. Though ask me again when winter sets in. So Warren," Guin said, turning to Sophie's husband. "I heard you got a big promotion. Are you still with the same firm?"

He said that he was, and Guin asked him about his projects. Then their server came over with their drinks and asked if they were ready to order. They said they needed a few minutes and picked up their menus. Though Guin and Sophie knew what they were having: the pumpkin waffles.

When brunch was over, Sophie told Guin that she and Glen had to come over for dinner and see the kids. Guin said that they would.

"Sophie and Warren seem nice," said Glen as they headed home.

"They are," said Guin. "I was stupid to let that friendship go."

"Well, now you can make up for lost time."

"Hey, would you mind taking a slight detour and walking home through the park? It's such a nice day, and I could use the exercise, especially after eating those pumpkin waffles."

Glen said he didn't mind at all, and they turned and headed to Fifth Avenue.

CHAPTER 11

Guin had still not heard from the basketball players or Aleksei Smirnov by late Monday morning, so she picked up her phone and called Ronnie. She hated to nag, but she was eager to speak to everyone who had been at the shoot before too much time went by.

Ronnie picked up after several rings but asked Guin if she could hold, not bothering to wait for Guin's reply. Guin was about to hang up when Ronnie finally came back on the line.

"Sorry about that," said Ronnie. "It's been an absolute zoo this morning."

"I understand. I'm just calling to see if you communicated with your cousin and Mr. Smirnov. I'm eager to speak with them—for my article."

"I did speak with them and gave them your information. They're all just so busy. I'll shoot them a text right now and tell them to get in touch with you."

"Thank you. I also had a few more questions for you."

"Can you text them to me? As I said, things are a bit crazy here this morning."

"I could stop by the office later."

"I appreciate that, but it'd be better if you just texted me your questions."

But Guin wanted to ask Ronnie her questions in person, so she could see how Ronnie reacted to them.

"I only need a few minutes. I'm going to be in Chelsea later, so it's no big deal," she lied.

Guin could hear Ronnie sigh.

"I'm getting a mani-pedi at one-thirty around the corner. If you really want to ask me whatever in person, you can meet me there."

"Perfect! I could actually use a mani-pedi myself. What's the name of your nail salon?"

"It's called Nails Plus."

"I'll meet you there at one-thirty."

Ronnie said she had to go and ended the call. Then Guin called the nail salon to see if she could get an appointment at one-thirty. As luck would have it, they were able to take her.

Guin was about to walk out the door to meet Ronnie when she received a text from a private number. It was Aleksei Smirnov. He apologized for not getting back to her but said that he could meet with her later that day if she was available.

Guin immediately wrote him back, asking him what time and where.

Smirnov suggested five p.m. at the office.

Guin asked if there was any way he could meet her a bit earlier, say at two-thirty or three. However, he was unavailable then. It was five or else they would need to pick another day.

Guin replied that she would meet him at the office of Mockingbird Beverages at five. She would just find someplace in Chelsea to camp out until it was time for their meeting.

Guin arrived at the nail salon a few minutes late, having encountered traffic on the way across town. She didn't see Ronnie and worried that she had canceled. Then Ronnie came through the door.

"What a day!" she said to Guin. "My phone has not stopped ringing. Speaking of…" She took it out, silenced it, and put it back in her bag. "Now I won't be disturbed."

Guin smiled at her. Then they both checked in, Guin asking if they could be seated next to each other.

They picked out colors, Guin taking a few minutes to choose, and then were seated in side-by-side pedicure chairs.

"So, what did you want to ask me?" Ronnie asked Guin as their feet soaked.

"It's about Margaux."

"What about her?"

"I keep thinking about who could have killed her."

Ronnie looked annoyed.

"The police have the killer. It was her ex, the photographer."

"I know. But I don't think he did it."

"Why not?"

"He just doesn't seem the type."

"You spoke with him?"

"I did. And he swore that Margaux was alive when he left, chatting on the phone with someone."

"He could have lied to you."

Guin was about to say that Glen would never lie to her, but she stopped herself. Instead, she told Ronnie that it didn't seem like he was lying.

"You were probably just taken in by his good looks."

"Isn't it possible that the police arrested the wrong person? I understand Margaux was being impossible, yelling at everyone that afternoon, and that a couple of people even walked out of the shoot."

"You're very well informed."

"I try to be. I also heard she was particularly tough on you."

"She was, but I understood. Château Margaux Mocktails meant everything to her. And after her last business failed, she felt she had something to prove. So everything had to be perfect."

"So you were okay with her behavior?"

"Of course not. I was appalled, and I tried to get Margaux to go easier on everyone. But as I said, I understood why she acted how she did. Anyway, I thought you wanted to ask me about Mockingbird Beverages. Why are you so obsessed with Margaux?"

Guin wanted to say that she wasn't obsessed with Margaux. Then again, maybe she was—or at least with finding out who really killed her.

"Sorry. As I think I told you, I used to cover crime, and this case intrigues me. It sounds like Margaux pissed off a lot of people that evening, and that maybe the wrong person was arrested."

"So who do you think killed Margaux, Ms. Former Crime Reporter?"

Guin knew sarcasm when she heard it.

"I don't know. Maybe it wasn't someone from the shoot but someone who wandered into the studio that evening, surprised Margaux, and wound up killing her. I heard there was a party for a rock band up on the roof with lots of people coming and going. Maybe one of them killed her."

"I guess that's possible," said Ronnie, though she didn't look convinced.

"Or it could have been someone from the shoot."

"Like who?"

"Well… like Fabio, for example."

"Fabio?" said Ronnie.

"I heard Margaux threw clothes at him and told him she'd rather be naked than wear the outfit he'd brought for her. I don't know about you, but that would make me pretty mad."

"Yeah, she made quite a scene. I didn't blame Fabio for walking out. But I can't see him killing her. He's known Margaux for years and is used to her moods. In any case, the police have their man."

"You mean Glen. You really think he killed her?"

"He had motive and opportunity."

Guin frowned. Time to change the subject.

"By the way, I'm meeting with Aleksei Smirnov later at Mockingbird Beverages. Thank you for arranging that."

"You're welcome."

"Will you be there?"

"I have an appointment."

"What can you tell me about him?"

"What do you want to know?"

"Do you two have a good relationship?"

"I would say so."

"And he's okay with you running the business?"

"More than okay. It was his idea. Frankly, I'm way more qualified than Margaux ever was." Which she had said to Guin before.

The nail technicians were almost done doing their toenails.

"I'm still waiting to hear from your cousin, Jordan. Is he still going to be a brand ambassador? And whose idea was it to sign him?"

"It was my idea. Margaux was looking for someone who would appeal to Millennials and Gen Zers, and I suggested Jordan."

"And who suggested giving him a piece of the business?"

"That was also my idea, though Margaux and I argued about how much to give him."

Their toenails were done. Time to move to the manicure stations.

Again, they were seated next to each other.

"Speaking of Jordan, I heard he walked out of the photo

shoot at one point. Something to do with something Margaux said to him."

"Who told you that? Was it Glen?"

"Does it matter? I read that Jordan had anger management issues and had been suspended a couple of games."

"That's all in the past. And if you must know, the reason Jordan briefly left the shoot was to avoid getting into it with Margaux. They taught him to do that in his anger management class."

"So Margaux did say something that upset him."

"Yes, but Jordan handled it—calmly."

"What about Jordan's friend, Shaq?"

"What about him?"

"What's he like?"

"Shaq's a total sweetie."

"He plays in the EuroLeague, yes?"

"He does, but he's hoping to get picked up by an NBA team. Personally, I'm hoping the Knicks sign him. He's a good influence on Jordan."

"Are you going to sign him to be a brand ambassador too?"

"I've discussed it with Aleksei, but he's not sure. Maybe if Shaq gets signed by an NBA team. But if he doesn't, we could always use him as a brand ambassador in Europe."

"Anyone else you're thinking of signing?"

"We have several people in mind. But I'm afraid I can't discuss it until we've signed contracts. I'm sure you understand."

Guin said that she did and decided she'd asked enough questions, at least for now.

CHAPTER 12

As the nail techs went to process their payments—before they applied nail polish to Guin and Ronnie's fingernails—Ronnie checked her phone.

"Everything all right?" Guin asked her, seeing Ronnie's frown.

"An issue with the bottles. Margaux insisted on using a custom size, so Château Margaux bottles would stand out on the shelf."

"That doesn't seem like such a bad idea."

"In theory, it isn't. But sourcing more bottles is proving to be a pain."

"Speaking of bottles… Why did you leave Diageo to go work for Margaux? Were you unhappy there?"

"I loved working at Diageo. I learned all about beverage marketing there."

"So why leave?"

"I liked the idea of working for a startup where I could be more involved in decision-making and help shape the brand. And mocktails are a category with lots of potential."

"That's true, but isn't there also a lot less job security working for a startup? And Margaux's previous business went bust after just a couple of years. Did you know about that when you went to work for her?"

"I knew about Margaux's athleisure business."

"And it didn't bother you that it went bankrupt?"

"Lots of entrepreneurs fail their first time out. What happened to Margaux could have happened to anyone inexperienced in running a business. But I believed in what Margaux and Aleksei wanted to accomplish with Mockingbird, and I doubted we would encounter the same issues."

"And did you get a sense regarding what working with Margaux would be like?"

Ronnie smiled. Or maybe it was a grimace.

"No. She was great during the interview, very enthusiastic about Château Margaux and eager to hear my ideas. It was only after I started working for her that I saw her other side."

"And were you ever tempted to quit, go back to Diageo?"

"I thought about it a couple of times. But I believed in the vision and wanted Mockingbird Beverages to be a success. I wasn't going to run back to Diageo just because my boss yelled at me a couple of times."

The nail techs had returned and were busy polishing Ronnie and Guin's fingernails.

"So, how's the rebranding going, other than issues with the bottles?" Guin asked Ronnie.

"Good. We're right on schedule."

"When do you anticipate rolling out?"

"We're planning a big New Year's Eve bash to introduce the world to Mockingbird Mocktails."

"Here in New York?"

"Yes, near Times Square. We want to give people an alternative to the usual drunken New Year's Eve parties."

"That's a great idea."

"I know. We've already gotten a bunch of athletes and celebrities to commit."

"Like who?"

"I can't name names just yet."

"Would you put me on the invite list? I think it would make a great story."

"Sure."

Their manicures finished, Guin and Ronnie headed to the nail drying stations.

"By the way," said Guin, after their nails had been drying for several minutes. "As I mentioned before, I still haven't heard from Jordan. Is he okay?"

"He's just busy."

"But you let him know that I wanted to speak with him."

"I did. I'll send him another text."

"I don't want you to mess up your nails."

"Don't worry," said Ronnie.

She gingerly retrieved her phone and spoke quietly into it.

A few minutes later, Guin heard Ronnie's phone ping. Ronnie tapped it.

"That was Jordan," she said a few seconds later.

"What did he say?"

"That he could meet you at his gym."

"When?"

"Now."

"Where's his gym?"

"Not far from here."

"Tell him I'll be there soon. What's the address?"

"I'll text it to you." Guin saw Ronnie typing. "You're all set," she said a few seconds later. "Just ring the buzzer and tell them who you are and that you're meeting Jordan Abara."

"Thank you."

"No problem. I should go."

They got up and left the nail salon together. As they stood outside, Guin noticed a liquor store across the street.

"Hey, Ronnie." Ronnie was looking down at her phone. "Did Margaux ever fall off the wagon?"

"Hm?"

"I asked if Margaux ever drank alcohol. That could explain her behavior at the shoot."

"Margaux and Aleksei made a promise to each other when they went into business: no booze. It was a deal-breaker."

"So Margaux was sober at the shoot."

"We told everyone there was no alcohol allowed."

Though that didn't answer Guin's question.

"What about drugs?"

"Drugs?"

"I'm just wondering if Margaux could have been on something. Her behavior seemed pretty outrageous for someone supposedly clean and sober."

Ronnie was looking down at her phone again.

"I have to go," she told Guin. Then she turned and walked away.

Jordan's gym was not your Planet Fitness or New York Sports Club. It was an exclusive gym for athletes and trainers and their well-heeled customers. However, you wouldn't know that from the street. The gym was housed in a nondescript building. If you didn't know it was there, you wouldn't. And to get to it, you had to be buzzed in.

Guin told the woman who answered the buzzer that she was there to meet with Jordan Abara. The woman then asked Guin for her name and, a few seconds later, let her in.

The gym was located on the second and third floors of the building, with the entrance on the third floor. There was an elevator, but Guin decided to take the stairs. The entrance, behind a glass door, was down the hall.

"Good afternoon," Guin said to the very fit-looking woman at the desk. "I'm here to see Jordan Abara. He's expecting me."

"Ms. Jones?"

Guin nodded.

"Would you mind letting me see your driver's license?"

"Sure," said Guin, reaching into her bag and withdrawing her wallet. "Here you go."

"Thank you," said the woman. She looked down at the license and then back at Guin. Then she handed the license back. "Mr. Abara will meet you at the juice bar. Just go through the curtain. You can't miss it."

"Is there a bathroom I could use?" Guin asked her.

"There's one in the women's changing room. Through the curtain to the right."

"Thank you."

Guin went through the curtain and found the women's changing room. It was pretty bare bones. Not what she expected. When she was done, she headed over to the juice bar, stopping to look out at the two-story fitness center.

She and Glen had been talking about joining a gym since moving back to New York. But they hadn't done anything about it, content with going for runs and walks in the park. However, she would talk to him again about joining a gym as when the cold weather and snow hit, they'd be less inclined to exercise outdoors. Assuming, that is, that they'd still be in New York come wintertime.

As Guin headed to the juice bar, she saw Jordan coming out of the men's locker room. She knew he was tall, but seeing him up close made her feel like a munchkin.

She smiled as she went to greet him.

"You must be Jordan," she said.

"And you must be Ms. Jones."

"Please, call me Guin. Thanks for meeting with me."

"Sure. Would you like a juice or a smoothie?"

"I'm good."

"You sure? They make the best smoothies and juice drinks."

"Are you going to have something?"

"I'm going to have a kale tonic."

"Is it good?" It didn't sound that good to Guin.

"I know, you hear *kale* and think, how good can it be? But it'll surprise you. You should try it."

"Fine. I'll have a kale tonic."

"Two kale tonics," he said to the woman behind the juice bar.

Guin reached for her wallet when the drinks were ready, but Jordan told her he had it. Guin protested, but he informed her that they didn't take outside money.

They took their kale tonics to a nearby table and sat.

"Ronnie said you wanted to talk to me about her mocktails."

"That's right," said Guin. "I understand Margaux Boucher wanted to hire you to be a brand ambassador."

Jordan nodded as he took a sip of his kale tonic.

"Are you going to do it?"

"I was planning on it."

"Even though Margaux's no longer with the company?"

"I was never doing it for Margaux. I was doing it for Ronnie."

"You two are close?"

"She's like a sister to me—an older, slightly annoying sister," he added with a smile.

Guin smiled back at him.

"I'm curious. You must get loads of offers. Why be a brand ambassador for a startup that no one's ever heard of? Was it just because of Ronnie?"

Jordan took another sip of his kale tonic before replying.

"I believe in the message."

"The message?"

"That you don't have to drink alcohol to have a good time. That's something important to me as a Muslim and an athlete."

"You don't drink alcohol?"

"Drinking alcohol is considered *haram*, forbidden, in Islam."

"Yet some Muslims drink it."

Jordan frowned.

"Have you tried Mockingbird's mocktails?"

"I have. I wouldn't agree to endorse anything I hadn't tried."

"And?"

"I liked them. They're good."

"So you feel comfortable promoting them."

"Like I said, I wouldn't promote something I didn't believe in."

"What about Margaux Boucher?"

"What about her?"

"Were you comfortable with the way she treated you? I understand she said some pretty harsh things to you at the photo shoot." Though Guin didn't know what Margaux had said to Jordan.

"Who told you about that? Was it Ronnie?"

"Does it matter? What did Margaux say to you?"

"Ronnie didn't tell you?"

"Not in so many words."

"I'd rather not discuss it."

Guin decided not to push.

"I understand you walked out at one point."

"I came back."

"Why?"

"I owed it to Ronnie. The shoot was important to her."

"But you had second thoughts about signing on to be their brand ambassador after that."

Jordan didn't say anything.

"But now that Ronnie's in charge, you're okay with being a brand ambassador."

Again, Jordan didn't say anything.

"Have you met Ronnie's new boss, Aleksei Smirnov?"

Jordan nodded as he took a sip of his kale tonic.

"What do you think of him?"

"He seems like a good guy."

"You ever go to one of his parties?"

"No. Though he invited me and Shaq to one this weekend."

"Shaq as in your friend who plays in the EuroLeague."

"For now. He's trying to land a spot here."

"With the Knicks?"

"With whoever'll sign him."

"He's a forward?"

"Yeah."

"And you guys were at UConn together?"

Another nod.

"Getting back to Mockingbird, can you tell me about the photo shoot?"

"I told you, I don't want to talk about it."

"I didn't mean why you walked out. I'm just curious to know if Margaux did or said anything to upset anyone else."

"Oh yeah. She was out of control: throwing things and hurling insults at people."

"Who did she throw things at?"

"That stylist, the one who brought all the clothes for us to wear. She threw a dress at him and told him she'd rather be naked. Like I said, she was crazy."

"And how did the stylist react when Margaux threw the dress?"

"He walked out."

"Did he come back?"

"Eventually."

"She throw things at anyone else?"

"No, but she hit that photographer."

"She hit him? What happened?"

"She was yelling at Ronnie, and the photographer tried to stop her. So she hit him."

"Margaux hit the photographer?" Jordan nodded. "Did he hit her back?"

"No, but I bet he wanted to. I would have hit her. But he just grabbed her wrists."

"Then what happened?"

"She calmed down."

"Did he threaten her?"

"Threaten her?"

"Threaten to kill her."

"Not that I heard. Though…"

"Yes?" said Guin, leaning forward.

"Margaux got this call during the shoot, and it sure made her angry."

"Who called her? Do you know?"

"I've no idea. But I heard her say, *don't you dare threaten me.*"

"You heard her say that? You're sure?"

"Pretty sure."

Jordan finished his kale tonic and looked down at his smartwatch.

"I've gotta go."

"Oh, okay. Thanks for taking the time to meet with me."

"No problem."

He got up and Guin followed suit.

"If I have more questions, what's the best way to reach you?"

"Talk to Ronnie."

"You don't have an email?" Guin doubted he'd give her his cell phone number.

"I do, but I don't check it that often. If you've got any more questions, just send them to Ronnie. She'll make sure I get them."

Guin wasn't so sure about that, but she would just have to trust Ronnie.

CHAPTER 13

Guin's meeting with Aleksei Smirnov wasn't for another hour. Not really enough time for her to go home. She thought about going to a coffee shop. Then she had a better idea. Her brother-in-law's art gallery was just a few blocks away. So she headed there.

Guin entered the gallery and looked around. She didn't see anyone at first. Then she spied a young woman seated at the desk in the back and went over to her.

"Excuse me," Guin said to the young woman. "Is Owen around?"

"He's in his office."

"Would you tell him Guin's here?"

"Is he expecting you?"

"No, but I'm his sister-in-law."

"Ah. I'll let him know."

The young woman disappeared, and Guin looked around. Owen's gallery specialized in contemporary art, not Guin's favorite. But she took a look around the gallery just the same. Owen usually showcased two or three artists at a time, doing several shows a year. However, on occasion, if an artist was popular enough, he'd give him or her a one-person show. Currently, Owen was showcasing the work of a photographer and a collage artist.

The photographer, a man named Bill Cermac, specialized in photographing musicians, mainly jazz musicians, in black and white. Guin liked his photographs and wondered how much Owen was selling them for.

She had started to look at the collage artist's work when Owen appeared.

"Guin! This is a pleasant surprise."

Guin turned to her brother-in-law and smiled.

"I happened to be in the neighborhood and thought I'd stop by."

"Welcome. Let me know if you have any questions."

"Actually… I was wondering how much that photograph over there was."

"The one of the three jazz musicians?"

Guin nodded.

"Let me check." Owen returned with a binder in his hand. "It's three thousand dollars."

"A thousand for each musician?"

Owen smiled.

"You interested?"

"You know Glen loves jazz. And it's a great photo. I was thinking it might make a nice birthday present. His birthday's next month."

"If you want it, I'll give you a deal."

"Thanks. I'll think about it and get back to you."

"Don't take too long. We've already sold several of Bill's photos, and the exhibit just opened."

Guin looked again at the photograph of the three musicians on the opposite wall.

"So, what do you think of Miriam Margolis's work?" Owen asked her. "I saw you looking at it."

Miriam Margolis was the collage artist.

Guin turned back to the collage she'd been looking at.

"They're… interesting."

"Interesting good or interesting bad?"

Owen knew Guin's feelings about contemporary art.

"Just interesting. I kind of like this piece and the one next to it. But I'm not sure about those two."

"Those are more recent pieces," said Owen, pointing to the two Guin said she didn't like. "These two are earlier works."

"I like the way she uses color in these two. The two over there are darker, both in mood and color."

"True."

"Where did you find them? Bill and Miriam, that is."

"I came across Bill's work in Paris. He's Czech but divides his time between Paris and Brooklyn. I saw a couple of his photos in a gallery over there and reached out to him. He had a small show in Brooklyn a few years back but nothing here since then."

"I really like his work. And Miriam?"

"Her family is from Belarus. They immigrated here when Miriam was a baby. Miriam grew up in the Bronx and then lived in Mexico for several years before moving to upstate New York. She did those colorful pieces you like when she was living in Mexico."

"Ah. And the dreary ones when she moved to upstate New York?"

Owen smiled.

"Correct."

"And how did you find her?"

"A friend put me onto her. She had a show last year at a gallery in Ithaca that got good reviews."

"And you were impressed enough with her work to give her a show here."

"I have a soft spot for artists who grew up or live here. Not enough galleries showcase local artists, in my opinion."

"Though you feature artists from around the world."

"I like to think I feature the best of both worlds."

Guin heard a cell phone ringing. It was Owen's. He pulled it out of his pocket and told Guin he needed to take the call, but he shouldn't be long. While Owen excused himself, Guin circled the gallery again. It wasn't that big, just three rooms, plus an office in the back.

Guin looked over at the young woman she had seen earlier. She was still seated at her desk, looking intently at something on her computer. Guin went over to her, and the young woman looked up.

"Hi," said Guin. "I didn't catch your name."

"I'm Daphne."

"Are you new? I don't think I've seen you here before."

"I just started."

"Well, welcome," said Guin. "Owen's a great guy. Though I may be a bit biased. And he always finds interesting artists to showcase."

"I know. I used to come here when I was in high school and dreamed of working here one day."

"Are you in college?"

Daphne smiled.

"I'm getting my MFA at SVA," which Guin knew stood for the School of Visual Arts.

"So you want to be an artist?"

Daphne nodded.

"And have my own gallery."

Guin mentally wished her good luck with that. She knew how hard it was to be a successful artist and run a successful gallery. She was about to say something to Daphne when Owen reappeared.

"Sorry, that was a client."

"No worries. Anyway, I have an appointment I need to get to."

"Business or personal?"

"A bit of both."

"Before you go, how's Glen doing?"

Guin had told her brother about Glen's arrest—and told him not to say anything to their parents. However, he had clearly told Owen. Guin just hoped that Owen was the only person Lance had told.

"Good. Better than I would be doing in the same circumstance."

"Has he found a good lawyer?"

Guin glanced over at Daphne. She seemed to be engrossed in whatever she was looking at on her screen, but Guin didn't want to discuss Glen's situation in front of her.

"Ah. Got it," said Owen. "Well, let me know if you need anything. You know Lance and I are here for the two of you."

"I know," said Guin. "Is he back from San Francisco?"

"He gets back Wednesday."

"Let's have dinner or brunch when he's back."

"Let's." Owen's phone was ringing again. He pulled it out and frowned. "I need to get this."

"No worries," said Guin. "I need to head out. See you and Lance soon!"

Owen headed back to his office and Guin turned to Daphne, who was still looking at her computer.

"It was nice chatting with you," Guin said. "Good luck with everything."

Daphne looked up and thanked Guin.

Before leaving the gallery, Guin took one last look at the photo of the three jazz musicians. Should she buy it for Glen? She stood staring at it for a few more seconds, decided that she would sleep on it, and left.

Guin took the elevator up to the twelfth floor and headed to Mockingbird's office. The door was unlocked, and she saw a man seated in one of the office chairs, his back to her. He was typing something on his phone. Guin waited for him to notice her, but he didn't seem to be aware she was there. Guin waited a minute and then cleared her throat to get his attention. He whirled around to face her.

"Hey! Ronnie didn't tell me Amy Adams would be paying us a visit!" he said with a smile.

Guin mentally rolled her eyes. Though it wasn't the first time someone had told her that she resembled the actress.

"Sorry to disappoint you, but I'm not Amy Adams."

"I know," said Smirnov, still smiling. "You're that reporter. Please, won't you have a seat?"

Guin sat.

"Ronnie said you wanted to include us in an article you were doing on new startups."

"That's right. My condolences, by the way. I heard about your partner."

"Thank you. Margaux will be greatly missed. Though, as I'm sure Ronnie told you, we're moving forward with the product launch despite what happened."

"She told me. And that you're changing the name of the mocktail line from Château Margaux to Mockingbird Mocktails."

"Correct. And did she tell you that we've inked deals with several restaurants and clubs to carry them?"

"She did not. I'm impressed. That was fast."

Smirnov smiled again.

"We've been busy."

"Ronnie said you were planning a big launch party for just before New Year's."

"That's right, but we're planning on supplying clients with our mocktails before then."

"Wow. New Year's Eve is just a couple of months away. Aren't you worried about getting everything done in time? You just started the rebranding process."

There was that sly smile again.

"Our suppliers have assured us that we should be a go by Thanksgiving."

"Wow," said Guin a second time. That seemed awfully quick.

"So, what can I tell you about Mockingbird?"

"Well, I guess my first question is: Why enter the zero-proof beverage business?"

"As Ronnie probably told you, Margaux and I met at AA and felt an immediate connection. Then, during one fateful meeting, several people talked about how being sober had killed their social lives, how they couldn't go to clubs or parties anymore because they couldn't drink.

"And Margaux mentions that she would just tell the bartender to make her whatever cocktail she wanted without the alcohol and just pretend it was the real thing—and how she'd give the drinks cute names, like a faux-jito instead of a mojito, or a mocktini instead of a martini. Everyone loved the idea. And I guess you could say, Mockingbird Beverages was born."

"So whose idea was it to actually create a line of mocktails, yours or Margaux's?"

"Both of ours. However, I was busy with my DJ business. So we decided Margaux would be in charge."

"You weren't at all concerned by her track record and the fact that she was a recovering alcoholic?"

"I'd be lying to you if I said I wasn't a little bit concerned. But that's why we hired Ronnie. I insisted we hire someone with premium beverage experience to help Margaux get the business up and running."

"How did you find her? Ronnie, that is."

"She answered an ad."

"And now that Margaux's gone, Ronnie's in charge?"

"Correct."

"About the name, was it Margaux's idea to call it Château Margaux Mocktails?"

"It was."

"And you weren't concerned about being sued by the Château Margaux wine estate in France?"

"Margaux said she'd handle it."

"Did she?"

"Apparently not."

"Is that why you decided to change the name?"

"One of the reasons."

"The other being Margaux's death?"

Smirnov was looking down at his phone.

"Do you think Margaux would have approved of the name change?"

"Hm?"

"I asked if you thought Margaux would be okay with the name change."

"She's dead so…"

"I'm curious, why weren't you at the photo shoot?"

"I was working."

"On a Tuesday afternoon?"

"I was preparing for a party that evening."

"All afternoon?"

"DJing is serious work. You think we DJs just wing it? No. At least not the good ones. There's a lot of preparation involved. Before I DJ a gig, I do a full run-through in my studio."

"Who was the party for?"

"I'm afraid I can't tell you that."

"Can you tell me where it was?"

"Sorry."

"Where's your studio? Is it close to here?"

Smirnov smiled at Guin.

"Are you interested in a tour? It's quite impressive."

"I'm sure. I was just wondering why you couldn't take time away from practicing to visit the photo shoot. I would think you'd want to be involved with something so important."

"I trusted Ronnie. She was my eyes and ears."

"So she reported what was going on?"

He was looking at his phone again.

"So you knew about Margaux's behavior."

"Hm?"

"I asked if Ronnie told you about Margaux's behavior, how Margaux was driving everyone crazy, trying to micromanage everything."

"That was just Margaux being Margaux."

"You weren't concerned? I heard people left the shoot."

"Just temporarily."

"And when did you hear about Margaux, that she had…" Guin searched for the right word.

"You mean that she'd been murdered?" Guin nodded. Though the police didn't know that Margaux had been murdered when they found her. "The next morning. Ronnie called me as soon as she heard."

"Do you know who found her?"

"The cleaning lady. She had come in to clean the studio that morning and found Margaux there, face down on the floor."

"Did she know Margaux was dead?"

"It was obvious."

"Was it the cleaner who called the police?"

"No, she went to tell the studio manager. He was the one who called."

"And was he the one who contacted Ronnie?"

"He was."

"And Ronnie phoned you as soon as she heard."

"She did."

"It must have been quite a shock."

"It was. Margaux and I had been through a lot together."

"You two ever date?"

"Me and Margaux? God no."

"Why not?"

"We were too much alike. I loved Margaux, but we would have killed each other."

"You ever fight?"

"Of course. But we always kissed and made up."

"So now that Margaux's gone, will you be taking a more active role in the business?"

"Perhaps. I still have my DJ business to run."

"You're not worried about the business floundering without Margaux there to guide it?"

"Ronnie's more than capable of handling things."

"You have a lot of confidence in her. But she's only one person."

"She's put her heart and soul, as well as her life savings, into Mockingbird. She wants more than anyone for it to succeed."

"She invested her life savings into the business?"

He nodded.

"So she owns a part of the business?"

"She does. Not as big a part as me and Margaux, but a percentage."

Guin wanted to ask him how big a part and what happened to Margaux's shares now that she was dead, but Smirnov's phone was vibrating across the table. He picked it up and told Guin he needed to wrap things up.

"I just had a few more questions."

"Send them to me," said Smirnov, looking down at his phone.

"How do I reach you?"

"Here," he said, handing her a card.

"Thanks," said Guin.

"I need to make a call," he told her. "I trust you can see yourself out?"

Guin thanked him for his time and left.

CHAPTER 14

Guin thought about her meeting with Aleksei Smirnov on her way home, replaying what he had told her. There was something about him that rubbed her the wrong way. He was so cocksure. Yes, he had answered her questions and seemed friendly. But his smile didn't seem genuine. And she didn't believe him about being too busy to stop by the shoot.

Guin was so lost in thought that she nearly missed her stop.

The cats were waiting for her when she got home. They seemed annoyed. Guin walked to the kitchen and saw that their food bowls were empty. While it was possible Glen had fed them, and that the cats had immediately devoured their food, she knew it was more likely Glen hadn't left his office and wasn't aware of what time it was.

She went to his office and knocked on the door. No response. She didn't hear anything, so she opened the door a crack and peered in. Glen was in front of his computer with headphones on, watching a jazz concert. Guin went over and tapped him on the shoulder.

He flinched but then smiled when he saw her.

"Busy working?" Guin teased.

"I was taking a break."

"Did you feed the cats?"

"No. Why? Was I supposed to?"

Guin sighed.

"I'll go feed them."

"Is something wrong?"

"No. I'm just a bit frustrated."

"About?"

"About who could have killed Margaux. Speaking of that, you reach out to any more defense attorneys?"

As far as Guin knew, he had only reached out to one of the lawyers on Tom's list.

"I did. I have an appointment with her tomorrow."

"You contacted Imani Williams?" That was the only woman on Tom's list.

"I did. I know you liked her."

"I just said that she had an impressive resume. What time is your appointment?"

"At noon. She had a last-minute cancellation."

"Great. I don't have anything going on tomorrow at noon."

"You don't have to go with me."

"I know I don't have to, but I'd like to meet her."

"Don't you trust me?"

"Of course I trust you! But this is a very important decision. This is the person who will be defending your life."

"That's a bit melodramatic."

"It's the truth. Let me come with you. I promise you won't even know I'm there."

Glen snorted.

"What?"

"Nothing. Just promise me you won't grill her."

"I wasn't planning on grilling her. Though, if she can't take being grilled by a reporter, she's not the person you want defending you."

"Why don't you wait and see if I like her first."

"I'm going with you."

Glen sighed.

"Fine. But it's my call regarding who's the best attorney to represent me."

"Of course."

Something was rubbing up against Guin's legs. It was Spot. As soon as he saw Guin looking down at him, he started to meow.

"I know," she said. "You're hungry. Let's go to the kitchen, and I'll feed you and Fauna."

She went to the kitchen, Spot and Glen following her. Fauna was waiting for them. Guin opened a cabinet and took out a can of wet food. Immediately, both cats began to meow. Guin divided the contents of the can between the two bowls and then gave the cats fresh water.

"Speaking of eating," said Glen as he watched the cats chow down, "what are we doing about dinner?"

"I don't know. I don't really feel like cooking."

"Neither do I."

"Shall we order in something?"

"I'd be fine getting a pizza and a salad."

Guin smiled. Glen was always good with getting a pizza and a salad. Though in Manhattan, you could get nearly anything you wanted delivered to your door, unlike on Sanibel.

"Where do you want to order the pizza from?" There was no shortage of pizza places within a few blocks of their apartment.

"Mariella's?"

"Grandma's or traditional?"

"Hm… Would you be okay getting a grandma's?" A grandma's was a rectangular Sicilian-style pizza.

"That's fine. A house salad or a Caesar's?"

"Either's fine."

Guin took out her phone to order.

"Hm, the app's saying forty-five minutes for delivery. You want to just go there?" Mariella's was only a few blocks away.

"Sure. I haven't been out of the house all day."

Guin tsked.

"You need to get out and walk. At least around the block. It's not good to sit all day. Actually, I've been thinking we should join a gym. It's going to be cold soon. And I doubt we'll want to run in the park when it's below fifty degrees."

"Would you go if we joined a gym?"

"If I liked the place, I would. Maybe we could go check out some gyms this weekend?"

"Maybe."

Guin insisted they go for a run the next morning, to work off some of the pizza and tiramisu they had eaten the night before. While they ran, Guin told Glen about her next assignment, which she was looking forward to researching. It was on the rise of specialty bookstores. And she had an appointment later that morning with the owner of a bookstore that specialized in romance novels.

"They only sell romance novels?"

"Yup."

"And they can make a living doing that?"

"I'll find out."

As soon as they got home, Guin went to take a shower. Then she fixed herself breakfast and scrolled through the paper on her phone as she ate. A little after nine, she headed to the bookstore, which was in Brooklyn. She'd meet Glen at Imani Williams's Midtown Manhattan office at noon.

Guin loved bookstores. When she was growing up on the Upper East Side of Manhattan, there was a little bookstore across the street from her apartment that she would visit at least once a week. Everyone at the bookstore knew Guin, and they would recommend books to her.

Years later, while she was off at college, she was devastated to hear that her little bookstore had closed. So Guin was thrilled to learn that indie bookstores were making a comeback.

Lover's Lane, however, was not your typical indie bookstore. In fact, the place looked more like a bordello, albeit a very fashionable one, than a bookstore. Guin loved it. And clearly customers did too according to the reviews.

Guin got there a little before her interview and was surprised to see several people—three women of varying ages and a young man—browsing the titles. She went to talk to them, explaining she was doing an article on specialty bookstores, and asked if they would be okay answering a few questions. One of the women begged off, but the other two and the young man were happy to chat with Guin.

When she was done speaking with them, she sought out the owner, who, it turned out, was the woman behind the cash register. As the owner was the only one working that morning, and couldn't leave the cash register or her customers unattended, Guin interviewed the woman at her post—and had to stop recording every time a customer came over to pay or to ask the owner a question.

By the time Guin was done with the interview, it was after eleven. Time for her to head to Imani Williams's office.

Guin took the train from Park Slope to Manhattan, arriving a little before noon. Glen was already there.

"How was the bookstore?" Glen asked her. "You buy any books?"

"Just one. The bookstore was great. I may have to go back. How were your calls?"

"Good! Photog just landed another corporate client!"

"That's great! Can you tell me who?"

"A real estate firm. They want someone to redo all their agents' headshots. If the photographer we send them does a good job, I'm hoping they'll hire us to do their listing photos too."

"I'm sure they will."

Just then a tall, well-dressed woman came over to them.

"Mr. Anderson?"

Guin recognized Imani Williams right away. Though her headshot didn't do her justice. Maybe, if Glen hired her, he could take a new headshot.

Glen smiled at the attorney.

"Ms. Williams, I presume?" Ms. Williams looked over at Guin. "Ah, yes. This is my wife, Guinivere Jones. She wanted to meet you."

"Ms. Jones."

"I hope you don't mind me tagging along," said Guin.

"Not at all. Come, I reserved a conference room."

The couple followed the attorney down the hall.

"I didn't realize she was so tall," Guin whispered to Glen.

Ms. Williams led them to a small conference room and asked if they'd like anything to drink.

"I'm good," said Glen.

"Me too," said Guin.

"Very well," said Ms. Williams. "Please, have a seat."

Glen took the seat next to the attorney, Guin on his other side.

"So, how can I help you?" said Ms. Williams.

CHAPTER 15

Glen told Imani Williams about Margaux and being arrested and asked if she could help him.

"Did you kill her?" she asked him.

"Of course not!" he replied. "She was alive when I left the studio."

Guin saw the attorney studying Glen.

"Tell me about this photo shoot."

As he spoke, Ms. Williams took notes on a legal pad, which Guin found old-fashioned but endearing.

"And then I left," he finished.

"And you didn't see anyone from the photo shoot outside the studio or hanging around the building?"

"I did not. But I was focused on getting out of there and getting home."

"What about other people? Did you see anyone on the third floor as you left?"

"I didn't see anyone, but I could hear people in the stairwell. And there were people in the elevator heading up to the roof. A band was shooting music videos up there."

"Did you happen to notice if there was a video camera in the elevator?" Guin asked him. She hadn't thought to ask about that before.

"I don't know."

Guin saw the attorney scribbling something.

"You said the police claimed your fingerprints were

found on the bottle by Ms. Boucher's body."

"That's right. But lots of people handled those bottles."

"Who specifically?"

"Pretty much everyone, until Margaux yelled at everyone to stop handling the bottles. She didn't want people to get their fingerprints on them. Though they had several backup bottles."

"So everyone handled the bottles, but the police only found your prints on the bottle they found next to Ms. Boucher's body?"

"That's what the detective led me to believe."

"Any idea why only your prints were on the bottle found next to Ms. Boucher?"

"None. As I said, several people handled the bottles."

"You ever hit your ex-wife when you were married to her?"

"Never!"

"You ever want to?"

Guin wondered what Imani Williams was driving at.

"I won't lie to you. I thought about it once or twice, but I never did. I would never hit a woman."

"What about a man?"

Glen didn't say anything.

"What time did you leave the studio?"

"Around eight-forty-five."

"And where did you go?"

"Straight home."

"What time did you get there?"

"A little after nine-thirty."

"Did you stop anywhere between the studio and home?"

"Just to get my car. I had parked it at a nearby garage."

"You drove to the studio?"

"I had camera equipment."

"And you drove straight home from the garage?"

"I did."

"And you parked where?"

"I have a space at a garage a couple of blocks away from the apartment we're renting."

"Do you have receipts showing when you left the first garage and arrived back at the other one?"

"I think I have the receipt from the garage by the studio building. But I wouldn't have one for the one by our apartment as I'm a monthly renter. However, you could call the garage. They probably logged in my SUV."

Guin watched as the attorney wrote.

When she was done writing, Ms. Williams asked Glen about the people at the shoot, to describe them and whether any of them had a reason, in his opinion, to harm Margaux. Glen gave descriptions of everyone who'd been there and told Ms. Williams some of the things he and/or Eric had overheard Margaux say to them.

"And don't forget about Fabio and Jordan walking out after Margaux yelled at them," said Guin.

The attorney looked over at her and made a note on her legal pad.

"How tall was your ex-wife?" Ms. Williams asked Glen.

"Around five-nine."

"And how much would you say she weighed?"

"I have no idea. She'd lost weight since the last time I saw her and she was thin to begin with."

Ms. Williams put down her pad.

"Do you have any questions for me?"

"Do you believe me?"

The attorney studied Glen, not saying anything for several seconds.

"Did you tell me the truth?"

"I did."

Ms. Williams continued to study Glen.

"I believe you. But I'm not the one you have to convince. If the case goes to trial, you'll have to convince a jury that you're innocent. And it won't be easy."

"But Glen didn't do it!" said Guin.

The attorney looked at her, and Guin felt her face grow warm.

"Will you help me?" Glen asked her.

"If you hire me, I'll do everything in my power to defend you."

"And how do you plan on doing that?" asked Guin.

"Our firm works with several private investigators who are experts at ferreting out the truth."

"So your private investigator will talk to everyone who was at the shoot?"

"As well as anyone who may have known about it and people who were at the Studios at Hudson Yards that evening."

"I've already interviewed several people who were at the shoot," said Guin. "None of them had nice things to say about Margaux."

"May I ask why you spoke with people who were at the shoot?"

"My wife's a reporter," said Glen. "And she was involved with several murder investigations back on Sanibel, where she used to live."

"I see. And did the people you spoke with know that you were Mr. Anderson's wife?"

"No. We don't have the same last name, and I told them I was interviewing them for different articles I was working on for the *New York Times*. I'm a stringer there."

"I appreciate you wanting to help," said Ms. Williams. "But I think we should leave the investigative work to the professionals."

Guin felt chastised, but she understood. Although she planned on continuing to investigate, professional investigator or not.

"So you believe you can get Glen off?"

The attorney looked at Glen.

"If what you've told me is the truth, yes, I believe I can. But know this: I require total honesty from my clients. If I find out you've lied to me, withheld important information or evidence, I'll drop the case."

"I understand," said Glen.

There was a knock at the door, and a young woman poked her head in.

"I'm sorry to disturb you, Ms. Williams, but there's an urgent call for you."

"I'll be right there." The young woman nodded and disappeared. Then Ms. Williams turned to Glen and Guin. "If you have any more questions, you know how to reach me." She then rose, and Glen and Guin did the same.

"Thank you for your time," said Glen.

Glen and Guin were both hungry after their meeting with the attorney, so they stopped to have lunch at a nearby café.

"So," said Guin as they waited for their food. "What did you think of Ms. Williams? How did she compare with the other attorney?"

"To be honest, I liked Bob Rutherford better. He was less intimidating."

"I didn't meet him, but I know what you mean about Ms. Williams. Does that mean you're going to go with Bob?"

"I haven't decided who I'm going to hire. I need to think about it."

"What was it about Bob that you liked?"

"He was more approachable. He made me feel comfortable, as though he was an old friend."

"And how does Tom know him?"

"They play pickleball together."

"Ah."

"And Ms. Williams?"

"A colleague of his recommended her."

"Did you talk to Tom about them? He have anything to say?"

"Just that they were both excellent attorneys."

"What about the other attorneys on his list? Did you reach out to them?"

"I did. The two others weren't able to take on my case right now."

"So it's down to Bob and Ms. Williams. Though I suppose we could look for more attorneys if you're not happy with either of them."

"I'm sure both of them would do a good job."

"So, who do you think you'll go with?"

"I told you, I need to think about it."

They headed home after lunch. Guin said she would go to the supermarket when they got off the subway and get something for dinner. And Glen promised to cook that weekend.

As Guin roamed the aisles of the grocery store, thinking about what to make for dinner, she kept thinking about their meeting with Imani Williams. Guin hadn't gotten the warm fuzzies from the attorney, but she liked the fact that Ms. Williams was no-nonsense and commanded respect. On the other hand, an attorney who was friendly and approachable might go over better with a jury.

Guin sighed and stared at the meat and poultry. What to get? She picked up an organic free-range chicken and a ribeye steak from a ranch that claimed to use humane, sustainable farming practices. Then she went in search of vegetables.

She was heading to check out when she swerved into the frozen food aisle and picked up a couple of containers of gelato.

When she got home, she put away the food and headed to her office. Tomorrow she would be visiting two more bookstores, one that specialized in children's books and another that specialized in history, both nonfiction and fiction. In the meantime, she would transcribe her interviews with the owner of Lover's Lane and the customers she had spoken with. She would also read up on Imani Williams and Bob Rutherford.

"Mm, what smells so good?" said Glen, stepping into the kitchen. "Are you roasting a chicken?"

Guin was always amazed by what a good sense of smell Glen had.

"I am."

"When will it be ready? I'm starving."

"It needs fifteen more minutes."

Glen went to the pantry.

"Don't snack," said Guin. "Dinner's almost ready."

"I was just going to get a cracker."

Guin sighed.

"Fine. Have a cracker."

"No, I'll wait."

"You want some wine? I opened a bottle of white. It's in the fridge."

Glen went to retrieve it.

"Can I pour you a glass?"

"Sure."

He got out two glasses and poured white wine into them.

"Here," he said, handing Guin a glass. "Did you make rice?" He was looking at a little pot on the stove.

"I did. And there's carrots, onions, and potatoes with the roast chicken."

"Mm."

"So, how did your calls go?"

"Fine."

"You talk to Raj?"

Glen spoke with Raj at least once a day, or so it seemed.

"I did."

"You tell him about Ms. Williams?"

"I did."

"And? Who does he think you should hire?"

"He told me to go with my gut."

"And what does your gut say?"

"That it wants roast chicken."

Guin shook her head.

"That was delicious," said Glen when they were done. "Thank you."

"You're welcome. I'm glad you liked it. And I got gelato for dessert. That is if you're not too full." Glen had had a second helping of chicken, rice, and vegetables.

"I always have room for gelato. What kind did you get?"

"Cappuccino chip and pistachio."

"Mm. I think I'll have a little bit of both."

"Let's clean up first."

"I'll clean. You have a seat."

"You sure?"

"Positive. You cooked. I should clean."

"Thank you."

Guin sat and watched as Glen cleaned. Not that there was that much to clean up. Guin was one of those cooks who cleaned as she went. But she appreciated her husband's willingness to clean and watched as he rinsed their plates, put them into the dishwasher, and then cleaned the roasting pan.

"I'll wipe down the counters after we've had some gelato," said Guin. "Shall I serve it up?"

"Please."

She scooped some gelato into two bowls and passed one, along with a spoon, to Glen.

"So," she said after they had had a few bites. "Now that you've been fed and have had time to think, which attorney are you leaning towards hiring?"

Glen swallowed a spoonful of gelato.

"My head says I should go with Imani, but my heart is saying Bob."

"Mm," said Guin, taking a bite of pistachio. "Tough one."

"Who do you think I should go with?"

"I didn't meet Bob, but I looked into him and Imani."

"And?"

"They both have impressive resumes and track records. But I'm leaning towards Imani."

"Really? I got the sense you didn't like her."

"I don't have to like her. I just got the feeling that she doesn't like to lose. And I liked that about her."

"I'm sure Bob doesn't like to lose either."

"I wish I could have met him."

"You were out when I Zoomed with him."

"You could have told me you were meeting with him."

Glen didn't say anything for several seconds.

"So you think I should hire Imani?"

"I do, but the decision is up to you."

They finished their gelato, and Glen put their bowls and spoons in the dishwasher.

"I need to wipe down the counters," said Guin. "Then you want to watch something?"

"What did you have in mind? No offense, but I'm not in the mood for one of your murder mysteries."

"I understand. What do you want to watch?"

"You pick."

"Just no mysteries."

They went into the living room, and Guin turned on the TV. But they couldn't agree on what to watch.

"I have a better idea," said Glen.

"What?"

"How about we act out a scene from one of your favorite romance novels?"

"Which one do you suggest?"

"You pick."

Guin grinned at her husband.

"I know just the one. Shall we go to the boudoir?"

"Lead the way."

CHAPTER 16

Guin spent the next day visiting bookstores and then typing up her notes. She was just finishing up when Glen knocked on her door.

"Yes?" she said, turning around.

"Do you have a minute?"

"What's up?"

"Do you have time tomorrow to meet with the private investigator?"

"Private investigator? Does this mean you hired an attorney?"

"I did."

"And? Which one did you hire?"

"Imani Williams."

"And here I thought you were going to go with Bob Rutherford. Why did you choose Ms. Williams?"

"I spoke with Tom about her and Bob this morning."

"And he suggested you go with her over his pickleball partner?"

"He didn't suggest anything. He said the decision was up to me and that both would do a good job."

"So why did you choose Ms. Williams?"

"I guess I liked that she asked a lot of questions, like someone else I know," he said, looking at his wife.

Guin smiled.

"Well, I have no doubt she'll do a good job. So, what do you know about this investigator of hers?"

"Not much. Just his name."

"Which is?"

"Adam Leong."

"How do you spell that?"

"L-E-O-N-G. Why?"

"Just curious. Is he from Singapore?"

"I don't know. Why?"

"I used to work with an Astrid Leong. Her family was from Singapore. And I know she had a brother. Though they're probably not related. Leong's probably a common Asian last name. Anyway... So, Ms. Williams's investigator wants to meet with us tomorrow—us as in you *and* me?"

"He didn't specifically say the two of us, but I thought you'd want to meet him."

"I do. Did he suggest a time?"

"No. He just asked if we were available tomorrow. I guess he wants to get the ball rolling."

"What time were you thinking?"

"I'm pretty busy tomorrow, so I was going to see if we could meet with him on the early side, say at eight or eight-thirty, or else late afternoon."

"First thing works for me. Where's his office? Or could we meet with him here?"

"I'll ask him."

"Do, and let me know what you decide."

"I will." Glen's smartwatch was flashing. "I have to go. I have a call."

"You still able to make dinner?"

"I was planning on it."

"Cause if you're too busy..."

"I said I would cook tonight."

"Okay, but if you get tied up..."

"Do you not want me to cook tonight?"

"I love when you cook. I just know how busy you are. And we have other options."

"Thank you, but I'm looking forward to cooking. It takes my mind off of work. Speaking of…"

"Go," said Guin.

He left Guin's office, and Guin immediately did a search online for Adam Leong.

"So, did you speak to the private investigator?" Guin asked Glen over dinner.

"I did."

"And?"

"He'll be here at eight-thirty tomorrow."

"Great. I'll be interested to hear his thoughts on the case. He has an interesting background."

Glen raised an eyebrow.

"What?" said Guin, taking a sip of wine.

"You looked into him?"

"Of course I did."

"And what did you find out?"

"First of all, I was right about him being from Singapore. I should ask if he's related to Astrid. Anyway, he went to college at the University of California–Irvine where he studied Criminology. Then he worked for the LAPD for a while before moving to New York and going into private practice."

"Interesting."

"I thought so."

"You learn anything else about him?"

"Just that he's good-looking and appears to be single."

"Hm. Should I be concerned?"

Guin smiled.

"Not at all."

"You want some dessert? We still have some gelato, and there's biscotti."

"I'm pretty full. Maybe just some herbal tea."

"I'll boil some water."

The doorbell rang at exactly eight-thirty the next morning. Guin liked that the private investigator was punctual. Glen was on a call with Raj, so Guin went to answer the door.

"Mr. Leong?" she said. Though she knew it was him.

"You must be Ms. Jones."

Guin nodded.

"Won't you come in?"

As soon as he stepped inside, the cats rushed over and began to sniff his legs.

"I hope you like cats," said Guin. But she could tell that he did as Leong was petting them.

"They probably smell Choo-Choo," he told her.

"Choo-Choo?" said Guin.

"My cat."

"Why did you name him Choo-Choo?"

"He's long and black and sounds a bit like a train."

Guin grinned. She could just picture Choo-Choo.

The private investigator straightened, and Guin saw that his legs were covered with cat fur.

"I have a lint roller."

"That's okay."

"You sure?" said Guin, looking at his pant legs.

Leong looked down.

"Maybe before I leave."

"No problem. Just remind me. Can I get you something to drink? Some coffee, or tea, or water?"

"Thank you, but I'm good."

Guin had led him into the living room, and they were about to sit when Glen appeared.

"Sorry to keep you," he said.

"Shall we all have a seat?" said Guin.

Glen and Guin took a seat on the couch. The private investigator sat in a nearby armchair, and Guin watched as he removed a tablet from his briefcase.

"Would it be better for you if we sat at the dining table, so you could type more easily?"

"Wherever you are more comfortable."

"Let's go sit at the table," said Guin, not wanting Leong to have to type in his lap.

They moved to the dining area, and Guin waited for the private investigator to say something. When he didn't, Glen asked him what he needed from them.

"Let's start with the victim, Margaux Boucher," said Leong. "What can you tell me about her?"

"What do you want to know? She was my ex-wife, as you probably know. And I hadn't heard from her in years—until she submitted a request on Photog to hire me to do her photo shoot."

"How long were the two of you married?"

"Five years. Though we dated for two years before that."

"And why did you divorce?"

"She was having an affair with her tennis instructor."

"Alex Morgan."

"So you know about him."

"Go on."

"There's not much else to say. Margaux told me she had met someone and wanted out of our marriage."

"And you agreed to give her a divorce?"

"Not at first. I suggested we go to couples counseling, but Margaux said it wouldn't help."

"Did that upset you?"

"It did. I wasn't a quitter. But Margaux was adamant. She wanted out. She didn't believe I could change. Said I'd become a workaholic, and she wasn't wrong. And although she could be difficult, I loved her."

"What do you mean by difficult?"

"Margaux was prone to mood swings. One day she was on top of the world, the next day she could barely get out of bed. She could also be anxious and quite combative."

"Was she bipolar?"

"I don't know. Looking back, she could have been. I wasn't around that much the last year or so of our marriage and just avoided her when she was in one of her moods."

"Did she ever see a therapist?"

"Tennis was her therapy. She spent hours at the club we belonged to. She always seemed to be in a better mood after being there."

And screwing the tennis pro, Guin said to herself.

"Did you ever fight?"

"Occasionally."

"Did you ever hit her?"

"No. Never."

"Did she ever hit you?"

Glen didn't say anything.

"Mr. Anderson?"

Glen sighed.

"Margaux would get worked up and would want to fight with me, but I'm not really a fighter. So to get my attention, she would hit me. I suppose to get a rise out of me."

"But you never hit her back?"

"No. Never."

"What else can you tell me about her?"

"She was beautiful. And smart. And she could make me laugh."

When she wasn't yelling at you and hitting you, Guin thought.

"And you say you hadn't heard from her between the time of your divorce and when she hired you for her photo shoot?"

"Correct."

"Any idea why she wanted to hire you?"

"According to her assistant, Ronnie Banerjee, Margaux had been making amends, or trying to, to the people she had hurt. It was part of her Twelve Step Program. Apparently, Margaux was an alcoholic."

"You didn't know?"

"I mean, I knew she drank, but not more than anyone else we knew. I didn't think she had a problem. But again, I wasn't around a whole lot the last year of our marriage. And then she launched her athleisure business."

"Which failed," Guin couldn't help adding.

"And why did you agree to do the photo shoot?"

"I thought it would be good for business. My company, Photog, has been trying to land corporate clients, do more commercial work, not just headshots and parties."

Guin watched as Adam Leong wrote on his tablet.

"And how did you feel about your husband working with his ex-wife?" the private investigator asked Guin when he was done.

"I didn't have a problem with it. A gig is a gig."

"Had you ever met Ms. Boucher?"

"No."

"Were you jealous of her?"

Guin regarded him.

"Not at all," she replied. "As I said, I didn't know her. But I know Glen. And I know he would never cheat on me."

The investigator turned back to Glen.

"Tell me about the photo shoot."

A little before nine-thirty, Glen's smartwatch started flashing.

"I need to go," he told Adam Leong. "I have a conference call."

"That's fine. I got what I needed for now. Though if you have a few minutes, Ms. Jones, I'd like to ask you a few questions."

"Sure," said Guin. She turned to Glen. "Go, do your

call." He hesitated. "Go!" she said. "I'll be fine."

Glen got up and headed to his office, glancing back at his wife and Adam Leong.

CHAPTER 17

"How long have you and Mr. Anderson been married?" the private investigator asked Guin.

"Six months now. But I've known Glen for around three years. We worked together at the *Sanibel-Captiva Sun-Times* in Southwest Florida before we started dating. And we rarely fight," she added.

"Ms. Williams said that you were a reporter."

"That's right. I'm a stringer for the *New York Times*. Before that, I was a general assignment reporter for the *San-Cap Sun-Times*. I covered everything, including crime. And I was a business reporter here in New York before that."

"I understand you interviewed several of the people who were at the photo shoot."

"That's right."

"May I ask why?"

"To find out who really killed Margaux."

"You think your husband is innocent."

"I *know* he's innocent. And it's not just because I'm married to him. Ask anyone who knows Glen. They'll tell you he doesn't have a violent bone in his body. He'd never hit someone over the head with a bottle."

"Even if provoked?"

"Even if provoked. Glen's one of the most zen people I know. Very little gets to him."

"I see. So you believe someone who was at the photo

shoot killed Ms. Boucher."

"That's the most logical assumption, even though everyone had supposedly left before Glen did. But you know what happens when you assume."

The investigator gave her a quizzical look.

"You make an *ass* out of *u* and *me*. Anyway, I wanted to speak with everyone who had been there and hear what they thought about Margaux, her behavior that evening."

"Who did you speak with?"

"Margaux's assistant, Ronnie Banerjee, who's currently running the company; Ronnie's cousin, Jordan Abara, who plays for the Knicks and has anger management issues—or had; the two stylists, Fabio Bertolini—he was Margaux's personal stylist—and Dionne Davies, the product stylist."

Guin watched as Leong wrote on his tablet.

"I also spoke with Margaux's partner, Aleksei Smirnov, though he wasn't at the shoot."

"And do you think one of them killed Ms. Boucher?"

"I don't know. If it was someone who was there, my main suspects would be Fabio and Jordan. They were both pretty upset after Margaux yelled at them. And I could see them snapping and hitting her with a bottle. Though Fabio claimed he never lost his temper, and Jordan said he'd learned to control his."

"What about the other basketball player?"

"Shaq? I haven't spoken with him. But I doubt he killed her."

"And why's that? Did she not yell at him?"

"She yelled at everyone. But everyone said that Shaq was a sweetie, very chill."

"Yet even the most chill people can snap if provoked."

True, thought Guin.

"You think Shaq could have killed her?"

"I think I need to speak with him and everyone else who was there."

"But I…" Guin stopped. "I'd love to come with you and watch you work."

"I work alone."

The investigator put his tablet back in his briefcase.

"No more questions for me?"

"No more questions."

"May I ask you a few questions?"

The investigator waited.

"I read that you were originally from Singapore. By any chance are you related to an Astrid Leong who lives here in New York?" Though Guin didn't know if Astrid still lived there.

"Leong is a common last name, at least in Singapore and Malaysia. And I'm not aware of any cousins named Astrid here in New York."

"Speaking of New York, what brought you here from LA?"

"Work. And now, Ms. Jones, I must go. I have another appointment."

"Of course. Before you go, would you like a lint roller? I have one in the living room. It'll only take a second."

Guin didn't wait for a reply, just got up to fetch the lint roller.

"Here," she said, handing it to him.

"Thank you."

As he removed the cat fur from his pants, Guin asked him if he had met with Detective Spinosa. Though that would have been awfully fast.

"I have an appointment to speak with Detective Spinosa this afternoon," he said, straightening and handing Guin the lint roller.

Guin took it and wished she could go with him, but she doubted he would let her. He had made it clear that he worked alone.

"When you talk to him, ask him about Margaux's phone."

"What about her phone?"

"Glen said that Margaux was on the phone when he left. So that would prove that he couldn't have killed her."

"Not necessarily."

Guin frowned.

"Anyway, will you let us know about her phone and what else you find out?"

"Ms. Williams will update you."

The private investigator headed to the door.

"Do you have a card?" Guin asked him.

The investigator removed his wallet and withdrew a card, handing it to Guin.

"Thank you," she said. "I'll let you know if I find out anything."

"I would prefer you let me handle the investigation from here."

"Of course," said Guin. "Thank you for meeting with us."

She opened the door for the investigator, closing it behind him. If he really thought she would just sit back and do nothing, he had another thing coming.

Guin sat in her office looking at Adam Leong's card. She would have liked to have attended his meeting with Detective Spinosa. She just hoped that he discovered something useful.

Guin stared at the investigator's card for a few more seconds and then put it in a drawer. She had work to do. She was in the middle of typing when Spot jumped on her desk and began to meow.

"What?" said Guin, looking at the big, mostly white cat.

"Meow!" repeated Spot.

"I already fed you," said Guin.

"Meow," said Spot.

"Do you want me to pet you?"

Spot butted her arm with his head.

"Fine," said Guin, scratching his chin.

Spot purred.

Guin petted him for another minute and then picked him up and placed him on the floor.

"I need to work," she told him. "Go play with Fauna."

Spot looked up at her and meowed, but Guin ignored him.

It was nearly one o'clock when Guin finished the first draft of her bookstore article. She messaged Glen to see if he wanted to join her for lunch in the kitchen. He said he would meet her there in five minutes.

Guin was poking around the refrigerator when Glen came in.

"What are you thinking of having?"

"I was thinking of making myself a grilled cheese. You want one?"

"Sure."

Guin took out bread, cheese, and butter.

"So, how did your talk with the investigator go?" Glen asked her as she melted butter in the cast-iron pan.

"Fine."

"What did he ask you?"

"He wanted to know about the two of us and the people I had interviewed, what I thought of them."

"What did you tell him?"

"I told him we were madly in love and that we never fought."

"That's not entirely true."

"You mean you're not madly in love with me?"

Glen smiled.

"That part is true. But you can't say we've never fought."

"It's not like we've had any knock-down-drag-out fights, more like disagreements."

"True."

"I didn't know Margaux hit you."

"Yes, well…" He seemed uncomfortable.

"It's okay. We don't have to talk about it. But it must have been hard being married to someone so volatile."

"She wasn't like that all the time."

Guin didn't say anything.

"She was clever, like you. And adventurous. And she had a great laugh."

"Did she have any siblings? What about close friends?"

"Why the sudden interest in Margaux?"

"Just curious, I guess. Here," she said, handing him a plate with grilled cheese.

"Thank you. Looks good."

"You want some water?"

"Sure."

Guin poured them each a glass of water and then sat down next to him.

"So, what did you think of Mr. Leong?" Guin asked her husband.

"He seemed a bit reserved. I couldn't really get a read on him."

"I thought the same thing."

"You didn't learn anything from your private chat?"

"Just that he's probably not related to Astrid."

"I meant about the case."

"Right. Just that he's meeting with Detective Spinosa later. I'd have loved to have gone with him, but he said he prefers to work alone."

Glen's smartwatch was flashing.

"You have another call?"

He nodded.

"In a few minutes."

"How was your call with Raj this morning?"

"Okay. He's really hot to open an LA office."

"So, let him. It's not like he expects you to run it."

"No, but I'd oversee it. And we're still trying to fix those bugs in the scheduling software."

"So, is he looking for someone to run it?"

"He's put out some feelers. But he's currently focused on getting the Paris office up and running."

"Hold up. Paris office? You didn't mention that Photog was opening a Paris office."

"I didn't?"

"I would have remembered that. I'd be down with moving to Paris if Raj needs someone to run the Paris office."

"You would?"

"Sure. I mean, I wouldn't want to live there forever, but for a year or two…"

"Good to know, but he already hired someone to oversee Paris."

"Oh well. So is Raj planning on expanding Photog across Europe and the US?"

"That's the plan."

"He's very ambitious."

"He is."

"And he's okay with you being in New York?"

"For now."

"What about your parents?"

"What about them?"

"I know you video chat with them, but don't you worry about them being in Florida and us being up here? We were only supposed to be here for six months."

"They like their assisted living place and have friends there. Besides, it's only a two-and-a-half-hour plane ride. And it's not like we'll be here forever."

"You sure about that?"

Glen's smartwatch was flashing again.

"I need to go," he said, downing the last bite of his sandwich. "Thanks for lunch."

He gave Guin a quick kiss and then headed to his office.

CHAPTER 18

Guin thought about going back over her bookstore article, but she would wait until tomorrow to do it. She also had a new assignment to tackle, but she wasn't in the mood to start it. She wondered if Adam Leong was meeting with Detective Spinosa right now. She thought about texting him, but she would wait. Instead, she decided to do a little digging into Margaux's past.

She tried to recall the name of Margaux's athleisure company and typed *Margaux Boucher athleisure company* into the search box. Immediately, Alex + Margaux popped up. Guin clicked on the link to the Alex + Margaux website, but the website had been taken down. However, there was no shortage of articles about the company and its feuding founders.

Guin started with an older article that raved about the company and had photographs of the photogenic co-owners. They looked happy and in love in the photos and talked about theirs being the perfect partnership. So what had gone wrong?

Guin continued to read about the business, how it had quickly taken off, its clothing worn by professional tennis players and other athletes as well as some celebrities. Then, less than two years in, there were rumors of financial trouble. Not long after came the lawsuits, with both partners accusing the other of mismanagement.

Finally, just two years after Alex + Margaux had debuted,

it declared bankruptcy. Guin searched for articles about the lawsuits. It seemed like they'd been settled, but she couldn't find much information. So what had happened to Margaux's partner, Alex Morgan? Did he still harbor bad feelings toward Margaux? And was he still in New York? Guin had read that he was British. Had he gone back to England?

She did a search for him. However, there appeared to be dozens, if not hundreds, of Alex Morgans out there. Guin narrowed her search, adding the words *tennis* and *New York*, though she had no idea if he still played tennis or lived in New York City. Still, it was worth a shot.

"This has to be him," she said, coming across an article about a country club in Bronxville, a wealthy suburb located just outside the city in Westchester, that had recently hired "world-renowned tennis pro Alex Morgan" to be its new Director of Tennis.

Guin clicked on the link. There was a picture with the article. It was definitely Morgan. So, did he live in Bronxville now? Not that Bronxville was that far from Manhattan. Morgan could have easily hopped a train to Grand Central and taken the subway or walked to the Studios at Hudson Yards, assuming he knew about Margaux's new business and the photo shoot.

But even if he did, was he still mad at Margaux, mad enough to seek her out and kill her? It had been two years since Alex + Margaux had blown up, and over a year since they had settled. Well, there was only one way to find out.

Guin picked up her phone and called the number for the country club, asking to be connected to the tennis pro shop. A few seconds later, a cheerful-sounding woman answered.

"Tennis pro shop! This is Tammy. How may I assist you?"

"Hi, Tammy," said Guin. "I'd like to speak with Alex Morgan. Is he available?"

"He's giving a lesson right now. Is there something I can

help you with? Are you looking to arrange a lesson with Alex? He's booked through the weekend, but he has a couple of openings next week."

"Actually, I'm a reporter. And I wanted to speak with him for an article I'm working on."

"Oh! I'm sure he'd be happy to speak with you. You want to give me your name and number? I'll give him the message when he's done with his lesson."

"That would be great." Guin gave Tammy her name, spelling it for her, along with her number.

"Got it! I'll be sure to give him the message."

"Thanks," said Guin.

She ended the call and put down her phone. Then she looked at the photo of Alex Morgan on her monitor. Could he be the killer?

Guin was eating dinner in the kitchen, Glen having gone out with some former colleagues, when her phone started ringing. She looked down at the caller ID. The number had a New York City area code, but she didn't recognize the number. She was going to let the call go to voicemail but decided at the last minute to pick up.

"This is Guin," she said.

"Guin Jones?" said a man with a British accent.

"That's right. Who is this, please?"

"This is Alex Morgan. Sorry to call so late. Been a bit of a crazy day. I received a message that you called."

"Yes. Thanks for ringing me. I was hoping we could arrange a time to chat in person. It's for an article I'm working on. By any chance do you have some time tomorrow or over the weekend? I'd be happy to come to your club." Though she needed to finish her bookstore article and get going on the new one.

"I'm a bit busy this weekend. However, let me check my schedule. Can you hold for a moment?"

"Sure."

He returned less than a minute later.

"Ah yes, I had a last-minute cancellation tomorrow at eleven. Would that work?"

Guin bit her lip. It would mean losing half a day of work, but she was eager to meet with Margaux's former partner.

"That's fine. Eleven tomorrow it is."

"What's the article about, by the way? Tammy didn't say."

"I'm doing a piece on where to play tennis in and around New York," Guin quickly made up.

"Ah. Though you know you have to be a member to play at our club."

"Not a problem," Guin lied. She hated to lie, but she couldn't tell him the truth. "I'll see you tomorrow at eleven."

"I look forward to it."

Guin finished her article on the specialty bookstores and sent it to her editor before heading to Grand Central Terminal to take the train to Bronxville. As she rode the train, she thought about what she would ask Morgan. She figured she'd start off asking him about his background, how he got into teaching tennis, and then segue to his business, the one he started with Margaux. Then she would casually ask him about Margaux.

Guin got off the train at Bronxville and thought about taking a cab to the club. However, the club was only a mile from the train station, and it was a beautiful early fall day. So she decided to walk, even though it might mean arriving at the club a few minutes late.

Guin had only been to Bronxville once, to have dinner

with friends of her ex-husband, Art. And that had been years ago. But the town was small, and, using her phone, Guin was able to guide herself to the club.

She arrived at the tennis pro shop a couple of minutes after eleven and went over to the young woman behind the desk. Could this be Tammy?

"Good morning," Guin said to the young woman, smiling at her. "I'm here to see Alex Morgan."

"The women's locker room is in the clubhouse," said the young woman, noticing that Guin wasn't dressed for tennis. "You can change there."

"I'm not here for a lesson. I'm here to interview Mr. Morgan."

"Oh, you must be that reporter! Alex said to expect you. He's running a few minutes late. You can wait for him over there or you can wait in the clubhouse."

Guin glanced out the large window that looked onto the tennis courts. She recognized Morgan right away. He was in his early forties with wavy dark brown hair and was quite fit.

"Okay if I watch?"

"If you like."

Guin went over to the window and watched as Morgan hit balls to a woman who looked to be in her sixties. She wasn't bad. A few minutes later, the lesson was over, and Morgan and his client came into the pro shop.

"Same time next week, Mrs. Jensen?" said the young woman.

"I'll be away next week," Mrs. Jensen replied. "Put me in for the week after."

"Will do."

"Thank you, Tamara."

"No problem, Mrs. Jensen."

Mrs. Jensen left the pro shop, and Morgan came over to Guin.

"You must be Ms. Jones," he said, smiling at Guin.

Guin thought he had a rather nice smile.

"And you must be Mr. Morgan," said Guin, smiling back at him.

"Please, it's Alex. Do you mind giving me a minute to freshen up?"

"Actually, I could use a bathroom myself."

"Let's go to the clubhouse." He turned to Tammy. "If my twelve o'clock shows up early, tell her I'm in a meeting."

Tammy nodded, and Morgan led Guin to the clubhouse.

"The ladies' locker room is just over there. Shall we meet here when we're done?"

"Sounds good."

Guin emerged from the ladies' locker room a couple of minutes later and waited for Morgan. He emerged from the men's locker room shortly after.

"Let's go have a seat in the bar and grab a drink," he suggested. "I'm parched."

Guin followed him to the bar.

Morgan smiled at the bartender.

"I'll have a club soda with a splash of cranberry juice and a touch of mint, Frank. And for you, Ms. Jones?"

"That sounds tasty. Make it two."

"Shall we have a seat? Frank will bring the drinks over."

Morgan led them to a table for two.

"So, how can I help you?"

"Well, as I said, I'm doing research for a story."

"On tennis clubs."

Guin had prepared a list of questions to make Morgan think she was doing an article on tennis clubs, but she suddenly felt guilty about lying to him. Something about the way he was looking at her.

"Actually…" she began. She was interrupted by Frank. He placed their drinks on the table and asked if they needed anything else.

"I'm good," said Morgan. "Ms. Jones?"

"I'm good."

Frank left, and they took a sip of their drinks.

"Mm," said Guin. "This is good. What do you call it?"

"I don't think it has a name. I made it up."

Guin took another sip.

"You were about to say something before we were interrupted," said Morgan.

"Right. I'm afraid I wasn't honest with you, Mr. Morgan."

"Oh?"

"I am a reporter. But I'm actually looking into the death of Margaux Boucher."

"Oh."

"I understand the two of you were quite close at one time."

"We were."

"And that you were in business together."

"We were."

"And that the business failed."

Morgan took a sip of his drink before speaking.

"What is it you want to know, Ms. Jones?"

"Tell me about your relationship with Ms. Boucher."

"My professional one or my personal one?"

"Your professional relationship." Though Guin was curious about their personal relationship too.

"It was bumpy."

"Bumpy?"

"Margaux was a perfectionist. Everything had to be a certain way, and it cost us a good deal of money and good will."

"What do you mean?"

"If Margaux wasn't satisfied with an order, she would refuse it or refuse to pay. She also changed suppliers several times. And don't get me started on how she treated the poor interns."

"So she was difficult."

"Very."

"Did that go for your personal relationship too?"

He smiled.

"I don't think Margaux had any complaints in that department. I knew what she liked and how to please her."

Guin could believe that.

"Getting back to your professional relationship, I read that Margaux accused you of financial mismanagement."

"You mean she accused me of embezzlement." Guin didn't say anything. "I did nothing illegal or improper. I was just trying to save the business from her mismanagement."

"What do you mean?"

"I mean that Margaux had good taste and ideas, but she wasn't very good with money. Correction: She was very good at spending it, not so good at managing it. So I set up a separate account to keep her from spending all of our money."

"And she accused you of embezzling."

"I did tell her what I was doing."

"And yet the business still declared bankruptcy."

"It was unfortunate, but there was really no other choice."

"Why didn't you two hire a CFO or someone to manage the financial side of things?"

"We had talked about it, but it would have cost money, money we didn't have to spend initially. And we foolishly thought we could manage everything ourselves."

"How much money did the business lose?"

"I don't remember."

"And did you have investors?"

"That was the worst part. I had convinced several of my clients from my former club to invest in the business."

"What about Margaux? Did she bring in any investors?"

"Just one: her stylist, Fabio."

"Fabio Bertolini?"

"You know him?"

"We've met. How much did he put in?"

"I don't remember. Maybe fifty?"

"Fifty thousand?"

He nodded.

That seemed like a lot for a stylist.

"And how much did you and Margaux put in?"

"We each put in a hundred thousand."

That was a lot of money, especially for a tennis pro. Though maybe Morgan came from money. Had Margaux? She would ask Glen.

"Were Fabio and the other investors angry when the business failed?"

"They were furious. It's why I had to leave my last club."

"Were you angry too?"

"Of course I was. I had put my heart and soul into the business. I didn't want it to fail."

"Is that why you sued Margaux?"

"She sued me first."

"But you blamed Margaux for the collapse of the business."

"I did. But I came to realize it was likely both of our faults. We were naïve thinking we could do everything ourselves."

"So you settled."

"We did. We both realized that the only people making money from the lawsuits were the lawyers."

"And had you spoken to Margaux since you settled the lawsuits?"

"We spoke regularly."

"You did? She wasn't angry at you for the way things ended?"

"We forgave each other."

"And did you know about her new business?"

"You mean Château Margaux Mocktails?"

Guin nodded.

"What did she tell you about it?"

"Just that she had started the business with a friend from AA and was very excited about it."

"That was it?"

"I don't think there was a lot to say."

"Did she tell you about the photo shoot?"

"Photo shoot?"

"For Château Margaux Mocktails."

"I don't think so." He looked down at his watch. "I need to go. I have a lesson."

"One last question," said Guin. "Do you know of anyone who might have wanted to harm Margaux, perhaps a disgruntled investor?"

Morgan looked thoughtful.

"Everyone was pretty angry when Alex and Margaux failed. But all of the investors I had recruited were well off and eventually moved on. The only one who was really hurt by the bankruptcy was Fabio. He wasn't rich like the others."

Interesting, thought Guin. *So why had Fabio continued to work with Margaux after losing so much money with her? Had she paid him back or offered him a piece of the new business?* She would ask him—or maybe Ronnie knew.

"I really must go," said Morgan, getting up.

"Thank you for your time."

He paused.

"Just so you know, I was quite upset when I heard about Margaux. We had our squabbles, but we had kissed and made up. She didn't deserve to die like that."

Guin studied his face as he spoke. He seemed sincere, but Guin couldn't shake the niggling feeling that he wasn't telling her the truth.

CHAPTER 19

Guin thought about her conversation with Alex Morgan on the train ride back to Grand Central. Had he told her the truth? Had he and Margaux really kissed and made up?

Guin took out her phone to check her messages. There was nothing important. She sent a text to Ronnie, saying she wanted to speak with her. Guin wanted to know what, if anything, Margaux's assistant knew about her boss's former partner.

And what about Fabio? He hadn't mentioned lending Margaux money. Had Margaux paid him back? Or maybe she had offered him a piece of the new business. Again, something to ask Ronnie. Or she could just ask Fabio.

Guin found his number in her contacts and sent him a text.

"Been thinking about what you said the other day and would love to go shopping with you. Let me know when you can slot me in." Then she remembered he had said she could schedule an appointment on the website. Well, she would do that if he didn't get back to her.

He wrote back a short time later, saying the first slot he had available was Tuesday morning at ten.

"Nothing sooner?" Guin replied. She didn't want to wait until Tuesday to speak to him.

"No," he texted, adding that he only had that slot because of a cancellation.

Guin sighed.

"Tuesday at ten it is. Thank you."

It was probably just as well. She needed to get going on the new piece she'd been assigned, about a stationery shop on the Upper East Side that was about to celebrate its 75th anniversary. While stationery stores had once proliferated around New York City, most of them had since closed. Yet this one had not only stayed open but had thrived. And over the years, it had counted many members of New York's elite as its customers.

Guin knew the shop, having walked by it dozens of times on her way to and from school. She had purchased notebooks, pens, and stickers there. It was also where her mother got her stationery. Or used to.

Guin hadn't visited the place in years and had no idea who currently owned or managed it. Time to pay a visit.

She exited the train and was trying to decide what to do. Should she go home or go to the stationery store? As she was deciding, her stomach let out a low growl. It was after one, and Grand Central had lots of good food options. After looking around, Guin bought herself a California roast turkey sandwich on whole grain bread and a bottle of sparkling water. Then she found a free table and took a seat.

She was scrolling through Instagram when she stopped on a photo recently posted on Smirnov's DJ Smirnoff page. She had followed him to see if she could figure out where he had DJed the evening of the shoot. He had posted a few pictures from what Guin assumed was the private party, but there was no location tag on the photos, and none of the people were tagged either.

The new photo was similar to his other photos: Smirnov DJing at some party, surrounded by happy partygoers or mugging with a celebrity friend. Guin typically had no idea who the people in the photos were, but she recognized the woman in this photo. It was Ronnie Banerjee. They looked like they were at a club, and the caption read, "Celebrating with one of my favorite people!" In the photo, Smirnov was giving Ronnie a big kiss on the cheek.

The next photo showed Smirnov with Ronnie, Jordan, and Shaq holding up a bottle of—was that a Château Margaux Mocktail bottle? Guin couldn't read the label. So, had Smirnov signed Jordan to become a Mockingbird Beverages brand ambassador? And what exactly was Smirnov's relationship with Ronnie? Was it more than professional? Then again, Smirnov often posted photos of attractive women kissing him or vice versa.

Guin checked her phone to see if Ronnie had replied to her text. She hadn't.

Guin finished her sandwich and threw the paper wrapper and the empty water bottle in a recycling bin. Then she headed to the subway.

Guin got off at West 23rd Street and walked to the building that housed Mockingbird Beverages's office. As she pressed the button for the elevator, Guin knew that there was a good chance Ronnie might not be there or would be too busy to speak with her. But she was already there. May as well go see if Ronnie was in.

The elevator finally arrived, and Guin pressed 12. She got out and headed to Mockingbird's office. She peered through the glass door and saw Ronnie speaking on her phone, pacing. Guin knocked on the door to get Ronnie's attention. Ronnie ignored her. Guin knocked again. This time Ronnie turned around.

She frowned when she saw Guin but came over.

"Yes?" she said through the door.

"We need to talk," said Guin. "It's important. May I come in?"

"I'm a bit busy. Send me a text."

"I promise not to take up too much of your time."

Ronnie sighed.

"Give me a few."

"Could I wait inside?"

"The door's open."

Guin let herself in and watched as Ronnie went to the back of the office to continue her conversation. Guin wondered who she was talking to.

Five minutes later, Ronnie returned.

"I only have a minute," she told Guin. "What's so important?"

"What do you know about Alex Morgan, Margaux's former partner?"

Ronnie made a face, as though she smelled something nasty.

"You ever meet him?"

"I have. He came to the office, demanding to see Margaux."

"Did Margaux invite him?"

"No."

"Why did he want to see her?"

"He wanted a piece of the business."

"You mean Mockingbird Beverages?"

"He felt Margaux owed it to him after bankrupting their previous business. Those were his words, not mine."

"So I take it Margaux wasn't happy to see him."

"Actually, she was, at first. She thought he had come to congratulate her on the new business."

"But that wasn't the case."

"As I said, he was looking to get a piece of Mockingbird."

"He told Margaux that?"

"Not at first. He made her think he was there to wish her well and get back together with her. He invited her to have lunch, and she foolishly went with him."

"What happened?"

"She came back in one of her moods. I'm pretty sure she

slept with him and that he then tried to sweet-talk her into giving him a share of the business. In any case, she was furious when she got back to the office."

"I take it she didn't offer him a piece of the business."

"Hardly."

"And when was this?"

"I don't know, two or three weeks ago?"

"So not long before the photo shoot. Did he know about it, the photo shoot, that is?"

"I don't know. It's possible she told him about it. Why?"

"Maybe he's the one who killed her."

"But he wasn't at the shoot."

"He could have come to the studio building, waited until everyone had left, snuck in, and then got into it with her."

"I don't know. I'm not a fan of Morgan's, but that seems unlikely. Besides, the police have Margaux's killer."

"You still think Glen did it, even though he defended you?"

"I'm not saying I didn't appreciate Glen standing up for me, but he was the only one who had motive and opportunity." Ronnie's phone was ringing, and she told Guin she needed to answer it.

"Please," said Guin. "I just had a couple more quick questions. I promise they won't take long."

"Make it quick."

Guin took out her phone and pulled up DJ Smirnoff's Instagram feed, going to the night of the photo shoot.

"Do you know where these photos were taken?" she asked Ronnie, holding up her phone.

"At a private party."

"I realize that. But do you know where the party was?"

"Some yacht over by Chelsea Piers. Look, I have to get on a call."

"Just one last question. Did Fabio invest any money in Mockingbird, or did Margaux offer to give him a share of the business?"

"Why do you ask?"

"I understand Fabio invested a lot of money in Margaux's previous business, the one that went belly up. Yet he still worked with her. Why is that?"

"You'd have to ask him. Look, I have to go. I trust you can see yourself out?"

She then turned and headed to the back of the office.

Instead of going home, Guin decided to pay a visit to the stationery store. The schools in the area were just letting out, and there were a half-dozen or so girls dressed in uniforms in the shop. Guin smiled at the sight. It reminded her of when she was that age.

She went over to the counter, where a man who looked to be in his seventies was ringing up a woman and her daughter. Guin waited for the man to finish and then asked if the manager was in. The cashier said that the manager was in the back.

It wasn't a large store. Or maybe it seemed small because of how much merchandise there was. There were shelves full of notebooks, others full of writing implements, a stationery section, a greeting card section, and even a section with hostess gifts. Guin found her way to the back of the store where there was a door with a sign that said Employees Only. Guin knocked on it. No answer. She knocked again and then opened the door a crack.

There was a casually dressed man, about half the age of the cashier, seated at a desk. He was staring at a computer screen and wearing what looked like noise-canceling headphones.

Guin knocked again, a bit louder this time. That seemed to get the man's attention. He turned and looked at Guin.

"Yes?" he said.

"Are you the manager?"

"What?" he said. Then he realized he had headphones on and removed them.

Guin smiled.

"I asked if you were the manager."

"I am. Can I help you?"

"I'm here to do a story about your store, its seventy-fifth anniversary. I'm with the *New York Times*."

"Oh!" said the man. "Please, come in."

Guin stepped inside, but she didn't see a place to sit as the one chair in the small office had boxes and catalogs on it.

"Sorry about the mess," said the manager. "I'm in the middle of a purchase order and have been going through samples. You can put that stuff on the floor." Though there wasn't much available floor space.

"I realize I should have called or written first," said Guin, still standing. "But I found myself in the neighborhood and thought I'd just stop by. If you're busy, I can come back another time."

"Now's just as good a time as any. Please, have a seat, Ms. ...?"

"Jones, Guinivere Jones. Though you can call me Guin. As I said, I write for the *Times*, and my editor asked me to do a piece on your store's seventy-fifth anniversary."

"Here," said the man, getting up and removing the boxes from the chair. "Please, have a seat."

Guin sat.

"It's funny," she said, glancing around. "I used to visit your store when I was a girl. Bought my notebooks, pens, and stickers here—and my first box of stationery. Being here brings back so many fond memories."

The manager smiled.

"Many people feel that way."

"I'm sorry, I didn't catch your name."

"It's Jason, Jason Abelman."

"Nice to meet you, Jason. And how long have you been running Madison Stationers?"

"Going on two years now. My father and mother technically own the store, but they moved to Florida last year."

"And they wanted to keep it in the family?"

"They did. My brother had no interest in the stationery business, so…"

"Had you worked here before becoming the manager?"

"I worked here as a kid and during summers when I was in college. It was required. And much as I loved the old place, I never imagined I'd be running it when I got my law degree."

"You're a lawyer?"

"I am."

"And you gave that up to manage the store?"

"More like I'm on an extended sabbatical," he said with a smile.

"What kind of law do you practice?"

"Mainly contract law. To be honest, I was feeling a bit burnt out when my parents approached me about taking over the store. I thought being here would be less stressful."

"And has it been?"

"Not really. But it's a different kind of stress. And, as you said, being here brings back fond memories."

"You said your brother didn't want to be involved in the family business. What does he do?"

"He's a doctor. Which is the next best thing to managing the family business, according to my parents."

He said it with a smile, and Guin smiled back at him.

"So, how have you managed to keep the business going for seventy-five years? Most stationery stores around the city have closed. Do people still buy stationery?"

"You'd be surprised. And we don't just sell stationery. We have pens, paper, cards, stickers, even hostess gifts."

"And who shops here? Is it mainly women of a certain age and students?"

"We get all sorts of people here. Though, as you surmised, it's mainly women of a certain age and students."

"People who live on the Upper East Side?"

"People who live around here, but we have customers from all over the world. We created an ecommerce site around ten years ago now. It was my idea. And today it accounts for about half of our business."

Guin hadn't known that.

"And to what do you attribute your success?"

"Several things. Our inventory is one thing. We stock items that customers can't get anywhere else. Also, there's the shop itself. It's an outlier, a bit of old New York. People look in the window and find themselves walking through the door and then buying something they had no intention of buying."

Guin could easily imagine that. Actually, she didn't have to imagine it. She had been one of those people.

"We also pride ourselves on making our customers feel like part of the family. By the way, that's my uncle up front, working the cash register. He's retired, but he works here a couple days a week. Says it keeps him young. Though I know it's probably to keep an eye on me."

Guin smiled at that.

"Was it your family who started the business?"

Jason nodded.

"It was my great-grandfather and his brother. They fought in World War Two and opened this shop shortly after the war. It's been in the family ever since."

"And has a member of your family always worked here?"

Another nod.

"We've hired people outside the family to help out over the years. But everyone in the family was required to spend some time here, even if it was only during a school vacation.

Of course, when we used to sell candy, us kids happily volunteered to help out."

Guin smiled again.

"So, any special plans for the seventy-fifth anniversary?"

"We're having a small party for long-time customers and some of our vendors. We'll also have some specials. Nothing big or flashy though. We're just grateful to still be here."

"Have you ever thought of moving?"

"We nearly did a couple of times, but in the end we stayed put. This location is special. We have women who come in and tell us that they used to go to school around here and bought their supplies from us or their first box of stationery."

"I'm one of those women. I used to come here as a girl. And I'm pretty sure my mother still gets her stationery from you."

"What's your mother's name? Is it Jones?"

"No, it's Martin, Carol Martin."

Jason turned to his computer and began to type.

"Ah, we have an order for her."

"For stationery?"

He nodded.

"I was about to call her and tell her it was in."

Guin's mother was one of the few people Guin knew who still wrote thank-you notes and letters to friends.

"Speaking of my mother, did you invite her to the party?" She hadn't mentioned anything. Though why would she have?

"Let me check." Jason returned to his computer. "She's on the list, but she wrote to say that she couldn't attend."

"Oh. When's the party?"

"Next weekend."

"Ah. Would it be okay if I go in her stead? I'd love to chat with some of your customers. Will your parents be there?"

"They will. And you're welcome to attend." He opened a drawer and rummaged inside. "Here's an invitation."

Guin looked at it. The party was being held at a nearby restaurant from six to eight the following Saturday.

"Thank you. I don't think I have anything that evening. May I bring my husband? He's a photographer. He could take pictures of the event."

"He's welcome to attend, but he doesn't need to take pictures."

"Great. I'll let you know if we can come. Do you have a card?"

Jason opened the drawer again and handed Guin a business card.

"Thank you." Guin then reached into her bag and withdrew one of hers. "And here's mine."

He looked at it and then put it down.

"Well, it was nice to meet you, Guinivere."

"And you, Jason. I'll probably have some more questions for you. Okay if I email you?"

"Sounds good."

"And I'll let you know about the party."

Guin toured the store before leaving, stopping in the greeting card section. She picked up a couple of birthday cards as well as a couple of blank note cards. You never knew when you might need a card. She also picked up a calligraphy pen.

There was no one waiting in line at the cashier, so Guin figured she'd ask Jason's uncle a couple of questions.

"Hi there," she said to him.

"Hello yourself," he replied.

"I'm doing an article on the store's seventy-fifth anniversary, and I'd love to ask you a few questions if that's all right."

"Ask away."

"When did you start working here?"

"When I was a kid. Everyone was required to work here back then."

"So you'd work here after school?"

"And on weekends and school vacations."

"What about during college?"

"During college too."

"And after?"

"After I went into advertising."

"So you didn't work at the store?"

"No, I got a job at an advertising agency."

"Why did you decide to come back?"

"Retirement wasn't all it was cracked up to be. And I missed the place."

"So you work here a couple of days a week?"

"That's right."

"And what do you think of Jason, of the job he's doing?"

"Asher—that's my brother—is lucky to have him. Jason's a good boy, very conscientious."

"You think he's doing a good job?"

"He's breathed new life into the old place."

Guin noticed that there was a woman behind her waiting to pay.

"Sorry," Guin said to her. "I'm almost done." Then she turned back to Jason's uncle. "Could you ring these up?"

He took the cards and the calligraphy pen and rang them up, placing them in a little brown bag.

"Thanks," Guin said as she handed him some money. "I'm sorry, but I didn't catch your name."

"It's Sam, Sam Abelman."

"Nice to meet you, Sam. I'm Guin."

"Nice to meet you, Guin."

He handed Guin her change, and she thanked him and left.

CHAPTER 20

Guin went straight to her office when she got home, eager to put down her thoughts on her meetings with Alex Morgan, Ronnie, and Jason Abelman. She was busy typing when she heard a knock on her door.

"Come in!" she called, not turning around.

"Are you busy?" said Glen.

"Just give me a sec." Guin finished the sentence she was typing and turned around. "Yes?"

"I just received a call from Imani's office. They expect to receive the information from the DA's office Monday."

"That's great."

"And she wanted to know if I could meet with her Tuesday afternoon."

"And you are telling me this because…?"

"I thought you'd want to go with me."

"I thought you didn't want me involved."

"I didn't say that. I said I didn't want you investigating. So, are you free Tuesday afternoon?"

"I have something Tuesday morning, but I don't have anything currently scheduled for that afternoon. Just let me know when."

"Will do." He peered over at Guin's computer. "Who's Jason Abelman?"

"He runs Madison Stationers. They're celebrating their seventy-fifth anniversary."

"Wow. That's impressive. You don't see a lot of stationery stores anymore."

"I know. They're having a party to celebrate next Saturday, and I'd like us to go."

"Where's the party?"

"At a restaurant near the store, not far from here. You free?"

"I think so, but let me check. What time is the party?"

"It's from six to eight. I thought you could bring your camera, maybe take some photos?"

Glen raised his eyebrows.

"I thought maybe if you took some photos at the party and they liked them, maybe they'd hire you or Photog to take pictures of their store. They have an ecommerce site too. You did say you wanted more corporate clients."

Glen shook his head.

"What?" said Guin.

"You should be in PR."

"I've thought about it."

"Maybe we should hire you."

"Doesn't Raj have someone doing PR for Photog?"

"Not here. I was supposed to hire someone, but I've been so busy. You want the job?"

"Thanks, but no thanks. I don't know if us working together is a good idea."

"We worked together at the paper."

"Yes, but you weren't my boss then."

"Anyway, think about it." Glen's smartwatch was flashing. "Gotta go."

"Before you go, what do you want to do about dinner? Should we just order something?"

"Sure."

After a long walk with Glen in Central Park early Saturday morning, Guin spent the rest of the morning working on her piece about Madison Stationers, sending Jason a few follow-up questions along with her and Glen's RSVP for the party the following Saturday. However, her mind kept straying to Margaux's murder. What did the DA have on Glen? So far, the evidence against him appeared to be purely circumstantial. She sighed, frustrated that they would have to wait until Tuesday to find out.

She pulled up her notes on Alex Morgan. Where had he been the night of the murder? She needed to speak with him again and ask him—and if he had, indeed, asked Margaux for a piece of her mocktail business.

Guin picked up her phone and realized she had neglected to get his number or an email address, so she called the club and asked for the tennis pro shop. A man answered the phone and said that Mr. Morgan was giving a lesson. So Guin left a message, asking that he call her when he was free.

Sunday, she and Glen had brunch with Owen and Lance. Guin had forgotten, while living on Sanibel, how much New Yorkers loved to do Sunday brunch. Not that people didn't do brunch in Southwest Florida, but in New York it was a ritual.

They were meeting Lance and Owen at a brunch spot they'd been wanting to try in Gramercy Park, which was roughly halfway between their two places. There was a line, of course, the restaurant not taking reservations. But, fortunately, it wasn't cold out, and they only had to wait 20 minutes or so.

As they waited for their drinks, Lance asked Glen how he was doing. Glen said that he was trying not to think about the case, but that he and Guin were meeting with the attorney Tuesday. Then Guin asked her brother about San Francisco. After that, the conversation turned to Owen's current exhibit, which reminded Guin to ask him in private about the photograph of the jazz musicians, if it was still available.

An hour later, they were back outside, saying their goodbyes.

"Let us know how your meeting with the attorney goes," Lance said to Glen.

Guin sighed. She hadn't thought once about the meeting the last half an hour or so. But now she would likely obsess about it.

"You okay?" Lance asked her.

"I'm fine. Just nervous."

"You and Glen are going to be fine."

"I know we will, but that's not what I'm worried about."

He gave her a hug and whispered in her ear.

"Try not to worry."

Easier said than done.

Guin hadn't heard from Alex Morgan over the weekend, so she phoned the club again Monday morning. However, when she asked for him at the tennis pro shop, Tammy told her that he wasn't there.

"Will he be in tomorrow?"

"He's supposed to be. Is this regarding a lesson?"

"No, it's about my article," said Guin. "I'm the reporter who was there Friday, and I had some follow-up questions for him."

"I can give him a message."

"I left a message for him Saturday, but he didn't get back to me. Can you just give me his phone number or email?"

"Sorry. It's against club policy to give out employees' personal information."

"I understand." Though Guin was mentally kicking herself for not getting Morgan's contact information when she met with him. "Could you tell him that I called and give him my number?"

"Sure."

"While I have you on the phone, could I ask you a few questions?"

"What sort of questions?"

"What do people at the club think of Mr. Morgan?"

"What do people here think of him?"

"Do they like him? Is he popular with members?"

"Oh, yes! His clients love him. He's usually booked up weeks in advance."

"Has he ever dated any of his clients?"

"Has he dated them?"

"Yes."

"He's not supposed to," Tammy said slowly.

Which Guin sensed meant that he had.

"I need to go," said Tammy. "I'll tell Alex that you called."

Before Guin could say another word, Tammy had hung up.

Guin stared out the window. However, there wasn't much to see. Her office looked out onto another brick apartment building. She wondered how much a director of tennis at a Westchester club made, and if he was hurting financially from the failure of Alex + Margaux. Was that why he had asked Margaux for a piece of her new business?

Well, she would just have to wait to find out. In the meantime, she had some questions for Fabio.

It was Tuesday morning, and Fabio would be arriving any minute. He had wanted to view Guin's wardrobe and learn more about her before they went shopping. However, when Guin had said that was fine, she had forgotten about Glen.

Fabio didn't know that Glen was her husband. At least she didn't think he did. And she wanted to keep it that way. So she had asked Glen to make himself scarce between ten and eleven. She had also hidden all of the pictures of the two of them.

It was now a quarter past ten, and there was no sign of or word from the stylist. Was he blowing her off? Guin was about to text him when the doorbell rang.

"Fabio!" she said, opening the door. "You made it!"

"Traffic was beastly," he said, stepping inside.

"Did you take the bus?"

Fabio sniffed.

"Please. I took a car service." He glanced around. "Are you renting or do you own this place?"

"We're renting."

Just then the cats came over, and Spot started rubbing himself against Fabio's black pants.

"You have cats."

"I do," said Guin.

"You didn't mention them."

"Are they a problem?"

Fabio was scowling.

Guin picked up Spot.

"Sorry. He has a thing for men and black pants. I have a lint roller."

Fabio continued to scowl.

"Shall we go see my clothes?"

Guin led Fabio to the bedroom, putting Spot down before closing the door.

"My closet's over here," she told Fabio.

She opened the closet door and turned on the light. Glen had graciously given her the bigger closet, a walk-in, but bigger was relative. Neither of the two bedroom closets was very large.

"Hm," said Fabio, eyeing Guin's clothes.

Guin suddenly felt insecure. Were her clothes that bad?

She had spent half an hour that morning tidying her closet and organizing it. She had also dressed nicer than she usually would. Though that was in part because she and Glen would be going to the lawyer's office that afternoon.

Fabio turned to her.

"Is this everything?"

"I left some of my more casual, warm-weather clothes back in Florida," she said. "And I have t-shirts and jeans and some other things in a chest of drawers."

"Show me what you normally wear to interview people."

"That depends."

"What do you mean?"

"It depends on who I'm interviewing and where."

"Just show me some typical outfits."

Guin's brain momentarily froze, trying to think what she typically wore to interview people. Then she slowly reached for a dress, even though she rarely wore dresses to interviews, unless she was interviewing a CEO.

"Hm," said Fabio. "Yet you were dressed quite casually when you met with me."

"That was different."

"Why?"

"I was meeting you at a coffee shop. Look, to be honest, I don't usually dress up for interviews. Unless I'm interviewing a CEO or someone very important. But I always look professional."

"That's a matter of opinion. And what do you wear when you go out with your husband?"

"My husband? How do you know I'm married?"

Fabio looked down at Guin's left hand.

"Right. Well, to answer your question, it depends on where we're going."

"And your husband doesn't mind the way you dress?"

"He likes it. He's always telling me that I look beautiful no matter what I wear."

That was one of the things Guin loved about Glen. But there was that *hm* from Fabio again, as though he didn't approve of such behavior.

"Well, I can see I have my work cut out for me."

"How bad is it?"

"You need a whole new wardrobe."

"I do? I don't know if I can afford an entire new wardrobe."

"Well, at least some new work attire and something for when you go out at night."

"I told you, I mainly work from home. And it's not like my husband and I dine at four-star restaurants."

"I understand. But you want to make a good impression when you venture out, yes?"

"I suppose."

"Trust me, Guinivere, when I'm done with you, you'll thank me. So, shall we set a date?"

"A date?"

"To go shopping."

"Uh, sure?"

Fabio took out his phone and started scrolling.

"I'm rather busy this week, but I could do next Friday at ten."

"You're booked until next Friday?"

"It's possible I could have a cancellation, but it's unlikely."

Guin had no idea what she would be doing the following Friday.

"Can I get back to you?"

"Fine," he replied. "But don't take too long."

CHAPTER 21

Fabio announced that he needed to go.

"Would you like to use a lint roller?" Guin said, noticing the white fur on his black pants.

Fabio frowned.

Guin hurried over to her nightstand and retrieved the lint roller.

"Here," she said, offering it to him.

He sighed and took it. As he removed the cat hair from his pants, Guin asked him if he often suggested clients purchase a new wardrobe.

"No," he replied.

Great, thought Guin. Just what she wanted to hear.

"So what do you typically advise clients to purchase?"

"It depends. Some of my clients have been out of the workforce for years and are looking for a new work wardrobe. Others are looking for something for a special event. And then there are those who realize they need a new look but don't know where to start," he said, looking at Guin.

"What about Margaux? What was she looking for?"

"It constantly changed."

"Was it hard to shop for her?"

"It could be. But I enjoyed a challenge."

"You said before that you worked for her athleisure business. What exactly did you do there?"

"I was a consultant."

"Meaning?"

"She consulted with me on fabrics and designs."

"Did she take your advice?"

"When it suited her. And now, Ms. Jones, I really must go," he said, handing Guin the lint roller.

Guin followed him out of the bedroom.

"I heard that you invested quite a bit of money in Margaux's athleisure business. And that you were furious when the company declared bankruptcy."

Fabio stopped and turned to face her.

"Who told you that?"

"Alex Morgan, Margaux's former partner."

At the mention of Morgan's name, Fabio scowled.

"I wouldn't believe a word that comes out of that man's mouth."

"Why not?"

"Alex Morgan is a scoundrel. He seduced Margaux and a lot of other lonely women with that faux British charm of his and then stole from them."

Guin was going to say that Morgan's charm may have been put on but that he really was British. However, she held her tongue.

"You believe he stole from Margaux?"

"He's the reason the business failed."

"Margaux wasn't at fault too?"

"Margaux's fault lay in her trusting that man."

"So you weren't angry with her?"

"I was angry with her for being so naïve."

"Did Margaux offer you a piece of her new business, perhaps as a way of paying you back?"

"She did."

"So she gave you a share of Mockingbird Beverages?"

Fabio frowned.

"She was planning to."

"But?"

"She died before we could sign the official paperwork. And now, Ms. Jones, I must take my leave. I have another appointment."

"Thank you for coming over. I'll let you know about next Friday."

Guin opened the door for him and then quickly shut it after he left so the cats wouldn't run out.

A minute later, Glen emerged from his office.

"Is he gone?" he asked Guin.

"He is."

"How did it go?"

"Not great. Fabio said I needed a whole new wardrobe."

"A whole new wardrobe? Why? What's wrong with your current wardrobe?"

"He doesn't think I dress professionally enough. And he thinks I need to look more glamorous when we go out at night."

"Did you tell him that you mainly work from home and that we rarely go out to eat at fancy restaurants?"

"I did. But he has a point, Glen. I haven't really updated my wardrobe in years. It was different on Sanibel. No one dressed up there. But this is New York. And I should dress up a bit more, at least when I go do interviews and go out to eat."

"If you say so. But I think you look just fine."

"Thank you."

"What else?"

"What do you mean, what else?"

"I mean I doubt the only reason you met with Fabio was to discuss your wardrobe."

"I may have asked him about Margaux's athleisure business and if she had offered him a share of her new business."

"And?"

"He blamed Alex Morgan for the collapse of the athleisure

business, and said that Margaux had offered him a share of the new business."

"Why would Margaux have offered him a piece of Mockingbird?

"Fabio had invested a lot of money in Margaux's athleisure business, which, as you may know, went belly up."

"So?"

"I guess this was her way of paying him back."

"So she gave him a share of the business?"

"She was going to."

"Going to?"

"She died before they signed the paperwork."

"You look skeptical. You don't think Margaux was going to give him a piece of the business?"

"I don't know. From what you and the others said, she wasn't treating him like a potential partner. I should ask Ronnie about it. She would probably know. Though…"

"What? I know that look."

"What if Margaux promised Fabio a piece of the mocktail business and then reneged on her offer or was dragging her feet? Maybe Fabio wanted to have it out with her or she told him they'd discuss it after the shoot. So Fabio waits until everyone has left and returns to the studio to talk to Margaux. But Margaux doesn't want to discuss it with him or she tells him she's changed her mind. Fabio snaps and hits her over the head with a mocktail bottle."

"I don't know, Guin. It sounds a bit far-fetched to me."

"But not impossible. Hey, do you know if Margaux had a will?"

"I don't. Why?"

"You never discussed what would happen if one of you died?"

"It never came up. We were both young and in good health. And we didn't have any children."

"Did Margaux have money?"

"What do you mean?"

"I know she didn't work when she was married to you, but she had money to start Alex and Margaux. Did that money come from the divorce or did she have family money?"

"Margaux had a trust fund. Though I don't know how much was in it."

"You didn't ever discuss finances?"

"Not in depth. We had a joint account, which we both contributed to, but otherwise we were free to spend our money however we liked."

"What about after the divorce? Did you have to pay her alimony?"

"We had a prenup. Margaux had insisted. We sold the apartment and agreed to split the proceeds. And I let Margaux keep the furniture and artwork, all of which she had picked out anyway."

Guin thought that was very generous of Glen, but she didn't say anything.

"So as far as you know, she didn't have a will."

"I didn't say that. She may have. But if she did, I would imagine she'd have updated it after the divorce."

"Good point."

"Why are you interested in whether Margaux had a will or not?"

"I'm just wondering who benefitted from her death—and who got her shares in the business. It could be a motive."

"A motive?"

"For murder."

CHAPTER 22

At one-thirty, Glen and Guin headed downtown to meet with Imani Williams. Guin had done some more digging into both Alex Morgan, who hadn't called her back, and Fabio, but she hadn't come up with any new information or anything incriminating about either one of them. Hopefully, Ms. Williams's investigator had.

"Ms. Williams will be with you shortly," the receptionist informed Guin and Glen.

A few minutes later, the young woman they had seen poke her head into the conference room at their last meeting appeared.

"Mr. Anderson? Ms. Jones?"

"Yes?" they said in unison.

The young woman smiled.

"I'm Lauren, Ms. Williams's assistant. She's finishing up a call, but she asked me to take you to the conference room."

Lauren led them down the hall to the conference room and asked if she could get them something to drink.

"Some water would be great," said Glen, smiling at the young woman.

"Still or sparkling?"

"Still is fine."

"Can I get you something?" Lauren asked Guin.

"I'll have a bottle of sparkling water, thanks."

"I'll be right back."

Lauren returned a minute later with two bottles of water and informed them that Ms. Williams would be in soon.

"Sorry to keep you waiting," the attorney said as she entered the conference room a few minutes later. She was accompanied by Adam Leong.

"No problem," said Glen.

The attorney and the private investigator sat.

"So, shall we get to it?" she said.

Guin noticed that Ms. Williams had a large file folder with her, which she proceeded to open.

"According to the information the police received from witnesses, you were the last person to leave the studio the night of Ms. Boucher's death, other than the victim," she said to Glen.

"Yes, but any of the people who had been there could have come back after Glen had left," Guin said. "Or someone who hadn't been there but knew about the shoot could have shown up at the studio after Glen had gone or gotten there earlier and waited until everyone had left."

"That's true," said Ms. Williams. "But everyone who was there claimed not to have hung around."

"They could be lying," said Guin. She turned to Adam Leong. "Did you speak with everyone who was there?"

"Not everyone," he replied.

"What about people who were in the building that evening? Maybe someone who was there saw something or someone."

"Adam has been busy trying to locate people who were in the building that evening," said Ms. Williams. "However, as you can imagine, due to the party on the roof, there were a lot of people milling about. And it would be impossible to find everyone who had been there that evening."

"Have you found anyone who was there that evening?" Guin asked the private investigator.

"I have," he replied.

"And? Did any of them see someone enter or leave the studio after Glen left?"

"None of the people I've spoken with were on the third floor that evening."

"Or so they claimed. What about the bottle the police found next to Margaux? Do we know for sure that was the bottle that killed her?"

"The police believe that was the murder weapon," said Ms. Williams.

"But they don't know for sure."

"The bottle fits the injury to the victim's skull, and Glen's fingerprints were found on it."

"What about other prints? Glen said several people handled the bottles."

"The report just mentions Glen's prints."

Guin frowned and turned to her husband.

"Is it possible you touched a bottle that no one else did?"

Glen looked thoughtful.

"I don't remember. It's possible but unlikely. I'm pretty sure Dionne handled all of the bottles, as did Margaux. I'm surprised their fingerprints were found on the bottle."

"Exactly!" said Guin, turning back to the attorney. "Maybe Dionne killed Margaux and then wiped the bottle!"

"Then how do you explain your husband's prints being on it?" said Adam Leong.

Guin frowned again.

"Maybe she switched the bottle with another one."

Ms. Williams looked skeptical.

"What about crime scene photos?" said Guin. "Did the DA's office supply them?"

"They did."

"I assume they show the bottle. Can we see them?"

Ms. Williams reached into the file folder and withdrew a small stack of photos.

"These are the photographs taken at the scene, shortly

after the cleaning woman found Ms. Boucher," she said, placing the stack of photos between Guin and Glen.

"May we take a look?"

"Go ahead," said the attorney.

Guin reached for the photos and started to go through them.

"The bottle didn't break?" Guin asked the attorney looking at the photo of Margaux face down on the floor, the unbroken bottle next to her.

"Apparently not."

"Isn't that unusual?"

Neither the attorney nor the private investigator said anything.

Guin went through the photos one more time.

"Did you notice anything odd?" she asked her husband.

"Other than Margaux being dead? Not really."

"Nothing seemed disturbed?"

"I'd need to study the photos more closely—and compare them to the ones I took."

"Can we keep the photos?" Guin asked the attorney.

"I'll have my assistant send Glen the .jpgs."

"Great. Thank you. About the cleaning woman, have you spoken with her?" Guin asked the private investigator.

"Not yet," he replied. "She took a leave of absence shortly after finding the victim."

"However, we have the statement she gave to the police," said Ms. Williams.

"What did she say to them?"

"That she went to clean the studio that morning and found Ms. Boucher lying on the floor, unresponsive."

"Did she know that Margaux was dead?"

"She said it was obvious."

"And what did she do after she found the body?"

Aleksei Smirnov had told Guin what had happened, but Guin wanted to see if his account jibed with the cleaner's statement.

"She went to find the manager of the studios."

"She didn't call 911?"

"She felt it was better to have the manager do that."

Guin wondered if the cleaner was undocumented.

"And what did the manager do when she told him she had found a dead body in one of the studios?"

"He went to see for himself and then called the police and Ronnie Banerjee."

"And did the cleaner notice anything about the condition of the studio? Did it look like there had been a struggle? Was anything missing or disturbed or damaged?"

"I'll have Lauren send Glen a copy of the police report along with the photos," said Ms. Williams.

"That would be great," said Guin. "Does it say what evidence they have? Is it just the bottle?"

"The bottle—and witnesses told the police that Glen argued with Ms. Boucher during the photo shoot and grabbed her," said the investigator.

"He grabbed her wrists so she'd stop hitting him!" said Guin. "It was self-defense!"

"They also had a history," said Ms. Williams.

"So?" said Guin. "Margaux had a contentious history with at least one other person who was there—as well as with Alex Morgan."

"Alex Morgan as in her former business partner?"

"And lover," said Guin. "Things didn't end well between them, professionally or personally. And Mr. Morgan was trying to get Margaux to give him a piece of her mocktail business and may have known about the photo shoot."

Ms. Williams and Adam Leong exchanged a look.

"I'll speak with him," said the private investigator.

"He's in Bronxville. Works at a club there as the director of tennis. He can be quite charming, but don't let that fool you."

"You met with him?" asked Ms. Williams.

"I did. I wanted to ask him about Margaux. He admitted that they fell out over the business, but he said that they had kissed and made up. And he implied that Margaux was going to give him a piece of the mocktail business. But both Ronnie Banerjee and Fabio doubted that."

"I see," said the attorney.

"So, what are your next steps?"

"Before we get to that," said Ms. Williams, "I want to go over a few things with your husband. That is if that's all right with you."

"Of course," said Guin.

The attorney turned to Glen.

"Why did you agree to stay after everyone had left the photo shoot?"

"I told you, Margaux asked me to. She wanted to see the photos I had taken."

"But you don't usually show clients the raw files, do you?"

"No, but… I thought it wise to placate her."

"And was that the only reason you agreed to stay after everyone had left?"

"What do you mean?"

"Do you still have feelings for your ex-wife?"

"Margaux? I mean, I feel bad about her dying like that, but that's all. It was over between us years ago."

"Were you angry about the way she treated you that evening? Maybe it brought up some unresolved feelings from the past."

"I'm a professional. I try not to let my client's stress affect me."

"But she was your ex-wife."

"That's true. But I'm happily married to Guin now."

Guin smiled.

"Why didn't you ask your assistant to stay with you?"

"It had been a long day, and I didn't really need Eric to stay.

I figured I'd show Margaux some of the photos, so she'd know that she had nothing to worry about, and then go."

"So the two of you were alone in the studio, looking at photos on your camera. Did you argue?"

"No. I wasn't there for very long."

"How long were you there for?"

"I don't remember exactly. I was showing her photos when her phone rang. She answered it, started to get upset, and I left."

"Do you know who called her?"

"No."

"And did you see anyone when you left the studio?"

"You mean from the photo shoot?"

"Or anyone else."

"Not on the third floor. Though I saw people entering and leaving the building as I left."

"And you said you heard people in the stairwell," said Guin.

"Right."

"And you went straight home?" the attorney asked him.

"I got my car from the garage by the studio and drove it back to the garage near my building."

"And what time did you leave the studio?"

"Around eight-forty-five."

"Yet you didn't get your car until five after nine."

"So?"

"The garage where you said you parked was less than two blocks from the studio building. What took so long?"

"I got a bottle of water at a bodega, and then there was a wait to get my car."

Guin looked at Imani Williams. Did she believe Glen? It was hard to tell.

"What was the time of death?" Guin asked the attorney.

"The medical examiner believes death occurred sometime between eight-thirty and midnight."

"That's a pretty big window. Anyone could have gone into the studio and killed her between the time Glen left and midnight."

The attorney didn't say anything.

"What about CCTV cameras?" said Guin. "Was there one in the studio or on the third floor?"

"No," said Adam Leong.

"What about an emergency exit? There must have been one."

"Just the fire escape," said the private investigator.

Guin frowned.

"What about a will? Do you know if Margaux had one?"

"We're looking into it," said Ms. Williams.

"What about the autopsy report?"

"We haven't received it yet. The medical examiner's office is a bit backed up."

"Will you let us know when you get it?"

"You'll be the first to know."

Was that sarcasm Guin detected?

"And now, if there's nothing else? I'm afraid I have another meeting."

Guin had more questions, but she could sense that Ms. Williams was eager to go.

"Thank you for your time," said Glen.

"Just send us copies of the crime scene photos and the police report," said Guin.

"I'll have my assistant do it this afternoon."

"Thank you."

The attorney left, and the private investigator was about to when Guin stopped him.

"Do you have a minute?"

"I have an appointment."

"This will only take a couple of minutes." She turned to Glen. "Could you wait for me by reception?"

Glen opened his mouth and then closed it.

After he'd gone, Guin turned to Adam Leong.

"Tell me the truth. How bad is it?"

CHAPTER 23

"What do you mean?" said the private investigator.

"From the way Ms. Williams was going on, it didn't sound good for Glen."

Guin felt Adam Leong studying her.

"Did you find something, something that could hurt Glen's case?"

"I haven't found anything that could hurt his case."

Well, that was encouraging.

"What about something that could help him?"

"Not yet."

"But you'll continue to look."

"We're doing everything we can to help your husband."

"We? I thought you worked alone."

"I meant Ms. Williams and I."

"Right. If you do find something incriminating, will you let us know?"

"I'm sure Ms. Williams will."

"Do you think Glen is guilty? I know what people said, and that his prints were found on that bottle, but I know he couldn't have done it. He doesn't have a violent bone in his body. And I should know."

The investigator smiled.

"You love your husband very much."

"I do. So, do you believe he's innocent?"

"My opinion doesn't matter. The prosecution will focus

on the evidence and eyewitness accounts."

"But the evidence is all circumstantial. And no one actually saw Glen hit Margaux with a bottle, did they?"

"No. But the DA will say that your husband argued with his ex-wife and in a fit of rage hit her with a bottle, resulting in her death."

"But that's not what happened."

"Were you there?"

"No, but… There must be some way to prove he didn't do it. You need to talk to everyone who was there—and Alex Morgan. Someone is lying. I know it. And have you asked the people who manage the studio building about CCTV cameras?"

"I did. As I said, there wasn't one in the studio, unfortunately. And now, Ms. Jones, I'm afraid I must go. Ms. Williams and I will keep you and Mr. Anderson informed of anything we find out."

"Thank you."

Guin followed him out of the conference room.

"You okay?" Glen asked her. "What did you have to say to Adam that you didn't want me to hear?"

Guin sighed.

"I just wanted to know if he had found anything incriminating."

"And had he?"

"No. But he hasn't found anything that could help you either."

"It's still early days, Guin."

"That's what he said. I just don't understand how you can be so calm."

Glen smiled.

"I may seem calm, but inside I'm terrified."

"You are?"

He nodded.

"Now let's get out of here."

Guin asked Glen later that afternoon if he had received the police report and crime scene photos from Ms. Williams's assistant. But he said that he hadn't. Guin frowned.

"It hasn't been that long," Glen told her. "She's probably busy."

"Okay. But if we haven't received the files by tomorrow morning, will you follow up with her?"

"You could follow up with her."

"But you're technically the client. It would be better if the email came from you."

"Fine. If I haven't received the files by midday tomorrow, I'll follow up with them. Just remind me tomorrow in case I forget."

"I'll put it on my calendar. So, what are we doing about dinner? You still feel like cooking?"

"I enjoy cooking. What do you feel like?"

"Well, we have that steak. And there's a potato and a sweet potato."

"Steak and potatoes it is."

Glen's phone was ringing.

"I need to get this," he said. "Hey, Dev." Dev was Photog US's coder.

Guin waited a few seconds and then left.

Guin messaged Glen late the next morning, asking if had received anything from the attorney's office. Glen said that he hadn't, and Guin insisted that he write or call Ms. Williams's office. A few minutes later, Guin received an email from Glen. He had cc'd her on his email to the attorney and her assistant.

"Thank you," Guin messaged him.

They were having lunch in the kitchen an hour later when Guin received an alert on her phone. Lauren had sent them an email. Guin quickly opened it.

"Lauren sent us the files!" she announced. "Shall we go look at them together?"

"Let's finish lunch first."

Guin was eager to review the files, but she waited for Glen to finish eating.

"You done?" she said when he had taken the last bite of his sandwich.

"I am. But I need to get on a call."

"Really?"

"Sorry. But you can look at the files without me."

"Are you sure? You don't want me to wait so we can look at them together?"

"I don't know how long I'll be. And I know how you are about waiting. I'll look at everything when I'm free."

"Okay."

Guin quickly rinsed her plate and put it in the dishwasher. Then she gave Glen a quick kiss and headed to her office.

She decided to look at the crime scene photos first. There were multiple photos of Margaux, taken from different angles, as well as a couple of wide-angle shots of the room. Guin studied each one.

There didn't appear to be any blood on or by the body, which Guin thought odd. Though she couldn't see Margaux's face. Next to Margaux was a mocktail bottle. Guin zoomed in. The bottle appeared to be full or nearly full, and Guin didn't see any blood on it. That too seemed odd.

She wondered why the bottle hadn't broken on impact—and why the killer hadn't taken the bottle with him or her. Surely, Glen wouldn't have left the bottle lying there if he had killed Margaux with it. That alone should prove his innocence. Though the prosecutor would likely say he panicked and fled without the bottle.

So who had killed Margaux—and was that, in fact, the

bottle that killed her? Guin had noticed a box with bottles in the background of one of the photos and zoomed in. The box was the kind you got at a liquor store with spaces for twelve bottles. Guin counted the bottles in the box. There appeared to be ten. If the bottle on the floor was number eleven, where was the twelfth bottle?

She messaged Glen, saying she had a question to ask him, but he didn't get back to her. He must still be on his call. She looked at the box of bottles again and then at the bottle beside Margaux. Were all of the bottles the same or were they different?

Guin went through the photos one more time as she waited for Glen to get back to her. Then she opened the file with the police report. She was just starting to read it when Glen finally messaged her back.

"What's up?" he wrote.

"Can you come here? It's important."

"Give me a few minutes," he replied.

Five minutes later, he knocked on her door.

"Come in," she said.

"What's up?"

"Take a look at this photo," she said, pulling up the photo showing the box of mocktail bottles.

"What about it?"

"Take a look at the box."

He squinted and Guin zoomed in on the box.

"Okay. What am I supposed to be seeing?"

"How many bottles of mocktails were at the shoot?"

"There were a dozen. But we didn't use all of them."

"Why not?"

"We didn't need to."

"And were all of the bottles the same?"

"What do you mean?"

"I mean, did all of the bottles look alike? Did they all have the same labels and liquid? I can't tell from the crime scene photos."

"The actual bottles were the same, but they had different mocktails and labels."

"What were the different kinds again?"

"There was the Faux-jito, the Mocktini, the Cosmockpolitan, and the Fizzy Navel.

"So were there three of each flavor?"

"Correct."

"Why three?"

"One bottle to pour from and another to use for the product shots and to use in the background of the shots showing people drinking the mocktails."

"And a spare in case you needed to pour more mocktails or a bottle broke?"

"Exactly."

"Any idea what flavor the one on the floor is?"

Glen looked at the photo.

"It looks like there's greenish liquid inside, so it's probably the Faux-jito."

"And did any of the bottles break during the shoot?"

"Not that I recall."

"Did you throw out any of the bottles?"

"I doubt anyone threw one away. Margaux would have had a fit. They were prototypes, and she didn't even want people touching them. Why?"

"One bottle appears to be missing." She zoomed in on the box again. "See."

"Hm."

"Any idea which one it could be?"

"No. They all look the same from the little bit you can see. Does it matter?"

"Maybe. And look at the bottle on the floor." Guin zoomed out. "Doesn't it seem strange to you that the bottle that supposedly killed Margaux looks pristine? It's almost like someone placed it there."

"It does seem odd."

"And why would you leave a bottle with your fingerprints on it next to her?"

"Good point. I wouldn't."

"Let's say you did hit Margaux with a mocktail bottle and she keeled over. What would you have done?"

"First of all, I want to reiterate that I did not kill Margaux. But to play along, if I had hit Margaux with a mocktail bottle, and she keeled over, as you said, I would have immediately called an ambulance."

Guin rolled her eyes.

"Of course, you would have. But let's say that you panicked and got the hell out of there. What would you have done with the bottle? Pretend you're not you."

Glen looked thoughtful.

"I would have taken it with me and probably dumped it somewhere."

"Exactly."

Unfortunately, it was too late to check the garbage cans around the studio building. The garbage had been picked up days ago.

"Any idea where the rest of the bottles are?"

"You don't think the police have them?"

"Good point. We should ask Imani. But if they don't, who would have them?"

"Probably Ronnie."

Guin would shoot her an email.

"While you're here, let me show you the rest of the photos."

"I have to get on another call in a few."

"Just take a quick look."

Guin showed Glen the photos.

"You notice anything?"

"Other than the dead body?"

Guin made a face.

"Not really."

"I think I need to pay a visit to the studio building."

"Why?"

"I want to take a look at the crime scene."

"The shoot was over a week ago. I doubt there's anything there to see."

"You never know."

Glen's smartwatch was flashing.

"I need to go."

"Hey, when you have a minute, can you send me your photos from the shoot?"

"I already sent you a link."

"Was that to all of the photos?"

"No, but…"

"Send me a new link to all of them, even the bad ones."

"Why?"

"I want to compare them to the crime scene photos."

"I don't know how helpful they'll be."

"Just send me what you've got."

Glen sighed.

"I'll send you a link."

His smartwatch was flashing again.

"I need to go."

"Go. We can go over the police report later."

CHAPTER 24

Glen sent Guin a new link to his photos from the shoot. There were a lot of pictures, as he had warned her. Guin focused on the shots showing the mocktail bottles. Then she pulled up the photos from the crime scene. It looked to be a Faux-jito bottle by Margaux's body, as Glen had thought.

Guin alternated between Glen's photos and the ones the police photographer had taken, wondering what had happened at the studio after Glen had left. If only there had been a CCTV camera. Though maybe there was one elsewhere on the third floor.

Guin opened the police report and read through it again. There was nothing about a CCTV camera. She opened her browser and did a search for the Studios at Hudson Yards. There was a link to its website, which Guin clicked on.

The building was located on West 36th Street, near the Hudson River. It contained seven loft-style film and photography studios as well as a roof deck with views of the New York skyline. In addition to offering studio space, the Studios offered clients the use of camera, film, lighting, and sound equipment, as well as furniture and props, for a fee.

Guin looked at the photos of the different studios, which had been staged with furniture, and wondered which one Margaux—or Ronnie—had rented. There appeared to be two on the third floor. She compared the photos online to the ones Glen had taken and the crime scene photos. But she couldn't tell which one had been used for the Château Margaux Mocktails shoot. She would check out both.

She clicked on the Contact Us link. There was a phone number and email address for someone named Reggie. Guin picked up her phone and called the number.

"The Studios at Hudson Yards," a man answered. At least it sounded like a man. It could have been a woman with a deep voice.

"Is this Reggie?" Guin asked.

"It is. May I help you?"

"Yes, I'm interested in checking out your studios."

"Is this for a photo shoot or a video shoot?"

"A photo shoot," she replied. "Though does it matter?"

"All of our studios can be used for both. It's just that some are better for recording sound."

"Ah. Well, I'd love to see your photography studios and the roof deck."

"I'd be happy to schedule an appointment. When did you want to stop by?"

"Do you have some time tomorrow?"

"Let me see… I could do ten tomorrow or else three."

Guin checked her calendar.

"Let's do three."

"Great," said Reggie. "And your name?"

"It's Guinivere Jones."

"Do you mind spelling that for me?"

"Just put down Guin, G-U-I-N. Do you need me to spell Jones?"

"No, that's all right. And a contact number?"

Guin gave it to him.

"I look forward to seeing you tomorrow at three, Ms. Jones."

Glen had been busy. So it wasn't until dinner that evening that they were able to discuss the police report. As Ms. Williams had said, everyone who had been at the photo shoot had said that Glen had stayed behind to speak with Margaux—and that they had seen the two of them arguing earlier that evening. Several had also seen Margaux slap Glen and Glen grab her by the wrists.

"But no one heard you threaten her or actually saw you hit Margaux with the bottle," Guin said. "So there's that. We should go through the crime scene photos together. Shall we look at them in your office on your big monitor?"

They went to Glen's office and he pulled up the crime scene photos.

"Do you remember touching any of the Faux-jito bottles?" Guin asked him.

"I don't. But that doesn't mean I didn't. I remember adjusting a couple of the bottles, to better see the labels. One could have been a Faux-jito bottle."

Guin stared at the bottle on the floor.

"Don't you find it curious that the bottle didn't break? In the movies and on TV shows, when a person hits someone with a bottle, the bottle always breaks."

"That's because they're made of spun sugar, not glass."

"Still. It seems odd to me."

Guin unlocked her phone and typed *If I hit someone's head with a bottle will the bottle break?* into her browser.

"What are you doing?" Glen asked her.

"Looking something up. Huh."

"What?"

"It says here that a bottle with a lot of liquid in it is more likely to break than an empty bottle. Yet that bottle sure doesn't look broken to me. And it appears to be full of Faux-jito."

"It does."

"Do you think Imani and Adam know that about bottles?"

"I have no idea."

"Well, someone should inform them in case they don't."

"Would you do it?"

"You don't want to?"

"I need to do a little work."

"But it's late."

"You discovered the thing about the bottles. You should be the one to tell them."

"Fine," said Guin. "I'll send them an email with a link to the article and the photo."

"Thank you," he said.

The next afternoon, Guin took the 6 train to Grand Central and then transferred to the 7, taking it west to Hudson Yards. Then she walked the few blocks to the Studios.

The Studios was housed in an old six-story brick building, the kind that still had the original metal fire escape stairs on the exterior. As Guin approached the front door, she noticed what appeared to be a security camera. She wondered if it worked. If so, there was probably a recording of who had entered and left the building the night Margaux was killed.

She tried the door, but it was locked. And Reggie hadn't given her the code to the electronic lock. She pressed the button for the Studios and a male voice answered.

"It's Guin Jones," Guin replied. "I have an appointment with Reggie."

"Come to the second floor," said the male voice. Then he buzzed her in.

There was an elevator near the entrance. Were there also stairs? There had to be. Guin found a door marked Stairs and tried the doorknob. The door was unlocked. She opened it and peered in. The stairwell was poorly lit and had a funny smell. Had someone been smoking pot in there?

She thought about turning around and taking the elevator, but she needed to check out the stairway. Hopefully, the door to the second floor wasn't locked. Though if it was, she'd just turn around.

She checked the door to make sure she wouldn't be locked in the stairwell in case the second-floor door was locked. The door was unlocked. She headed up the stairs and was relieved to find the door to the second floor was also unlocked.

She opened the door and emerged into a brightly lit hallway. She saw the office down the hall and headed there. On the way, she saw a door with Studio 2 printed on it.

The office door was made of glass and had The Studios at Hudson Yards printed on it, making it a bit difficult to see inside. Guin tried the door, but it was locked. She knocked on it and was buzzed in.

Guin saw a man on a cell phone. He held up a finger to indicate he'd just be a minute.

As she waited, Guin glanced around. On the walls were pictures of magazine covers and spreads, as well as a handful of ads. Had they all been shot at the Studios? Probably.

"Ms. Jones?"

Guin turned around.

"Reggie?"

Reggie smiled.

"Sorry about that. It's been a bit crazy this afternoon."

Guin looked around, noticing the empty desks.

"You here by yourself?"

"I am. One of my colleagues called in sick and the other's at an appointment. So, how can I help you? You said you were interested in renting one of our studios?"

"That's right," Guin lied. "I saw pictures of the studios online, but it was hard to get a read for how big they were from the photos."

"I'd be happy to show you the different studios. What are you planning on shooting?"

"Which studio or studios do people typically use for ad campaigns?"

"It depends. Are we talking still photography or video?"

"Still photography."

"And would this be for a fashion shoot or…?"

"It's for a beverage shoot."

Guin looked for a reaction but didn't see one.

"Well, we have two studios that I think would do nicely."

"Is one of them on the third floor?"

"It is. The other's on the fourth. I'll take you to see both of them."

"Thank you."

Though Guin was really only interested in the studio on the third floor, where the Château Margaux Mocktails shoot had likely taken place.

"This way," said Reggie, leading her out of the office and to the elevator.

"We could just take the stairs," said Guin.

"Trust me, you don't want to take the stairs."

"Is there a problem with them?"

"Let me show you our elevator. It's quite impressive. You can fit a piano in it. Though you probably saw it when you came up."

"I actually took the stairs."

"Oh."

"Let's take the elevator. I'd love to see it."

Reggie pressed the button for the elevator, and it arrived a short time later.

"Wow," said Guin, sounding impressed. "It's big."

"As I said, you can fit a piano in here—as well as any camera equipment and props you might need. Let me show you the studio on the fourth floor first," he said and pressed the button for four.

The elevator slowly rose.

"Studio Five is just over here," he said, leading Guin down the hall. He entered a code to unlock the door and stepped inside. "As you can see, it gets lots of natural light."

"Mm," said Guin, glancing around. Then she listened politely as Reggie extolled the virtues of the studio and some of the campaigns that had been shot there.

"And we can provide whatever equipment, furniture, and props you might need."

"For a fee."

He smiled.

"For a fee. But our fees are very reasonable."

"I'm sure," said Guin. "It's very nice. Could we go see the studio on the third floor now?"

"Of course."

Reggie escorted Guin out of the studio, locking the door behind them.

"The door doesn't lock automatically?"

"It used to, but people were constantly locking themselves out of the studios, so we changed the locks. Now you have to enter a code."

"What if someone forgets to lock up or forgets the code?"

"We have someone who checks the doors every evening."

"To make sure they're locked?"

"Yes."

Guin tried to remember if the police report mentioned if the door to the studio had been locked the morning after the shoot. She would check when she got home.

Reggie went to press the button for the elevator, but Guin suggested they take the stairs as it was only one flight down.

"As you wish," he said. But Guin could tell that he would have preferred taking the elevator.

The layout of the third floor was identical to that of the fourth floor. There were two studios, one on either end, with the elevator and a unisex bathroom in between.

"And this is Studio Three," he said, opening the door to the studio.

He stepped inside and turned on the lights. Guin took a look around, studying the space. There were large windows that looked out onto the street, just as in the studio they had visited on the fourth floor. And just outside the windows was the metal fire escape. However, the layout of this studio was a bit different from the one above it.

There was currently no furniture in the studio, but Guin was pretty sure this was the one that the Château Margaux crew had used. Just to be sure, she asked Reggie.

"Is this where Mockingbird Beverages did their photo shoot?" she asked him.

Reggie frowned.

"Why do you ask?"

"I know one of the people who was involved with the shoot. That's actually how I heard about your studios. They raved about the space."

"They did?"

"Uh-huh. I also heard about what happened, about the woman who was found here the next morning. So horrible. The person who checks the doors at night didn't check inside the studio?"

"The door to the studio was locked and no one answered when he knocked."

"I see."

"I assure you, Ms. Jones, we take security very seriously here. That's why we have locks on all the doors and monitor who goes in and out of the building."

"About the locks on the doors, I assume you give clients the codes, yes?"

"On the day of their shoot, we send the person who reserved the studio the code for the front door and the one to the studio they'll be using."

"And how long are the codes good for?"

"Until midnight the day of the shoot."

"And do you have security cameras in the building?"

"We do."

"Though I didn't see one here."

"We don't have them inside the studios."

"But you have them in other places? I thought I saw one above the front door."

Reggie didn't say anything.

"What about your cleaning service? Does it have the codes?"

"The service we use is bonded and insured and never enters the studios when clients are there."

He didn't answer the question, but Guin decided not to push it. She could tell he was feeling tense.

"Could I see the roof deck?"

"Of course. We should take the elevator."

Guin watched as he locked the door to Studio 3 and followed him to the elevator.

He pressed the button marked R when they got in, and the elevator slowly rose. When they got out, Reggie led them to a metal door with Roof printed on it. It didn't appear to have an electronic lock. He opened it and led Guin out.

"Wow!" she said, slowly turning around. "What a view! I can see why people like shooting up here."

Reggie smiled at that.

"Yes, it's quite impressive."

"I heard there was a band shooting music videos here the evening of the Mockingbird Beverages shoot."

Reggie didn't say anything.

"Did everyone who attended the shoot have the code to the building or did you just leave the door unlocked? I heard there were a lot of people up here that evening."

Reggie's phone was ringing. He quickly answered it.

"Can I call you back?" he told the caller. "I'm with a

client." He put his phone away and told Guin he needed to get back to the office.

Guin took a final look around and then followed Reggie back through the door to the elevator.

"Thanks for the tour," she said as they waited for the elevator.

"My pleasure," he replied. "Are you interested in renting one of the studios I showed you?"

"I'll need to get back to you."

The elevator arrived. Reggie pressed 2, and Guin pressed 1. They rode in silence to the second floor.

"Thanks again," said Guin as Reggie got out. Then she watched as the door closed.

CHAPTER 25

Guin got out on the first floor and took the stairs back up to the third floor. She went to Studio 3 and tried the door. It was locked, as she had expected. She had tried to see what numbers Reggie pushed, but he had kept his back to her. She wondered how careful Margaux had been with the code. Though it was probably Ronnie who had been given it if she had been the one to rent the studio. Had Ronnie given the code to everyone at the shoot? She would ask Glen—and then Ronnie if he didn't know.

She walked down the hallway, looking up to see if she could spot a video camera. She didn't see one. Maybe there wasn't one on this floor.

She went over to the bathroom. It didn't have a lock on it. Could someone have hidden in there, waiting for Glen to leave? Eric had said he saw Fabio come in but didn't see him leave.

She left the bathroom and headed back to the stairs. Did they go all the way to the roof? There was only one way to find out.

Guin headed up. The stairs ended at a metal door. Guin turned the knob. It was unlocked. She opened the door and found herself in a small hallway and spied the door to the roof deck. She opened it and went out. The roof really did have a magnificent view, both of the Hudson River and the city.

She looked west and saw a pier in the distance, along with

several boats. Could Smirnov have been DJing on one of those boats? Though some of the boats looked to be a good size, none of them appeared to be a mega yacht.

She took a couple of pictures and then headed back inside. As she descended the stairs, she checked the door to each floor. The first door she encountered was locked. She frowned and went to the fifth floor. That door was unlocked, as were the rest of the doors. Were they always unlocked or just during the day? And why was the door to the sixth floor locked?

She exited the stairs on the first floor and made her way out of the building. She stood outside looking up at the metal staircase that spanned the exterior. Could the killer have hidden on a fire escape and then snuck back into the studio? Though wouldn't someone have noticed someone hanging out on a fire escape? Then again, maybe not. This was New York after all, where people did that kind of thing all the time. Well, at least on TV shows and in the movies.

Guin saw the security camera above the front door and took a photo of it. Had Adam Leong been to the building yet? She was eager to compare notes with him. She sent him a text.

"We should meet," she wrote. "I found some things that could help clear Glen."

He wrote her back a minute later saying he was busy and to just email her findings.

"I'd rather meet," she replied. "I'd be happy to come to your office. Do you have time tomorrow?"

"Meet me at eight at the Black Cat Café, the one on the Lower East Side."

Guin smiled.

"I'll be there!"

As soon as Guin got home, she went to Glen's office. She listened at the door, but it didn't sound like he was on the phone. However, he could be on a conference call or in a Zoom meeting and have his headphones on, so she knocked.

"Come in," he called.

Guin opened the door.

"Are you busy?" she said, glancing over at his computer. It didn't look like he was on a web call.

"I'm actually done for the day."

"Wow."

It was only five o'clock, and he usually worked until dinnertime.

"I know. Though I probably shouldn't get used to it. What's up?"

"I was just at the Studios at Hudson Yards and met with Reggie, the manager."

"Why did you go there?"

"I wanted to visit the scene of the crime."

"I doubt you found anything. I'm sure they cleaned the studio."

"That wasn't why I went. I wanted to see if there were any security cameras and how easy it would have been for someone to hide out and return to the studio. You were in Studio Three, yes?"

"We were. So, what did you discover?"

"I didn't see any security cameras, except for the one by the front door. And all of the studios had electronic locks. If the door to the studio was locked after you left, the person who killed Margaux would have needed the code to get in. Or else Margaux knew the killer and let him or her in. Do you remember locking the door?"

"I didn't."

"Did you have the code?"

"I did."

"And the one to the building?"

"That too."

"Did Ronnie give them to you?"

"She did."

"Did she give the codes to everyone?"

"I don't know. You'd have to ask her."

"So why didn't you lock the door when you left the studio?"

"I was in a hurry. And Margaux was still there."

"Did she lock the door?"

"I don't know. I think she was too busy arguing with whoever phoned her. She didn't even say anything when I left, even though we hadn't finished going through the photos."

"And you have no idea who she was talking to."

"As I think I said before, I believe it was the person who had called her earlier and upset her."

"Remind me why you thought so."

"I heard her say, 'I told you before.'"

"Right. And was that all you heard her say?"

"I wasn't really paying attention. I was eager to go, and then Ronnie phoned me and…"

"Hold up. Ronnie phoned you as you were leaving the studio? You didn't mention that before. Did you tell the police that?"

"I don't remember. Anyway, the call only lasted a few seconds."

"Why did she phone you?"

"She wanted to make sure I was okay. I think she felt bad about leaving me alone with Margaux."

"And what did you tell her?"

"I told her I was fine and was heading home."

"That's it?"

"That's it."

"Do you remember what time that was?"

"No, but I can check my phone. Why? Is it important?"

"It could be."

They were having dinner with Guin's family that evening. Guin had nearly forgotten about it. Maybe that was because she didn't want to deal with her mother. She thought briefly about claiming to be sick, but her parents were about to go off on their cruise, so she knew she should just suck it up and go.

She still hadn't told her parents about Glen being arrested. And she hoped Lance hadn't either. She had been checking the newspapers daily to see if anyone had written about what had happened, but she hadn't spotted anything. The only thing she had found online was a tribute to Margaux on her Instagram feed, no doubt written by Ronnie. So there was a good chance her mother hadn't heard about Margaux's murder.

A few minutes before they were to leave, Glen came into Guin's office, asking if he needed to change. He was dressed in jeans and a button-down shirt, his typical work-from-home attire.

"You know how my mother feels about jeans," said Guin. (Carol didn't think they belonged at the dinner table.)

"Though they're nice jeans. And it's not like Nicola's is that fancy," Glen replied.

"True."

"Do you want me to change?"

Guin looked at him.

"Maybe just put on a jacket or a nice sweater?"

"I was planning on it. Is that what you're wearing?"

Guin looked down. She was still dressed in the outfit she had worn to tour the Studios: a white button-down shirt, a pair of dark blue jeans, a tweed jacket, and cowboy boots.

"I should probably change. Both of us in jeans might give my mother a heart attack."

They arrived at the Italian restaurant and were told they were the first ones there.

"Do you want to get a drink at the bar?" Glen asked Guin. "You seem a bit on edge."

"Sure."

A few minutes later, Lance and Owen arrived.

"Mom and Philip aren't here yet?" said Lance. It was unusual for their mother to be late.

"She's probably making sure Philip's packed for the cruise."

"You're probably right."

"You want a drink while we wait?"

"Why don't we go to the table? They'll probably be here any minute."

They went over to the hostess and were led to their table. Lance signaled to their server and ordered a Negroni while Owen ordered a glass of pinot grigio.

"So, what's new? You solve Margaux's murder yet?" Lance asked his sister.

Guin made a face.

"Not yet. You haven't said anything to Mom, have you?"

"You told me not to. But you should tell her. What if she finds out? She'll be pissed that you didn't tell her."

Guin knew her brother was right, but…

"So, how's it going?" Lance asked.

"We received a copy of the police report and the crime scene photos," said Guin. "And I went to check out the Studios at Hudson Yards, where the shoot took place."

"Which studio did you use?" Lance asked Glen.

"Studio Three. Why?"

"Have you shot stuff there?" Guin asked her brother.

He nodded.

"A few times. Their roof deck is amazing."

"It is. Some band was shooting a bunch of music videos up there when Glen was doing the Château Margaux Mocktails shoot."

"Which band?"

"I forget their name," said Glen. "I just know they were loud. You could hear them a block away. I'm surprised the neighbors didn't call the police."

"What's this about the police?" It was Guin's mother.

"Nothing," said Guin.

Just then their server appeared with Lance and Owen's drinks.

"Can I get you something?" he asked Carol and Philip.

"Give us a minute," said Carol.

"Is everything okay?" Guin asked her mother. "It's not like you to be late."

"Just doing some last-minute packing. The weather's so iffy this time of year in Switzerland and Germany. I wasn't sure what to bring."

"It's a cruise. You can bring as much stuff as you like," said Lance.

"That's what I told your mother," said Philip.

"I was just trying to be practical."

Philip signaled to their server, who came right over.

"Yes?" he said.

"I'll have a Johnnie Walker Blue on the rocks," Philip told him.

"Madam?"

"And I'll have a glass of chardonnay."

The server asked her which one, and Carol said whichever one was the driest.

As soon as he left, Carol turned to her daughter.

"Now, what's this about someone calling the police? Did something happen?"

Lance glanced over at his sister.

"We were just talking about some band Glen heard playing up on a roof the other night. He said they were really loud and was surprised no one had called the police."

"Oh," said her mother, looking relieved. "For a minute I

thought you were going to tell me you had stumbled across another dead body."*

Guin, Glen, Lance, and Owen all exchanged a look.

"What?" said Carol. "I see that look. What aren't you telling me?"

"You should tell her," Lance said to Guin.

Guin scowled at him.

"It's going to come out eventually."

"Tell me what?" said Carol. "What aren't you telling me?"

"I was arrested for allegedly killing my ex-wife," said Glen.

"Excuse me?"

"He didn't do it," said Guin.

"I should hope not," said Carol. "Why were you arrested? And why didn't you want to tell me?"

"Guin didn't want to worry you."

"Really, Guinivere," said her mother. Then she turned back to Glen. "So why, pray tell, do the police think you murdered your ex-wife?"

"I was supposedly the last person with her before she died."

"What were you doing with her?"

"He was photographing her new line of mocktails," said Lance.

"Mocktails? What are mocktails?"

"They're zero-proof cocktails. Cocktails made without any alcohol."

"So they're what, juice for adults?"

Guin couldn't help smiling.

Just then their server came over with Carol and Philip's drinks and asked everyone if they were ready to order.

"We need a few minutes," said Lance.

Carol took a sip of her chardonnay and then turned back to Glen.

---

* Read the Sanibel Island Mystery series.

"And why did your ex-wife hire you to photograph her mocktails?"

"She wanted to make amends for the way she treated me during our marriage and divorce."

Carol stared at him.

"I don't understand you young people."

"Do you have a lawyer?" Philip asked Glen.

"I do."

"Is he any good?" asked Carol.

"*She* has an excellent track record," said Guin.

"Well, if you're not happy with her, I know an excellent defense attorney," said Philip.

"Do you mean Roger?" said his wife.

Philip nodded.

"You should meet with him, Glen."

"I already have an attorney," Glen said. "But thank you."

Carol turned to her husband.

"Maybe we should cancel our trip."

"No!" Guin said, a bit too loudly. "Don't cancel your trip!"

"But what if you need us?"

"The trial isn't for months. And, hopefully, there won't be a trial if we can find out who really killed Margaux."

"What do you mean by *we*?" said her mother.

"It's just a figure of speech. I meant the attorney Glen hired and her private investigator."

"Shall we look at our menus and decide what we're going to get?" said Lance. "I don't know about all of you, but I'm famished."

Guin mouthed *thank you* to her brother and then picked up her menu.

Guin was exhausted by the time she and Glen got home from dinner. Mercifully, they hadn't spent the evening discussing Margaux's murder. Lance and Owen had seen to that, bless them. They were both quite good at keeping Carol and Philip entertained, telling them tales of their various clients and the new restaurants they had dined at.

"I thought that went rather well, considering," said Glen as he removed his shoes by the door.

"Mm," said Guin. "I'm just glad they're not canceling their trip."

"Do you really think they would have done that?"

"I don't know. I just hope they have a good time and that my mother doesn't pester me for updates. Maybe they won't have wifi on the ship."

"Here's hoping. You want to watch something?

"Sure."

They went into the living room, and Glen turned on the TV.

"What do you want to watch?"

"How about some HGTV? I don't think I'm up for anything heavy."

House Hunters International was on. A young family was looking for a place to rent in Nice.

"I'd like to go to Nice," said Guin, curling up against her husband.

"That would be nice," said Glen.

Guin smiled.

"Maybe, when this is all over, we could go there."

"I'd like that," he said. "Though…"

"I know, you'll probably be too involved with Photog to take a vacation any time soon."

"That wasn't what I was going to say."

"What were you going to say?" she said, looking up at him.

"I forget."

"Uh-huh."

She leaned against Glen again and closed her eyes.

"You tired?"

"I probably shouldn't have had that second glass of wine."

"You want to go to the bedroom?"

"It's too early for bed. I'll be fine. I just need to rest my eyes for a few."

However, five minutes later, she was fast asleep.

CHAPTER 26

It was a good thing Guin had set her alarm, otherwise she might have missed her appointment with Adam Leong. He was waiting outside the coffee shop when she got there, looking at his phone.

"Good morning," she said. He put away his phone. "Thank you for meeting me."

"You said it was important."

"Shall we go in and get some coffee?"

Guin ordered a cappuccino and a scone, and Leong ordered a black coffee. When their coffees were ready, they took them to an empty table.

"So, I asked you to meet me because I discovered something that could be important. Several things actually." He waited for her to continue. "Did you read the email I sent you, the one about the bottle?"

"I did."

"And? I assume you saw the crime scene photos. The bottle next to Margaux was full of liquid. And, if you clicked on the link I sent you, you'd know that a bottle with a lot of liquid in it is more likely to break than an empty bottle. Yet the bottle next to Margaux wasn't broken."

"Maybe the bottle was an exception."

"Maybe. But isn't it also possible that it was a different mocktail bottle, an empty one, that killed Margaux?"

Guin searched Adam Leong's face, but his expression remained unreadable.

"Also, there were twelve bottles at the shoot, three of each kind of mocktail. Yet there were only ten bottles in the box shown in the crime scene photos. Plus the one by Margaux makes eleven. Where did the twelfth bottle go?"

"Maybe you couldn't see it in the photos."

Guin frowned. It was possible but unlikely. The police photographer had been quite thorough.

"Take a look at the crime scene photos again. I'm pretty sure there's a bottle missing. Also, do you know where the bottles are now? Do the police have them?"

"I'm not sure."

"Would you check? One of the bottles in the box could be the real murder weapon. Though…"

Leong waited for her to go on.

"Though if it was a different bottle that killed Margaux, the killer probably took the bottle with him—or her," she added, "rather than sticking it in the box."

Leong didn't say anything.

"What's your theory?"

"I'm not paid to have theories. I'm paid to uncover evidence."

"Well, the bottle is evidence. Can the DA prove beyond a reasonable doubt that the bottle on the floor was the one that killed Margaux, especially if Ms. Williams can show that it should have broken upon impact?"

"I wouldn't count on a jury finding your husband not guilty because of a bottle not breaking."

Guin frowned.

"What about Margaux's cell phone? She was on the phone when Glen left. That should prove he didn't kill her."

"Not necessarily."

"Did the police check her phone?"

"It's missing."

Guin frowned again.

"What about the door to the studio?"

"What about it?"

"The cleaning woman said it was locked when she went in to clean the studio the next morning. But Glen said he didn't lock it. Also, you need a code to lock the door. So whoever killed Margaux must have locked the door—and probably took her phone."

"Did your husband have the code to the door?"

"He did, but…"

"So he could have locked it after he killed her."

"Glen didn't kill Margaux!" Guin said a bit too loudly. "I thought you believed he was innocent."

"I'm just stating what the DA will say."

Guin's frown returned.

"Let's say Glen did kill her, which he didn't. Why would he take Margaux's phone?"

"I don't know."

"Wouldn't the police have searched our apartment if they thought he had it?"

"They probably thought he disposed of it."

"That makes no sense! Margaux's phone could prove he was innocent! You should ask Ronnie Banerjee about the phone and the codes, find out who besides Glen she gave them to."

"I already spoke with her."

"And did you ask her who she had given the door codes to?"

"I did."

"And?"

"According to Ms. Banerjee, only three people had the codes to the front door of the building and the studio: her, Ms. Boucher, and your husband."

"And you believe her? What about the two stylists and the basketball players?"

"They were buzzed into the building or entered with someone."

"How did they get into the studio?"

"It was unlocked."

Guin frowned.

"Well, someone locked the door to the studio after everyone had left, and it wasn't Glen."

The private investigator didn't say anything.

"What about CCTV footage? I know there was a camera above the door to the building."

"Unfortunately, the building experienced a brief power outage shortly after your husband left, which knocked out the security cameras."

"Isn't that a little convenient?"

"You think whoever killed Ms. Boucher caused the power outage?"

"It's possible."

"I'm sorry to disappoint you, but the police believe the outage was caused by the musicians."

"The musicians? You mean the band up on the roof?"

The private investigator nodded.

"They had a lot of equipment, and it was an old building."

"Though you would think the wiring would be up to date. Or they'd have surge protectors," said Guin. "How long was the power out for?"

"Not long. Maybe fifteen minutes."

"And the cameras didn't go back online when the power came back?"

"Apparently not."

"What about all the locks? Did they get fried?"

"They had battery backups."

"Hm… Well, even if the killer didn't cause the outage, it's possible he or she took advantage of it to sneak into and/or out of the studio. Did you find any more people who were there that evening?"

"I did."

"And did any of them report anything or anyone suspicious?"

"Other than the power going off? No."

"Have you spoken to Alex Morgan?"

"Not yet. He's been out of the country."

"Out of the country? Where did he go?"

"England. His mother had a bad fall and is in hospital over there."

"Who told you that? Did you call the club?"

"I did."

"And you believe he's really in England, caring for his mother?"

"Why would they lie?"

"They wouldn't, but he might have. Did you ask for his number?"

"I did. But it's the club's policy not to give out employees' personal information."

"Did you tell them you were with the police?"

"I'm not with the police."

"You could have lied."

"I don't lie."

Guin looked at him. Did he really never lie?

"So you don't find it all suspicious that Morgan leaves the country shortly after his former lover-slash-partner is murdered?"

The investigator didn't say anything.

"Maybe I spooked him."

"Spooked him?"

"Maybe he thought after speaking with me that it would be best to leave the country for a while."

"Why would he think that?"

"Why? Maybe he thought that someone besides me might figure out that he killed Margaux."

"You really think Alex Morgan killed her?"

Guin could hear the skepticism in his tone.

"It's possible. Maybe he was the one who called Margaux during the shoot. Everyone said she received a call that upset her. Maybe it was Morgan. She tells him she can't talk, she's at her photo shoot, and she hangs up on him. Then he calls her back later and insists on meeting with her. Or maybe he knows where the shoot is and goes over there to confront her.

"He goes there, they fight, and he winds up hitting her with a mocktail bottle. She falls to the floor, and, realizing he's accidentally killed her, Morgan flees, taking the bottle and her phone with him."

"What about the bottle found by the body and the fact that the door was locked the next morning?"

"Maybe the bottle they found by the body had been on the table, by the box of bottles, and rolled off? Or maybe Morgan placed the bottle there."

"And the door?"

"Maybe whoever checks the studios at night locked it."

Leong looked skeptical.

"You don't think Morgan did it."

"I find it unlikely."

"Did the person you spoke with at the pro shop say when Morgan would be back?"

"Next week."

"So you'll follow up with him then?"

"I was planning to."

"Good. What about Margaux's current business partner, Aleksei Smirnov? Have you spoken with him?"

"I have."

"He claimed to be DJing at some private party that evening, but he wouldn't give me any of the details. Were you able to confirm his whereabouts that evening?"

"As you said, he was working as a DJ at a private event."

"What about the rest of the people who were at the shoot? Have you spoken with everyone?"

"I'm meeting with the two basketball players on Monday. They've been unavailable."

"Your meeting with both of them, at the same time?"

"I am. Is there a problem?"

"What if they're covering for each other?"

The investigator didn't answer.

"When are you meeting with them?"

"Why?"

"I didn't interview Shaq, and I had a few questions for him. I could come with you."

"I told you, I work alone."

"I know what you said. But this might be my only chance to talk to him. Please?"

"And how would I explain you being there? I believe you said that you had already met with Mr. Abara."

"You could tell them I was shadowing you for an article." Leong frowned.

"Please? I promise not to say anything. You can ask Shaq my questions. I just want to hear what he has to say."

The investigator studied her.

"If I allow you to accompany me, you promise just to observe?"

"I promise. Does this mean I can go?"

He looked like he was thinking it over.

"Very well."

"Great! So, what time are you meeting them and where?"

"I'm meeting them at their gym at eleven. I'll text you the address."

"Is the gym near Madison Square Garden?"

"It is."

"It has to be the place I met Jordan at. I know where it is."

Guin saw Adam Leong's smartwatch flashing.

"I need to go," said the investigator.

"Thank you for meeting with me."

He gave a curt nod and got up.

Guin watched him leave, wondering where he was off to. She finished her cappuccino, even though it had grown cold, and her scone. Then she headed home.

CHAPTER 27

Guin arrived at the gym the following Monday a little before eleven. Adam Leong was already there, talking on his phone. She waited for him to get off before approaching.

"Good morning," she said as he finished stowing his phone.

"Good morning," he replied.

"So, what's our strategy?"

"Our strategy?"

"Do you want to ask your questions first, and then I'll ask mine?"

"I thought I was clear that I was to ask the questions and you were there merely to observe."

"Right. I forgot. So you'll ask Shaq my questions? I had a couple for Jordan too."

"What are your questions?"

"I just want to know if Ronnie gave Jordan and Shaq the codes to the studio building and the studio. I know what Ronnie said, but it's good to check. Also, I want to know if Margaux said anything inappropriate to Shaq, and, if so, how he reacted. And if he overheard or saw anything. And where the two of them went after the shoot."

"Is that all?"

Guin wasn't sure if he was being sarcastic.

"I think so."

Adam's smartwatch was flashing. It seemed to do that a

lot. He glanced at it and frowned.

"I need to get this." He stepped away and pulled out his phone. "Yes?" he said.

Guin tried to subtly eavesdrop, but between Adam's back being turned to her and the street noise, she couldn't hear what he was saying. A minute later, he pocketed his phone and returned to Guin.

"I need to go."

"What? Why?"

"I just received word that a suspect I've been trying to locate just turned up."

"A suspect?"

"Another case I'm working on."

"And you have to leave? What about the interview?"

The private investigator looked thoughtful.

"You conduct it."

"Me?"

"Is there a problem? You practically begged me to let you come here. Have you changed your mind about speaking with them?"

"Not at all. I'm just surprised. I thought I was only to observe."

Leong didn't say anything.

"What about your questions?"

"Just find out what they saw and heard and where they went. I'll follow up with them later."

"Okay," said Guin. "You sure you don't want to stick around, ask them yourself?"

"I would if I could. But this takes precedence." He looked down at his smartwatch. "I should go. Let me know what they say."

"I'll record the interview and send you the file."

Guin was seated by the juice bar, scrolling through the news on her phone, when Jordan and Shaq appeared. They were dressed in their workout clothes and looked a bit sweaty. Jordan seemed surprised to see her.

Guin smiled up at them.

"Good morning," she said.

"Where's Mr. Leong?" said Jordan.

"He had a work emergency and asked me to step in for him."

"You work for him? I thought you were a reporter."

"I've been shadowing Private Investigator Leong for an article I'm working on, and he suggested I take over. He gave me his questions."

The two men looked hesitant.

"Please, won't you have a seat? Or did you want to get a juice first? I can wait."

The basketball players exchanged a look, shrugged, and then sat.

"So, what did he want you to ask us?" said Jordan.

"First of all," said Guin, opening up the recording app on her phone, "do I have your permission to record this interview? It's so Mr. Leong can listen to it later."

Jordan and Shaq exchanged a look.

"We've got nothing to hide," said Jordan.

"So is that a yes?"

He nodded.

"If you both wouldn't mind stating your name and saying something like, 'You have my permission to record this conversation,' into the microphone?"

They did as Guin instructed.

"Excellent," she said when they were done. "So, just to confirm, you were both at the Château Margaux Mocktails shoot at the Studios at Hudson Yards on…" she gave the date.

The two men nodded.

"If you wouldn't mind saying your answer?"

"That's right," said Jordan, leaning over Guin's phone.

"And were you both given the codes?"

"The codes?" said Jordan.

"To the keypad on the front door of the studio building and the one on Studio Three. They both had digital locks."

"Oh that. Yeah."

"So Ronnie gave you both the codes?"

"She just gave them to me," said Jordan.

So Ronnie lied about only giving the codes to Margaux and Glen. Or maybe she had forgotten she had given them to Jordan. Though Guin thought that unlikely.

"But we didn't need them," Jordan added.

"Oh? Why was that?"

"Some people let us into the building."

"What about the studio?"

"The door was open when we got there."

"During our previous conversation, Mr. Abara, you said that Margaux Boucher, the head of Château Margaux Mocktails, acted erratically during the photo shoot and that she behaved inappropriately towards you and some of the other people who were there."

"That's right."

"In fact, she said something so inappropriate or objectionable to you that you walked out at one point."

"I did. But I came back."

"Can you tell me what she said to you?"

"I'd rather not."

Guin decided to let it go.

"Why did you return?"

"Ronnie asked me to."

"What did she say to you?"

"I don't remember."

Guin wondered why he was being so cagey. Had Ronnie told him not to say anything? Could he have had something to do with Margaux's death? She studied him, but he was hard to read. She looked over at Shaq.

"Mr. Onyema, did Margaux say anything offensive or inappropriate to you during the photo shoot?"

"Yeah, but I'm used to people like her."

"People like her?"

"People who judge people like us."

"You mean basketball players?"

Shaq and Jordan both smirked.

"I meant people with a different skin tone."

"Do you remember what she said to you?"

"She told me I'd never make it in the big leagues."

"Why'd she say that?"

"Said I was too clumsy and that basketball players were supposed to be graceful."

"Why'd she say that?"

"I knocked over some stuff while trying to follow her crazy directions."

"Nothing broke," said Jordan. "But Margaux totally flipped out. Chewed my man here out."

"Is that true, Mr. Onyema?"

Shaq nodded.

"If you wouldn't mind?" she said, looking down at her phone.

"It's true."

"Did that make you angry?"

"Sure, but I let it go."

"You didn't talk back to her?"

"What would be the point?"

"I told him he should have said something," said Jordan. "It's not right what she said to him."

"I told you, I could handle it," said Shaq.

"Did you say something to Margaux?" Guin asked Jordan.

Jordan clammed up, but Shaq spoke for him.

"He told Margaux she shouldn't say things like that, that I had an MVP, and that it was just an accident. He was pretty steamed."

"And how did Margaux react when you said that to her?" she asked Jordan. But again Shaq was the one who answered.

"She said, 'You people always stand up for each other.'"

Wow, thought Guin.

"Is that why you walked out? You felt she was disrespecting you?"

Jordan didn't answer.

"Tell me about the bottles used at the shoot. Did you touch any of them?"

"Did we touch any of them?" said Jordan.

"You know, pick one up and look at it? Maybe pour yourself a drink?"

"I don't remember," said Jordan.

"What about you, Mr. Onyema? Do you recall handling any of the bottles?"

"We wanted to check them out. But Ms. Boucher yelled at us to put them down. She didn't want anyone getting their fingerprints on them or breaking them. Though they had extras."

"And did either of you take a bottle home with you after the shoot?"

"No," said Jordan. "Ronnie said they needed the bottles. They were prototypes."

"So no one left with a bottle?"

"We weren't supposed to," said Shaq.

"And what time did the two of you leave the shoot?"

"I don't remember," said Jordan.

"It was around eight-thirty," said Shaq.

Guin looked at Shaq.

"How do you know it was around eight-thirty?"

"I remember because I was looking at my phone when the elevator opened. And then those girls asked us if this was the way to the roof."

"This was on the third floor?"

"Yeah. I think they were on something. They were kind of giggly."

"Do you know why they were going up to the roof?"

"There was some band playing up there, shooting a bunch of music videos."

"And what did you tell them?"

"We told them this was the third floor, that they needed to go up."

"Then what happened?"

"They asked us if we were going to the party."

"And what did you tell them?"

"We told them we weren't planning on it."

"Then what?"

"They invited us to go up with them."

"And did you, go with them?"

Guin saw Jordan subtly shaking his head, but Shaq didn't see him.

"I was pretty beat, but Jordan said we should go check it out."

"So you went up to the roof with them."

"Yeah."

"You see anyone else from the photo shoot there?"

Before Shaq could answer, Jordan said no.

Shaq gave him a look, but Jordan didn't say anything.

"How long were you there for?"

"Not that long. Maybe an hour?"

"Did the power go off while you were up there?"

"Oh yeah!" said Shaq. "I forgot about that. That was freaky."

"What do you mean by freaky?"

"I mean one minute they were playing music and everyone was partying, and the next minute nothing. All the lights went off and it was silent."

"Did people panic?"

"Not really. There were lights on in other buildings, and people had their phones. We thought the band must have blown a fuse or something."

"Do you remember how long the power was off for?"

"Maybe fifteen minutes?"

"And did either of you leave the roof during the power outage?"

"No," said Jordan.

"What time did you leave?"

"I don't remember exactly," said Shaq. "Around nine-thirty maybe? I know I was in bed a little after ten-thirty. I had a tryout early the next morning and wanted to be well-rested."

"What time did you get home, Mr. Abara?"

"I don't remember."

"And did either of you stop by the studio after you left?"

"No," said Jordan. "Why would we?"

"And you didn't run into anyone from the shoot up on the roof or outside the studio building?"

Shaq opened his mouth to say something, but Jordan cut him off.

"We didn't see anyone."

However, Guin had a feeling he was lying. Something about his body language. And the fact that he cut off his friend.

"About the shoot, I understand Margaux—Ms. Boucher—received a phone call while it was going on, a call that upset her. Do you have any idea who called her?" she asked them.

"It was some dude called Alex," Shaq replied.

Guin looked at him.

"Are you sure about that?"

"Pretty sure," said Shaq. "I heard her say *Alex*, like she was mad at him." Guin saw Jordan giving Shaq a look. "But I could be wrong."

Guin wondered what that was about. Had Alex Morgan phoned Margaux?

"What about the photographer?"

"What about him?" said Shaq.

"What did you think of him?"

"He seemed like a good guy."

"You think he killed Margaux?"

"She was pretty hard on him."

"Do you think he could have killed her?"

Shaq looked over at Jordan.

"We heard the police arrested him," said Jordan. "So he probably did it."

"You think the police are always right?" Guin asked him.

Jordan frowned.

"We need to go," he said.

"I had a couple more questions."

"Sorry. We have an appointment."

Guin didn't believe him.

"Could I at least get an email address or a number, so I can send you the rest of my—I mean Mr. Leong's—questions?"

"Mr. Leong has our info."

The basketball players got up, and Guin did too.

"Thank you for your time," she said.

She watched as they headed to the locker room. Then she left the gym. She stood outside checking her phone. Adam Leong hadn't texted her. Not that she really thought he would. He was busy. She would listen back to the interview and transcribe it, then send him the files.

She put her phone away and headed to the subway. As she walked, she replayed the interview in her head. She couldn't shake the feeling that Jordan Abara was hiding something. But what? She would listen to the recording as soon as she got home. Maybe she would discover something then.

CHAPTER 28

Guin listened back to the interview as soon as she got home, transcribing it. When she was done, she sent the audio file and transcription to Adam Leong. She was having lunch in the kitchen, scrolling through her social media feeds, when she received a text from Sophie, asking her to call when Guin had a minute.

Guin finished eating her sandwich and then picked up her phone and called Sophie back.

"Guin?"

"Hi, Sophie. What's up? Is everything okay?"

"Everything's fine. I just need your advice. You've been a freelancer for a while, yes?"

"I have."

"And you like it." She said it as more of a statement than a question.

"I do. But I also like having a steady paycheck and the benefits that come with traditional employment, like paid time off and health insurance. Why?"

"I've been thinking of going back to work now that the kids are older."

"I think that's a great idea, provided you want to," Guin added.

"I do. Though I don't want to work full-time. At least not yet. I thought I might dip my toe in the water first, see how I liked it before making a commitment."

"Good idea. Is there someplace you're thinking of working? You still in touch with some of your colleagues from *Vogue*?"

"I am. But most of them don't work there anymore. One of them, Jacqueline," which she pronounced *zhack-LEAN*, "just started working for this new magazine, FLAIR."

Guin hadn't heard of it.

"Is it a fashion mag?"

"Mostly, but they also highlight women in other fields, women who've got flair."

"I like it!"

"I do too. And the thing is, Jacqueline asked me if I'd be interested in freelancing for them."

"I hope you said yes."

"I said I'd get back to her, that I needed time to think about it."

"It sounds perfect," said Guin. "What's there to think about?"

"Well, the hours aren't set, and they vary. So I'd probably have to hire a sitter."

"Is that a problem? You have someone who watches the kids when you and Warren go out, yes?"

"I do, but she's a senior in high school. And she's not usually free in the afternoons. So I'd have to find someone who is."

"I'm sure you could find someone. Or maybe your parents could help out. Are they still here in New York?"

"They are, but they travel a lot. So I can't really count on them."

"And what is it you'd do at FLAIR?"

"I'd coordinate the fashion shoots and do some other stuff, basically be an assistant fashion editor. It's a bit of a step backward from what I was doing before but... I haven't worked in eight years, so..."

"It sounds like a great opportunity. And I'm sure, once

they realize how amazing you are, they'll promote you."

"I doubt that."

"Don't be so down on yourself! So did Jacqueline say how much they'd pay you?"

"Not yet. But I wouldn't be doing it for the money."

"Don't let them know that. And don't sell yourself short, Sophie. Just because you haven't worked in a bunch of years doesn't mean you don't deserve a decent wage. This sounds like the perfect way to get your feet wet."

"What if I drown?"

"You won't drown. You'll do swimmingly. So, have you told Warren yet?"

"Not yet. I wanted to talk to you first."

"I'm sure he'll be supportive. Have you two ever discussed you going back to work?"

"We have. And he seemed fine with it. But I worry about Noah and Izzy."

"What do you worry about?"

"What if they resent me for going back to work?"

"I doubt they will. Especially if you explain why you're going. And you said it wouldn't be full-time. How many hours a week are we talking about?"

"Jacqueline said it would vary, but she was thinking around twenty to start with."

"Twenty hours a week is totally doable. I think you should tell Warren about the gig and the two of you can figure out how to make it work. Trust me, if this is something you want to do, it'll be good for everyone."

"You really think so?"

"I do. And you'll be setting a good example for the kids, showing them you can work and be a great mom."

Though what did Guin know about being a great mom? She didn't have kids. However, she knew plenty of women who managed to balance careers with family. And this job sounded like the perfect way for Sophie to ease back into work.

"And if you're not happy, you can always quit."

"I guess. Okay. I'll do it!"

"Yay! You go, girl!"

Sophie laughed.

"I've missed you, Guin. Hey, by any chance are you free for dinner tomorrow?"

"Tomorrow? I need to check, but I think so."

"Check and let me know. A bunch of us moms are getting together, and I'd love to introduce you to the group. I think you'd really like them. They're all around our age."

Guin hesitated. Her experience with moms, especially ones her age, wasn't the best. They typically felt sorry for her because she wasn't able to have kids. However, Guin had made her peace with infertility long ago, and was, in some ways, grateful to be childless, especially after her first marriage imploded. Still, the idea of hanging out with a bunch of thirty- and forty-something moms didn't excite her.

"I appreciate the invitation but…"

"Before you say no, you should know that most of the women work full-time. I'm the oddball in the group. Well, me and Joy. And it's not like we sit around and bitch about our husbands and kids the whole time. In fact, only three of us have husbands. Susan's divorced, and Candy's gay. Please say you'll come. We're a really fun group. And it's a great way for you to meet some nice people."

Guin sighed. It probably wouldn't be a bad idea for her to try and meet people. She'd pretty much been a hermit since moving back to Manhattan, only going out with Glen or her family.

She had lost touch with most of her New York friends after the divorce and move to Sanibel. And she hadn't been motivated to reach out to anyone since moving back.

"Let me just double-check that we don't have anything tomorrow."

"Okay. Text me later."

Guin said that she would.

Guin hadn't heard back from Adam Leong and wondered what was up with him. Had he spoken to the suspect he'd been chasing? Had something happened to him? She sent him a text as she was waiting for dinner to be ready, asking if he had received her email.

"Everything okay?" asked Glen, coming into the kitchen. "You look frustrated."

"It's Adam. He was supposed to interview Jordan and Shaq this morning at their gym, but he got some urgent call about a suspect he'd been chasing and bailed, leaving me to do it."

"You think something happened to him?"

"I don't know. I sent him the audio file and my transcription early this afternoon. But I haven't heard from him. I just sent him a text."

"He's probably just busy. Sounds like Imani has him working on several cases."

"I guess," said Guin, looking down at her phone. The private investigator hadn't replied to her text.

"You making roast chicken?"

"I am. I'm just waiting for the timer to go off."

Roast chicken was one of Guin's go-tos.

The timer dinged, and Guin checked the chicken, making sure it was the right temperature.

"Smells good," said Glen.

"You always say that."

"Because it's true."

Guin took out the chicken, which sat on a bed of vegetables, and served it.

Over dinner, she told Glen about her call with Sophie.

"You should go to the dinner," he said. "It'll be good for you to meet some people."

"I know plenty of people."

"People you interview for work and your family don't count. You need a social life."

"Says the man who spends all day in front of his computer. And it's not like we don't go out and do stuff."

"I meant, you need a life outside of us and your family. You need friends, women you can hang out with and share stuff with."

"I have women friends. And I share stuff with Shelly all the time." Shelly was Guin's best friend on Sanibel Island. Though the two of them hadn't seen each other since Guin moved to New York.

"I meant here in New York."

"Sophie doesn't count?"

"Sophie's who I'm talking about. You said she was a good friend. I'm sure she wouldn't invite you to meet her friends unless she thought you'd get along."

"I suppose."

"What's the worst thing that could happen?"

Guin immediately thought of a few things, but she didn't say anything.

"Fine, if you think I should go, I'll go."

"Go. I bet you'll have a good time."

"How much do you want to bet?"

Glen gave her a look.

"Fine. No bet."

"Are you going to text Sophie, tell her you're in?"

"You want me to text her now?"

"Why not?"

"Fine," said Guin, taking out her phone. She sent Sophie a text, telling her she was a go for the dinner tomorrow.

"Yay!" Sophie wrote back. "Here are the deets." A few seconds later, she texted Guin the name of the restaurant and that they would be starting with drinks at six.

"You tell her?" asked Glen.

"I did."

"Where's dinner?"

"At some restaurant on the Upper West Side. We're to meet there at six for drinks."

"You don't look excited."

"I just don't want to spend the evening surrounded by a bunch of drunk moms bitching about their partners and their kids."

"I'm sure that won't be the case."

Guin gave him a look. Then she looked down at Glen's plate. It was empty except for some chicken bones.

"You done?" Though it was obvious he was.

"I am."

Guin scraped the plates and then loaded them into the dishwasher. She went to clean the roasting pan, which was soaking in the sink, but Glen said that he would do it.

"Go relax in the living room," he told her. "I'll clean up."

"Actually, I should do a bit of work. But I'll meet you in the living room in a bit."

"Don't work too much," he said.

"Says the person who works too much."

"Touché," he replied.

CHAPTER 29

Guin was in bed, about to turn off her phone, when she finally received a text from Adam Leong, thanking her for the audio file and transcription.

"Everything okay?" she texted him back. "You get your man?" But he didn't text her back.

"What's up?" said Glen, coming over. He had just finished brushing his teeth.

"Adam just texted me, letting me know he received the audio file and transcription."

"You don't look happy."

"I just wish he was more communicative."

"As I said earlier, he's probably just busy. And he doesn't have time to respond to every text or email he receives."

"I guess. I'll follow up with him tomorrow. I'm interested to know what he thought about what Jordan and Shaq had to say. Have you heard anything from Imani?"

"Not recently. The way I see it, no news is good news."

Guin wasn't so sure about that, but she didn't say anything. Instead, she turned off her phone and picked up her book. Glen didn't move.

"You're not coming to bed?"

"I will in a bit."

"You going to your office?"

"I need to check something. I won't be long."

Guin sighed.

"So much for not working so much. I think I liked it better when you freelanced and didn't work all the time."

"Though at least I don't have to spend my weekends photographing weddings."

"True. Now you spend your weekends working on Photog."

"I promise I won't be long."

"Yeah, yeah, yeah."

He went over and gave Guin a kiss.

Guin felt her eyes drooping as she read and put down her book. She looked at the clock on her nightstand and wondered what Glen was doing. He'd been gone for over twenty minutes. She thought about going to his office and dragging him out of there. Instead, she turned off the light and rolled over.

The next morning, as Guin was sipping her coffee, she sent Adam Leong another text, asking if he'd had a chance to listen to the interview. No reply.

"What's up?" said Glen.

"Nothing."

"I know that look. Something's bothering you."

"It's Adam. I sent him another text, but he didn't get back to me."

"I told you, he's probably busy."

"I know he's busy. I just worry that he's not busy working on your case."

"You're the one who wanted me to hire Imani. Have a little faith."

"Mm," mumbled Guin.

"So, what have you got going on today?"

"I'm working on a piece about candy stores."

"Candy stores? Sounds sweet!"

"Ha."

"So what about candy stores? I didn't think there were any anymore."

"That's kind of what the piece is about, the return of the candy store."

"Huh. So, you planning on checking out a bunch of candy stores?"

"There aren't that many to check out, but yes."

Guin had done a quick search and discovered that there were a half-dozen or so candy stores located around the city. A couple of them had been around for decades while several new ones had only recently popped up.

Some of the shops focused exclusively on candy while others also sold ice cream and/or chocolate. Guin couldn't wait to visit all of them (well, maybe not all of them) and sample their wares.

One of the new stores was located on the Upper East Side, near several schools. It had only opened a few weeks ago and didn't have a website yet, just a splash page. She had seen an article about it on one of the food blogs she followed.

As it wasn't far from their apartment, Guin decided she would go over there first and check it out. If she liked the place, she'd include it in the article.

She arrived at the store a little after ten, just after it had opened. The store was small. Or maybe it just felt that way because it was crammed with jars and barrels of different kinds of candies, many of which Guin recognized from when she was a kid. There were Pixy Stix and Smarties, Swedish Fish and different types of Gummis, bubble gum and Tootsie Rolls, red and black licorice in many different form factors, every flavor of jelly bean, Red Hots and ATOMIC FireBalls, and a case filled with fudge, chocolate bark, and chocolate truffles. Guin was the proverbial kid in the candy store!

"May I help you?" said an older gentleman coming over to her.

"To be honest, I'm feeling a bit overwhelmed."

He smiled at her.

"We often get that reaction. Was there something in particular you wanted to try? I saw you looking at the chocolate case."

"You give out free samples?"

"To special customers."

And Guin hadn't even told him she was thinking of writing about the store.

"Thank you, but that's all right. I can pay. I'm actually here researching a piece I'm working on about candy stores. I'm Guin, by the way." She fished in her bag for her card case and handed the man a card.

He looked down at it and then up at Guin.

"Nice to meet you, Guinivere."

"Guin is fine. And you are?"

"Pete Samuelson. I own the place."

"It's a great place," Guin said, looking around. "But I have to ask, why open a candy store?" *Especially at your age,* Guin silently added.

"Nostalgia. I grew up in this neighborhood and had fond memories of going to the candy store that used to be a few doors down from here. Every Saturday, after I received my allowance, I'd run over there and pick myself out a few pieces of candy. And I wanted other kids to experience the same joy I did."

"I love that," said Guin. "So, do you get mostly kids in here? I noticed that you're conveniently located near several schools."

He smiled.

"We get kids of all ages, from little ones coming here with their parents, to students, to college kids, even people your age and my age. I'd like to think there's something for everyone here. And who doesn't love a sweet treat?"

Guin smiled. She certainly did.

"So, have you been busy since you opened?"

"Oh, yes. This is the first quiet moment I've had this week." He saw Guin looking at the chocolate case again. "Are you sure I can't get you a little something?"

"That dark chocolate bark does look very tempting." Dark chocolate was one of Guin's weaknesses.

"You should try a piece. My daughter made it. It's eighty-five percent cacao. Or so she tells me."

"That's pretty dark. You said your daughter made it?"

Pete nodded.

"She's got a fancy chocolate shop in Chelsea. Makes all of her own chocolates and gives me some to sell here. You might say chocolate runs in our veins."

Guin smiled at that.

"Okay, I'll take a piece of the dark chocolate bark and four of the chocolate truffles."

Pete put the truffles in a little box and the bark in a small paper bag.

"Anything else?"

"No, that's enough. How much do I owe you?"

"It's on the house."

"I can't let you do that. It wouldn't be ethical."

"Very well." He quoted her a price, and Guin paid him.

"Do you have a card?" Guin asked him. "I'll probably have more questions for you after I've visited the other stores on my list. And the *Times* will probably send a photographer."

"The *New York Times*?"

Guin nodded.

"I thought I said. I'm a stringer for them, a freelancer."

Pete plucked a card from a stack partially hidden by the cash register.

"Here you go," he said, handing it to her.

Guin took the card and thanked him. Then she asked if she could take a couple of pictures.

"Be my guest."

Guin took out her phone and took several shots of the store. The place was a throwback to a bygone era.

Guin thanked Pete when she was done and said she'd be in touch. As she was leaving, a mother with a little girl entered. As soon as the little girl saw all of the candy, her eyes grew big. Guin smiled. She understood the feeling.

She went home and typed up her impressions of the store. As of now, she planned on including it. However, she would need to check out a few more stores before finalizing her list.

She had lunch at home and then took the subway to Greenwich Village where there was another candy store. It was located near the main campus of New York University. The store had a website and said that they shipped all over the world.

Guin thought the website was well-designed and was impressed by the different types of candy on offer, some of which she'd never heard of. She could probably write about the store without seeing it, but she was curious to see if the place looked as good as it sounded.

However, she arrived to find the place jammed with college students. And she was told the owner wasn't in. She probably should have called first. She squeezed around several students, attempting to take photos, but she quickly gave up. She would phone the store later or email them to schedule an interview and come back another time.

Guin was working in her office when Glen knocked on her door and came in.

"What's up?" she asked him.

"I just got a call from Imani's office. She wants to meet with me."

"Good news or bad news?"

"Her assistant didn't say. Just asked if I had some time tomorrow or the day after."

"What did you tell her?"

"I told her I would call her back."

"You have no idea why she wants to meet with you?"

"I do not."

"Well, it must be important. When are you thinking of going? Do you have time tomorrow?"

"In the late afternoon. Though I don't know if Imani is free then. Assuming she is, do you want to come with me?"

"Is that a trick question? What time tomorrow afternoon?"

"Four or five."

"Fine by me. I was planning on checking out a place in Park Slope for my penny candy article tomorrow, but I could go there late morning or early afternoon—assuming Imani can meet with us at four or five."

"How's the article going?"

"Pretty good. I found a great place here on the Upper East Side that just opened. I left a box of truffles and a bag of chocolate bark from there in the kitchen."

"I saw them, but I wasn't sure if they were for us or for your GNO tonight."

"They're for us. Though, now that you mention it, maybe I should have gotten something for Sophie and her friends. What about you? You working on anything exciting?"

"Just the usual. I'll phone Imani's assistant now and let you know what time the meeting is."

"Great. Thanks."

Guin stood in her closet staring at her clothes. She had looked up the restaurant for tonight's girls' night out. The place seemed chic but not stuffy. And it would be a chilly fall evening. Should she wear a dress? Jeans and a top? And what about shoes?

She thought about texting Sophie, asking her what she planned on wearing. Sophie was so effortlessly chic and probably had a closet full of fabulous clothes, like Carrie Bradshaw in *Sex and the City*. But she was probably busy feeding the kids dinner or getting ready herself.

Guin wished she had been able to go shopping with Fabio before the dinner. But she would have to wait until Friday.

After rejecting several possible outfits, Guin settled on a pair of "nicer" jeans and a white button-down shirt, which she would top with her black leather jacket. And she would wear her black cowboy boots. She quickly changed and then went to the bathroom to put on a little makeup.

As she looked at herself in the mirror, she thought some of her freckles had faded. Did freckles fade? Actually, her whole complexion seemed much paler than when she had lived on Sanibel, and she was rather pale to begin with.

Well, some foundation should fix that. She applied makeup, putting on lipstick last, and studied herself in the mirror again.

"Not bad," she said. Though what to do about her hair?

It was strawberry blonde and curly. Excessively curly. Guin liked to say her hair had a mind of its own. She thought about putting it up but decided to leave it down.

She took a final look at herself and then went to say goodbye to Glen.

"I'm off to dinner," she said.

"You look great," he replied, taking her in. "Very badass."

"Thank you," she said with a smile. She did look a bit badass.

"I hope you have a great time."

"I hope so too."

"And stay out as late as you want."

"These are moms, and it's a school night. I'm sure I'll be home by ten."

"You never know."

"I'd give you a kiss, but I've got lipstick on."

"I understand. Now go. I'll see you later."

Guin arrived at the restaurant a little after six. She spotted Sophie and her friends right away. They were at the bar, laughing.

"Guin!" said Sophie, spying her and smiling.

Guin made her way over to the bar. There were four other women, all around Guin and Sophie's age.

"Everyone, this is Guin, my best friend from high school," Sophie announced.

"Hi, Guin!" They chorused.

"Guin, this is Joy, Candy, Susan, and LaToya."

"Nice to meet you all," said Guin.

"Get yourself a drink," instructed Sophie, "and huddle in. Who knew the place would be so busy on a Tuesday?"

Guin ordered a margarita on the rocks, no salt.

"Guin just moved back to New York from Sanibel, Florida," Sophie told the group.

"Ooh, I love Sanibel!" said Joy. "I used to go there as a kid with my family and look for shells. What were you doing there?"

"I worked for the local paper as a general assignment reporter."

"That sounds fun," said Susan.

"It was," said Guin.

"Do you miss it?" asked Candy.

"I do."

"Though Guin's working for the *New York Times* now as a business reporter," said Sophie.

"I'm just a freelancer."

"Don't sell yourself short. I've seen those articles you've written."

The bartender handed Guin her margarita. She thanked him and took a sip. It tasted delicious.

"So, what brought you back to New York?" asked LaToya.

"My husband's job mostly. He's a photographer, and a friend of his asked him to run his new photography business, Photog, here in the States."

"I love Photog!" said Joy. "I used them to find a photographer for my daughter's bat mitzvah. She was great."

"I'm happy to hear that," said Guin.

"I've used them too," said Susan. "It's a great service."

Guin took another sip of her margarita and then asked the women what they did.

"I'm a stay-at-home mom, like Sophie," said Joy. "Though I was an investment banker before I had Phoebe and Daniel. Now I mostly volunteer."

"Do you miss being an investment banker?"

"Hell no! I was so tired of the old boys' club mentality and getting smaller bonuses than my lame male coworkers."

"Yet you married one of those lame male coworkers," Susan pointed out.

"Ethan wasn't like the rest of them."

The other women didn't comment.

"What about you?" Guin asked Susan.

"I'm a buyer at Saks."

"She's in charge of women's shoes, lucky duck," said Sophie.

"Do you get free shoes?" Guin asked her.

"I wish. But I do get a discount."

"What about you, Candy?"

"I'm an editor."

"Publishing house or magazine?"

"I work for McGraw Hill in educational publishing."

"Candy edits textbooks," said Sophie.

Guin looked over at LaToya.

"I'm in real estate."

"Residential or commercial?"

"Residential."

"LaToya's a star," said Sophie. "She's been a top producer five years in a row."

"Wow," said Guin. "Very impressive."

LaToya shrugged.

Guin listened and sipped her margarita as the women talked about various things.

"Hey, it's time for our reservation," Sophie said at seven.

The women paid their bar tabs and then headed to the hostess stand.

As she predicted, Guin was home before ten o'clock. Glen was in the living room, watching a documentary, the cats asleep on either side of him. He paused the TV when Guin came in.

"You have a good time?" he asked her.

"It was all right."

"Just all right?"

"Sophie's friends are very nice, and the food was good."

"I sense a *but* coming."

"No buts."

"They didn't talk about their kids all night?"

"They talked about them a bit, but we mostly talked about other stuff."

"That's good, right? So, you going to go out with them again?"

"They invited me to next month's GNO, and I told them I'd let them know."

"Why the hesitation?"

"I don't know. I had a good time, but it felt a bit weird. Anyway, I'm going to bed. You coming?"

Glen turned off the TV and got up.

CHAPTER 30

Guin was up by seven the next morning. She planned on visiting a couple more candy stores before she and Glen met with Imani Williams that afternoon. And she wanted to speak with Adam Leong. He still hadn't gotten back to her, and she was feeling frustrated.

She would call him after she had her coffee and breakfast.

A little after eight, she picked up her phone and entered his number. She was expecting the call to go to voicemail and was surprised when he picked up.

"Leong."

"It's Guin Jones."

He didn't say anything.

"Do you have a few minutes? I wanted to discuss my interview with Jordan and Shaq. Did you have a chance to listen to it or read the transcription?"

"I did."

"In retrospect, I probably should have filmed it. But too late now. So, what did you think? I got the feeling they were hiding something."

"What makes you say that?"

"When I asked them if they had run into anyone from the shoot after they had left, they said that they hadn't. But I got the feeling they were lying."

The private investigator didn't say anything.

"Also, Jordan said that Ronnie had given him the code

to the building. But you said that she said that she only gave the codes to the front door and the studio to Margaux and Glen. And speaking of codes, how did all of those people who were at the music shoot get in? They couldn't all have had the code to the front door. My guess is the front door was left open, or it was unlocked. Did you ask the manager about that?"

"I did. Apparently, someone had propped it open."

"So anyone could have wandered into the studio that evening. Another thing, you heard the part where Shaq said that he overheard Margaux on the phone that evening, talking to someone named Alex, yes?"

"I did."

"Do you think it was Morgan?"

"Mr. Onyema said he wasn't sure who Ms. Boucher spoke with."

Guin frowned.

"Speaking of Alex Morgan, did you call the club to see if he was back from England?"

"I did."

"And? Is he back?"

"He is."

"Did you speak with him?"

"Not yet. I'm meeting with him at the club later today."

"I'd like to go with you." Though she was supposed to go with Glen to see Imani Williams that afternoon.

"I don't think that's a good idea."

"Why not?"

"Per your own words, you spooked him."

Guin made a face. She recalled saying that she thought she spooked Morgan. But maybe she was wrong and his mother really did have an accident.

"Let me speak with Mr. Morgan," said the private investigator. "If he says anything of interest, I'm sure Ms. Williams will inform you and your husband."

"Fine. What time are you meeting with him?"

Guin heard a beeping on the line.

"I need to go," said Leong.

Before Guin could say another word, the call ended.

Later that morning, Guin visited two more candy stores, both of which were in Brooklyn, though one of them was more of an ice cream parlor that sold candy on the side. The one that was a pure candy store had been around for decades and looked like it. In fact, Guin wondered how long some of the candy had been there for. There was a young woman by the cash register who looked bored. And Guin decided not to ask to speak with the owner. Instead, she left and headed to the ice cream parlor.

The candy store with the ice cream parlor (though it was really the other way around) was bright and cheerful, with colorful cartoons on the walls, and Guin couldn't resist treating herself to an ice cream, getting a scoop of oatmeal cookie, one of the place's inventive flavors, on a sugar cone. It was delicious. When she was done, she asked the young man who had served her if the owner was around.

The young man looked a bit nervous, and Guin quickly explained that she was a reporter doing an article on candy stores for the *New York Times* and wanted to include them.

The young man looked relieved and told Guin he'd get the owner.

A couple of minutes later, the owner, a woman named Beth who looked barely out of college, appeared, and Guin spent the next twenty minutes asking her about the store. It turned out, Beth's parents had owned an ice cream shop in Michigan, where Beth had grown up. And when Beth graduated from Pratt, instead of getting a job in graphic design, she decided to open an ice cream parlor/candy store like the one her parents had in Michigan here in Brooklyn.

Guin loved Beth's story—and her store—and planned on including her in her article.

Guin returned home and transcribed her interview with Beth. Then, a little before four, she and Glen headed downtown to Imani Williams's office.

"And you have no idea what she wants to discuss with you?" Guin asked her husband as they rode the subway downtown.

"Nope."

"You didn't ask her?"

"I didn't see the point."

"You think it's bad news?"

"Why don't you wait and see what she has to say before assuming it's something bad?"

Guin bit her lip to stop herself from saying something.

They exited the train at 42nd Street and headed to the lawyer's office. They were told that Ms. Williams was on a call when they arrived, but her assistant would be out momentarily. Sure enough, Lauren came out a few minutes later and escorted Glen and Guin to the conference room.

"How long do you think she'll be?" Guin asked.

"Not long," said Lauren. "Can I get either of you something to drink?"

"I'm good," said Glen.

Guin's mouth and throat felt dry, no doubt from nervousness, but she said she was good too.

Lauren left, and less than five minutes later, Ms. Williams came in, accompanied by Adam Leong. Guin hadn't expected to see him. Wasn't he supposed to be meeting with Alex Morgan? Had he met with him already?

"Thank you both for coming," the attorney said to Guin and Glen.

"I take it you have news," said Glen.

"I do. We received a copy of Ms. Boucher's will."

Guin and Glen waited for her to go on.

"Did you know that you were the primary beneficiary?" she asked Glen.

"I didn't even know she had a will," he replied. "When is it from?"

"Six years ago."

"So when you two were still married," Guin said. She turned to Ms. Williams. "How much did she leave Glen?"

"Her estate is still being evaluated, but," she paused. "Between her apartment, investments, jewelry, and artwork, it's believed her estate is conservatively worth around three million dollars."

Guin was about to whistle but stopped herself.

"And she left everything to Glen?"

"Not everything. She wanted half of her estate to go to charity if they didn't have any children. And she had a handful of bequests."

"To anyone we know?"

The attorney listed the names of the various people Margaux had left bequests to. Glen was familiar with most of them. They were all friends or relatives of Margaux's.

"But that still leaves around a million dollars to Glen."

"Correct."

Under other circumstances, Guin would be thrilled with Glen inheriting a million dollars. But Margaux leaving a small fortune to Glen in her will could be construed as another motive for him killing her, even though Glen didn't need Margaux's money.

"And the DA could say that Glen knew about the will and the money and that's why he killed her," Guin said aloud. "Even though he didn't know about the will and doesn't need the money."

"Correct. There's more though," said Ms. Williams. Guin waited for her to go on, dreading what else she had to tell them. "Ms. Boucher recently drafted another will using an online service."

"Did that one also name Glen as the primary beneficiary?"

"It did not."

Guin breathed a sigh of relief.

"Who was the primary beneficiary in that will?"

"Aleksei Smirnov. But as far as we can tell, the new will hadn't been notarized and witnessed."

"So is it not valid?"

"New York probate courts do accept wills that were drafted online, but they need to be signed and witnessed. And the person must be considered to be of sound mind when drafting it."

"So it's not valid," said Glen.

"It's up to the court to decide," said Ms. Williams. "It's possible they will admit it."

"Did Smirnov know about the will?" Guin asked her.

"He claims he didn't."

"So this will, was it on her laptop?"

"Her laptop is missing. The police found a printout of the will when they searched her apartment."

"What happened to her laptop?"

"We don't know."

"Did someone ask Ronnie Banerjee about it?"

"The police and Adam spoke with her."

"And?"

"Ms. Banerjee claimed to have no idea where it was."

"Did Margaux have a laptop with her at the photo shoot?" Guin asked Glen.

"I don't know. I just saw her using her phone."

Guin frowned.

"I assume the police searched her apartment for the laptop."

"They did."

"And it wasn't there."

"Correct."

"So whoever killed her probably has it. Along with her phone."

The attorney and the private investigator both looked at Glen.

"Don't look at me. I don't have her computer. I'm not even sure she had one at the shoot. But if you don't believe me, search our apartment."

"So in this new will," said Guin, "Margaux left everything to her business partner, Aleksei Smirnov?"

"Not everything, she made several bequests to relatives and friends."

"The same ones as in the old will?"

"With one addition. She made a rather sizable bequest to one Fabio Bertolini."

"Fabio, as in her stylist? How much did she leave him?"

"A hundred and fifty thousand dollars."

This time, Guin did whistle.

"That's quite a chunk of change. Did she say why?"

"She wanted to repay him for investing in her."

"Ah. He had invested fifty thousand dollars in her athleisure business. This must have been her way of paying him back. I wonder if he knew."

"He claims he did not."

"Did Margaux leave anything to Alex Morgan in the new will?"

"She did not."

"What about anyone else who was at the photo shoot?" Guin immediately thought of Ronnie.

"Only Mr. Bertolini."

"I'll ask him about it when I go clothes shopping with him on Friday."

"You're going shopping with him?" said the attorney. "I'm not sure that's a good idea."

"Why not? He is a personal stylist, and I need some new clothes." *And some answers*, she said to herself.

"You should let Adam speak with him."

"Adam's so busy, and I can ask Fabio about the will while I'm trying on clothes."

The lawyer and investigator exchanged a look.

"I promise not to accuse him of murdering Margaux."

"Very well," said Ms. Williams. "Just be careful."

"I will. In any case, I'm meeting him at Bloomingdale's. I doubt he'd try anything there."

The attorney and investigator looked dubious but didn't say anything.

"Was there anything else you had to share?"

"We received a copy of the autopsy report."

"And?" said Guin. "Anything interesting?"

"As a matter of fact..." said the attorney. "The toxicology report revealed a high level of amphetamines in Ms. Boucher's system."

"Amphetamines? Was Margaux on any prescription drugs?"

"The police found a half-empty bottle of Adderall in her bag."

"Did Margaux have ADHD?" Guin asked Glen. That was typically what Adderall was prescribed for.

"Not that I was aware of," he replied.

"We're looking into it," said Ms. Williams.

"What about drugs to treat bipolar disorder?"

"There was nothing about mood stabilizers in the autopsy report, just amphetamines."

"Huh. Well, the Adderall could explain her erratic behavior that evening. Did the autopsy report reveal anything else?"

The attorney looked at Glen.

"The medical examiner found bruises on her wrists."

"I told you, I was trying to keep her from hitting me again. Ask anyone who was at the shoot. But I didn't kill her. I swear to you."

Guin believed him, but it didn't look good.

Guin saw the attorney looking down at her watch.

"I need to go," said Ms. Williams. "Do either of you have any questions for me?"

"Do you still think I'm innocent?" Glen asked her.

"Have you told me the truth?"

"I have."

"Then I believe you."

CHAPTER 31

Guin had meant to take Adam Leong aside and ask him about his meeting with Alex Morgan, but he had hurried away before Guin had the chance. She texted him instead, but he hadn't gotten back to her.

Guin spent the next day working on her candy store article, calling or writing to the stores she planned on including with some additional questions and typing a first draft. But her mind kept wandering to the new evidence Imani Williams had received. None of it looked good for Glen. However, if they could prove that Fabio knew about the new will and needed money, it would show that Glen wasn't the only one with a reason to kill Margaux.

Guin had still not heard back from Adam Leong that evening, so she sent him another text, again asking him if he had met with Alex Morgan and, if so, what Morgan had to say. But she hadn't received a reply by the time she went to bed.

The next morning, Guin ate a light breakfast before heading to Bloomingdale's to meet with Fabio. She had spent way too long deciding what to wear, wanting to look stylish but not fussy. Finally, not happy with any of her clothes, she put on the same outfit she had worn to the GNO dinner. Then she hurried out the door.

As she rode the subway to 59th Street, she thought about Margaux's will, the new one. She needed a subtle way to ask Fabio about it.

She got off the 6 train and made her way up the stairs to Bloomingdale's. She was to meet Fabio on the fourth floor. Guin knew that Bloomingdale's had their own personal shoppers, and that early in his career Fabio had been one of them. Did he have some kind of special arrangement with the store?

Fabio was there when Guin arrived, chatting with a nattily dressed Black man. They stopped talking as Guin approached, and Guin saw the two men eyeing her. Guin immediately felt self-conscious. Were they silently judging her—or her choice of outfit?

"Good morning," Guin said, forcing herself to smile.

"This is Anthony," said Fabio. "He'll be helping us today."

"Nice to meet you, Anthony."

Guin saw Anthony eyeing her.

"Is something wrong?" she said.

"Sorry, it's just…" He turned to Fabio. "You were right. The resemblance is remarkable. Though the hair is all wrong."

"Resemblance?" said Guin.

"You look just like Amy Adams, the actress. Or her cousin. You're not related to her, are you?"

"Not that I know of."

"And is that your real hair or a perm?" He went over to Guin and took a closer look at her hair. "Though it doesn't look like a perm."

"You think I paid someone to make my hair look like this?"

"And is that your natural hair color?"

"Please forgive Anthony," said Fabio, giving the personal shopper a stern look. "He clearly had too much caffeine this morning."

"It's all right," said Guin. "I'm used to people commenting on my hair. And for the record, the curls and the color are a hundred percent natural." She looked over at the rack positioned behind Anthony. "Are all of those clothes for me?"

"They are," said Fabio. "I told Anthony to pull a selection of things."

"Wow," said Guin, looking at all of the clothes. "Where do we begin?"

"Let's start with business attire and go from there. Anthony will put everything in the dressing room for you."

Guin wondered how Anthony liked being bossed around. But if he regularly worked with Fabio, he was probably used to it.

There were four different work outfits for Guin to try on, and Fabio insisted she come out and model each one.

Guin emerged from the dressing room a few minutes later dressed in a navy pencil skirt and white blouse. Fabio looked down at her bare feet.

"Let's get you some shoes." He went over to the rack and retrieved a pair of navy pumps. "Here," he said, handing them to her.

Guin put them on.

"Better?" she said.

"Much. Now turn around."

Guin did as she was told.

"I may want to hem the skirt a bit, but it suits you."

"So you like the outfit?"

"It's a huge improvement."

Guin studied herself in the three-way mirror. She liked the way she looked, but she had no idea where she'd wear the outfit. Certainly not on Sanibel. Though she wasn't on Sanibel. She was in New York City, where people dressed much chicer.

"Go try on the pantsuit," said Fabio.

Guin went back into the changing room and put on the pantsuit. The pants were way too long, as were the sleeves on the jacket, and Guin felt ridiculous as she emerged from the fitting room.

"Hm," said Fabio. "We could always hem everything, but I'm thinking we should pass on this one. Go try on the dress."

Guin tried on the wrap dress Fabio had picked out for her. She liked how silky the fabric felt and how it hugged her body but wasn't too tight.

She emerged from the dressing room.

"What do you think?" Guin said, twirling for Fabio.

"Hm…"

"You don't like it?"

"I'm just not sure about the color."

"Well, I like it," said Guin.

"Go try on the slacks and the top."

Guin returned to the dressing room and put on the slacks and the top Fabio—or Anthony—had picked out. Again, the pants were long, but otherwise she liked the way they looked. She didn't really have any dressy pants for fall or winter. And the blue top fit her well.

She came out of the dressing room and went over to Fabio.

"What do you think?"

He studied her.

"The pants are too long. But otherwise the outfit works."

"I thought the same thing," said Guin.

"I'll have Anthony get someone to hem them. Now go try on the evening clothes I picked out."

"I don't know if I really need evening clothes if I get the pencil skirt and the wrap dress."

Fabio gave her a look.

"Fine. I'll go try them on."

Guin put on the black dress first, but she didn't think it worked with her coloring, and Fabio agreed. Then she tried on the three other dresses.

"What do you think of this one?" she said, twirling around in the green dress.

"You should get it."

Guin looked at herself in the mirror. She liked the green dress, but she wasn't sure. She went back into the changing room and tried on the blue dress. It also looked good on her.

"I like this one too," she said.

"You should get both."

"I don't know if I need three dresses."

"You'll have them forever. We just need to get you a jacket. Hold on." Fabio went over to the clothing rack to look for one.

"So is this what you do with all of your clients?" Guin asked him. "You have Anthony or someone like him pick out a bunch of clothes and have your clients try them on?"

"Yes," he replied, examining the jackets on the rack. "Though every client's needs are different."

"And do most of your clients take your recommendations?"

"They do. Here, try on this jacket," said Fabio, handing her a blue blazer.

Guin tried it on. It was a bit big.

"Hm. Maybe in a different size."

"And did Margaux take your recommendations?"

"Sometimes."

"Did you know that she left you money in her will?"

Fabio stopped what he was doing and turned to look at Guin.

"How did you hear about that?"

"Did you know?"

"I had no idea she left me a dime until I received a call about it from some private investigator. Margaux didn't like to discuss money."

"So she never mentioned leaving you a hundred-and-fifty-thousand dollars in her will?"

"Never."

Guin tried to discern if he was telling the truth. It seemed like it.

"So she never talked about paying you back for all the money you lost with her?"

"I told you, she was planning on giving me a share of the mocktail business."

"But she didn't."

Fabio sighed.

"No."

"Was she ADD?"

"Margaux? More OCD or bipolar. Why?"

"Just curious. Where did you go after the Château Margaux Mocktails shoot?"

"To see a friend."

"And can this friend vouch for you?"

"Why all the questions about Margaux and that photo shoot? The police caught her killer. It was her ex-husband."

"You really think he killed her?"

"Well, I certainly didn't!"

"Everything all right?" It was Anthony, looking concerned. He turned to Guin. "Did you like the clothes?"

"Very much," said Guin. "You have good taste."

Anthony preened. Then he saw Fabio looking at him and turned serious.

"It was really all Fabio. He told me what to get."

Guin wondered if that was true.

"So, what did you decide?"

"I think I'm going to take the wrap dress and either the green dress or the blue one."

"You should take the pencil skirt and the white blouse— and the slacks and blue top too," said Fabio. "You can wear the skirt and the slacks for work or for going out."

He had a point.

"I'll go take another look at everything," Guin said and went back into the dressing room to change and examine the outfits.

She looked at the price tags. None of the pieces were

cheap. But Guin hadn't bought work or evening clothes in ages. And with all of the assignments she'd been doing for the *Times*, she had money to spend.

She changed back into her jeans and shirt and grabbed the pencil skirt, slacks, two tops, and two dresses she had decided to get and emerged from the dressing room.

"If I get the skirt and the slacks, will you hem them for free?" she asked Anthony. "Otherwise, I'm not sure."

Guin saw Fabio give Anthony a look.

"Of course," Anthony replied.

Guin smiled and handed Anthony her credit card. When she had paid, he arranged for someone from their tailoring department to come and measure the pencil skirt and slacks.

"I'm afraid I need to go," said Fabio as Guin waited.

"Go? You don't want to make sure the tailor measures correctly?"

Guin was teasing. Sort of.

"I'm afraid I have another appointment."

"Oh," said Guin, feeling strangely disappointed.

"But Anthony will make sure it's done properly. Won't you, Anthony?"

"Of course," Anthony replied.

Guin saw Fabio looking at her hair.

"Is there something in my hair?" she asked him.

"No, but..." He was frowning.

"What?" said Guin.

"I should make you an appointment with Maurizio. He specializes in difficult hair."

"I, uh..."

"And we should do something about your makeup."

Guin suddenly felt a bit queasy.

Fabio's smartwatch was flashing.

"I must go," he said. "Let me know if you want me to schedule an appointment for you. Maurizio's typically booked months in advance, but he owes me a favor."

"Um, I'll let you know."

"Don't wait too long," he told her. Then he was off.

Guin thought about her time with Fabio on her way uptown. He had been her chief suspect, but now she wasn't so sure about him. Sure, he could be lying about the will, but she didn't think so. And the police probably checked his alibi—or Adam had. She would ask him if he ever got back to her.

The train pulled into 77th Street and Guin got out. Miracle of miracles, Adam had finally gotten back to her! Though his text was brief. He'd written that he'd been insanely busy, but yes, he had spoken with Morgan. And if she wanted to know what Morgan had to say, she should ask the attorney.

Guin frowned.

CHAPTER 32

"So, how did things go with Fabio?" Glen asked Guin as they ate lunch together in the kitchen. "Did you buy anything?"

"Uh-huh," she said, suddenly feeling self-conscious about all the clothes she had purchased. Not that Glen would care.

"You want to give me a fashion show later?"

"Sure."

"What's up? You seem a bit blue."

Guin sighed.

"I don't think he did it."

"You mean you don't think Fabio killed Margaux?"

Guin nodded.

"Did you really think he had?"

"It was a possibility. Margaux was pretty hard on him at the shoot. Pretty hard on him in general. Maybe he got fed up with her fits. Plus, he lost a lot of money with her."

"Though didn't you say he blamed Alex Morgan for that?" Guin frowned. "So why do you think he didn't kill her?"

"He claimed he had no idea about the will and that he was with a friend at the time of the murder."

"He could be lying."

"I know. But I don't think so. I watched his face when I told him about the will and asked him where he'd gone after the shoot. It didn't seem like he was lying. Do you think he could have killed her?"

"Not really. He doesn't seem the type."

"Though there isn't really a type when it comes to killers. Oftentimes they're regular people who just snapped. And it sounded like Margaux caused a few people to snap that evening."

"True."

"Also, I finally heard back from Adam Leong. He met with Alex Morgan, but he wouldn't tell me anything. Said we should ask Imani. You didn't hear from her again, did you?"

"Not today."

"Which leads me to think Morgan didn't kill Margaux either. Even though Shaq thought he overheard Margaux speaking to someone named Alex on the phone and that she was pissed at him."

"It could have been Morgan she was speaking to. But that doesn't mean he came to the studio and killed her."

"I know. Which leaves Jordan. I'm pretty sure he's hiding something. I wonder if Adam spoke with him and Shaq. I bet Shaq knows something. Though there's also the possibility it could have been someone who'd been at the music video shoot up on the roof who killed her."

"You really think that someone got lost, wandered into the studio, got into it with Margaux, and hit her with a mocktail bottle?"

Well, when he put it that way.

Guin sighed.

"I know, it sounds unlikely. We just need to give a jury something, something that could create a reasonable doubt in their minds that you were the only one who could have killed her."

Glen leaned over and kissed his wife.

"What was that for?"

"For believing in me and working to clear my name."

"You'd do the same for me."

Glen looked down at Guin's plate. She'd barely touched her food.

"You should finish your omelet."

"I'm not that hungry."

"Have a couple more bites. You'll feel better."

Guin reluctantly picked up her fork and had a couple more bites.

"Happy now?"

"You're in a mood."

"Sorry. I'm just frustrated. Thanks for making lunch."

"Happy to do it." He looked down at his smartwatch. "I hate to ask, but do you mind cleaning up? I have to get on a call."

"Go. I'll clean up."

Guin was working on her candy store article, but she was having trouble concentrating. Instead, she opened the file containing the crime scene photos. There must be something in the photos, some clue, that she missed. She slowly went through them but didn't notice anything new. Then she went through the photos Glen had taken.

She stopped on a photo she hadn't paid much attention to before. Was that Margaux yelling at Dionne in the background? She zoomed in. It sure looked like it. She clicked on the next picture. The two women looked to still be arguing, and was Dionne clutching a mocktail bottle?

Guin had dismissed the stylist as a suspect as Dionne didn't have a history with Margaux and had no reason to kill her. Well, other than Margaux insulting and belittling her. Could Dionne have snapped?

Dionne had supposedly kept her cool at the shoot. But Glen's photos said otherwise. Had Dionne returned after everyone had left to give Margaux a piece of her mind? Maybe the two women had fought and Dionne lost control and hit Margaux with a mocktail bottle, not necessarily planning on killing her. Guin tried to picture it.

She typed Dionne's name into her browser and watched as the screen filled. There were multiple people named Dionne Davies. Guin narrowed her search, adding the word *stylist* to it. That was better.

She scrolled through the search results and was about to skip over an article from four years before about a soap opera actress accusing her partner, Dionne Davies, of sexual assault when she decided to click on it.

Guin read through the piece and then sat back in her chair. The Dionne Davies mentioned in the article sure sounded like the Dionne Davies she knew. And if the actress was to be believed, Dionne had assaulted her, causing the actress to go to the hospital.

Guin looked to see if there were other articles about the assault. There were, on various gossip sites. And Guin didn't give a lot of credence to stories on gossip sites. Still, there was often a grain of truth to them.

Guin thought about tracking down the actress and asking her about the story. But she wasn't sure the actress would talk to her. And even if she did, Guin wondered if she could trust the actress, actors having a flair for the dramatic.

No, Guin would ask Dionne about it—and about Margaux. Not that Dionne would cop to assaulting either her former paramour or Margaux. But Guin still felt she should have another chat with the stylist, show her the photos Glen had taken, and see how she reacted.

She found Dionne's card and entered her number into her phone.

"Davies."

"Hello, Ms. Davies," said Guin. "This is Guin Jones. I had some follow-up questions for you and was hoping we could meet to discuss them."

"I'm at a shoot," said the stylist.

Then why did she answer her phone? Guin wondered.

"Do you have time early next week?"

"You can't just email or text me your questions?"

"I'd rather ask them in person."

Guin heard the stylist sigh.

"You want to come to my studio first thing Monday? I'm pretty busy the rest of the week."

"Monday morning is fine. What time?"

"Can you be there at eight-thirty?"

"I can. Where's your studio?"

Dionne gave Guin the address in East Harlem.

"Got it. Thank you. See you Monday."

Guin ended the call and put down her phone. As soon as she did, it began to ring. It was Sophie.

"Hey, Sophie. What's up?"

"Do you have a minute?"

"Is everything all right?"

"Everything's fine. I just wanted to let you know, I took the job! And today was my first day."

"Good for you!" said Guin. "So, how was it?"

"I was nervous at first, but the shoot went really well. I was mostly there to observe and play gopher, which was fine. Carmen is a pro. And Calista was great, really sweet."

"Who are Carmen and Calista?"

"Sorry. Carmen is FLAIR's fashion editor and Calista Galanis is the woman we're profiling. She's a jewelry designer. She creates these gorgeous brooches for men and women."

"Do men wear brooches?"

"Oh yeah. They're *the* accessory for guys this year. All these actors and models have been wearing them on their lapels, many of them designed by Calista. She's credited with starting the trend."

"Huh." Who knew? Guin couldn't remember the last time she looked at a fashion magazine.

"Anyway, I wanted to thank you. I'm not sure if I'd have taken the gig if you hadn't encouraged me to."

"Well, I'm glad you had a good first day."

"I did. And I'm looking forward to next week too."

"What's next week?"

"We're profiling Angie Heart."

"Angie Heart the rocker?"

"The one and only."

"Didn't we see her at the Garden?"

"We did. With her band the Angels. And now I'll get to meet her!"

Guin could tell that Sophie was excited and was happy for her friend.

"Hey, I've got to go pick up the kids at school. But let's get together soon."

"I'd like that," said Guin. "Let me know when you're free."

"I'll text you some dates. Ciao for now!"

"Ciao!" said Guin.

The call ended, and Guin smiled.

Lance and Owen had invited Glen and Guin over for brunch that Sunday. They had just finished redecorating their apartment and wanted to show it off.

"Come in!" said Lance, opening the door.

Glen handed him a bottle of champagne.

"Ooh, champagne! *Merci beaucoup!*"

Guin and Glen gazed around the loft.

"Come, let me give you two a tour."

"Where's Owen?" said Guin.

"In the kitchen."

Owen, like Glen, loved to cook, which was a good thing as Lance was clueless in the kitchen.

"Shall we go say hello?"

"Let's," said Guin.

"Something smells good," said Glen upon entering the kitchen. "Did you bake bread?"

"I did," said Owen. "As a matter of fact…" He opened the lower oven and removed a perfect-looking boule of sourdough.

"It looks beautiful," said Guin. She turned to her husband. "You should make us bread."

"I will. I just haven't had time."

"What else did you make?" Guin asked her brother-in-law.

"A spinach and tomato quiche and an arugula salad."

"Sounds great."

"And we got some fabulous fruit tarts from this new patisserie for dessert," said Lance.

"Yum!" said Guin.

Though between the quiche and the pastries, Glen would have to roll her home.

"Shall I open the champagne?" said Lance. "Or should I wait until after the tour?"

"Let's wait until after the tour," said Guin.

"*Allons-y!*" said Lance—which Guin knew meant *Let's go!* in French.

Guin oohed and aahed as Lance led them around. The decorator had done a good job. Though Guin hated to think how much he had charged her brother and Owen.

They returned to the kitchen when they were done.

"You did a great job," said Glen.

"Thank you," said Lance. "We're pleased. So, champagne?"

"Sure," said Guin.

"You want it straight up or mixed with OJ?"

"I'll take mine straight," said Glen.

"Of course you do," said Lance with a wink.

"I'll have mine with some orange juice," said Guin.

"*Bien sûr,*" said Lance. Then he deftly removed the cork and began to pour.

CHAPTER 33

Brunch had been fun, a much-needed distraction. Guin liked that she now got to see her brother and Owen regularly. It was one of the perks of living back in New York. Actually, living in Manhattan had a lot of perks: there were lots of good restaurants and coffee places, and you could have practically anything delivered to your door; there were the museums; and shows; and Central Park. Though Guin wasn't looking forward to winter. She hated the cold.

Today had been chilly, only in the fifties, and Guin had felt herself shivering. And it was only early October. What would it be like in December? Though Glen had promised her that if they wound up staying in New York longer, they would fly back to Sanibel for Christmas and New Year's.

"So, what do you want to do about dinner?" Glen asked Guin as they rode the subway back to Manhattan.

"How can you even think about food after what we just ate?"

"It wasn't that much," said Glen.

"You had two pieces of quiche, two pieces of bread, two helpings of salad, and a fruit tart. You call that not much?"

"They were small pieces of quiche, and I hadn't had breakfast."

Glen was over six feet tall and quite trim and could seemingly eat whatever he wanted and not gain a pound, unlike Guin.

"Fine. What do *you* want to have for dinner?"

"I was thinking we could pick up a piece of fish at Whole Foods."

"I'm down with that," said Guin.

Monday morning, Guin took the train uptown to Dionne's studio, arriving there at eight-thirty. She hadn't been to East Harlem in years, and it had changed quite a bit since she'd last been there. For the better, she thought.

She pressed the button marked D2 Styles on the outside of the building. A few seconds later, Dionne buzzed her in.

Guin took the elevator up to the fourth floor and found Dionne's studio. There was a video doorbell, which Guin rang, looking into the camera. She heard locks being turned a few seconds later and the door opened.

"Come in," said Dionne, locking the door behind Guin.

The studio was a big open space that Dionne had divided into different areas. There were racks of shelves filled with all sorts of props in one section; what looked like a conference table and chairs near the bank of windows; a little seating area; a small photo studio; and a kitchenette.

Guin was impressed.

"Do you do photo shoots here?" Guin asked the stylist, looking over at the photo studio.

"Sometimes," said Dionne. "Mostly it's just me, testing stuff out."

"Testing stuff out?"

"I like to do a dry run before showing up to a shoot, see how what I arrange is going to look to the camera."

Guin noticed the photos hanging on the walls. They looked like product ads or magazine spreads, except they didn't have any text.

"You take those?" Guin asked her.

"Some of them. Others I just styled."

"They're really good."

"Thanks. So, why did you want to talk to me again?"

"I wanted to show you something." Guin took out her phone and showed Dionne the photos Glen had taken, showing her and Margaux arguing.

"So?" said Dionne.

"It looks to me like you and Margaux were having it out."

"So?"

"You told me you didn't get into it with her, that you just ignored her insults. But you look pretty angry in these photos."

"I didn't want to get into it with her, but she didn't give me a choice. She practically shoved me against that wall, insisting that I answer her. What was I supposed to do?"

"What about the bottle you're holding?"

"What about it?"

"Did you think about using it on Margaux?"

"What do you mean?"

"I mean, did you think about hitting her with it?"

"I may have for a split second, but I'm not that stupid."

"Did you ever hit that actress you dated?"

"You mean Melanie?"

Guin nodded.

"I read that you assaulted her."

"You read that on some gossip site?"

"Is it true that you hit her? She said she had to go to the hospital and got stitches."

"That was just Melanie being a drama queen."

"So you didn't hit her?"

"She hit me first."

"So you did hit her."

Dionne didn't say anything.

"Where did you go after the Château Margaux photo shoot?"

"Home."

"You didn't go up to the party on the roof, maybe get a drink someplace?"

"I went straight home. You want to see the Lyft receipt? I've got it here on my phone."

"That's okay," said Guin as Dionne pulled out her phone and started scrolling.

"Here," she said, thrusting her phone in Guin's face.

Guin felt her face grow warm.

"Is that why you wanted to speak with me," said the stylist, "to ask me about Melanie and Margaux?"

"I just..."

"I think you should leave."

Dionne went over to a table and began to arrange the props that were on it. Guin went over to her.

"Look, I'm sorry. I just..."

Guin was looking down when she noticed a liquor box under the table. It couldn't be, could it? She leaned down and pulled it out. Were those the Château Margaux mocktail bottles? She pulled out a bottle. It had a Château Margaux label on it.

"Where did you get these?" she asked Dionne.

"Ronnie gave them to me."

"Why? Didn't she need the bottles?" *And why did Ronnie have them instead of the police?* Guin wondered.

"She said she didn't need them anymore, because of the rebranding."

"But why give them to you?"

"She thought I could use them as props. I was planning on removing the labels, but I hadn't gotten around to it."

Guin counted the bottles. There were nine of them.

"What happened to the other bottles?"

"I've no idea. That's what Ronnie gave me. Now if you wouldn't mind leaving? I've got work to do."

"Thank you for your time," said Guin.

Guin took a quick look around the studio and then left.

As soon as she got outside, she sent a text to Adam, asking if he could meet with her later, that it was important. She was surprised when he got right back to her.

"I'm meeting with Imani at noon. I could meet you after."

"That would be great," wrote Guin. "What time?"

"I should be free by one."

"One it is. Shall we meet in front of the New York Public Library? It's right by her office."

"Fine."

"Great. I'll see you then!"

Guin had been standing in front of the library for fifteen minutes, but there was no sign of the private investigator. Was he blowing her off? Guin had checked her phone several times, to see if he had messaged her, but he hadn't. She was typing him a text when he finally appeared.

"You're here!" she said. "I was starting to think you were blowing me off."

"My meeting ran long."

"So, shall we go to Bryant Park and grab something to eat? I haven't had lunch. Have you?"

"I don't have a lot of time."

"We can grab a hot dog or a sandwich. Come."

He reluctantly followed Guin to the park, where they purchased sandwiches and drinks and took them to an empty table.

"So what is so urgent?" Adam Leong asked Guin once they were seated.

"I know you said to ask Ms. Williams about Alex Morgan, but can you just tell me what he said? Did he have an alibi for the night of the photo shoot?"

"He did."

"Where was he?"

"With a client."

"He was giving a lesson? I didn't think the club was open that late."

"He wasn't giving a lesson. At least not a tennis lesson."

Guin looked confused.

"I don't understand." The private investigator gave her a look. "Oh," she said, realization dawning. So much for the club's no dating clients policy.

"Did you confirm his story?"

"I did."

Guin frowned.

"What about the phone call Margaux received, the one from someone named Alex."

"It wasn't Morgan."

"You sure about that?"

"He showed me his phone."

Guin frowned again.

"What about his wanting a piece of Margaux's business?"

"He confessed that Margaux hadn't actually offered one to him."

"So you don't think he killed her."

"I do not."

There went another suspect.

"So, what did you want to tell me?" he asked Guin.

"A few things. As you know, I met with Fabio Bertolini."

"To go clothes shopping."

"Yes. And I asked him if he knew about Margaux's new will, and he said he didn't. He also had an alibi for that evening. And while he could have been lying, I don't think he was. I watched his face and body language. It looked to me like he was telling the truth."

"You're an expert in physiognomy?"

"Physiognomy?"

"Reading people's expressions."

"No, but I'd like to think I can tell when someone's lying." Which is why she wanted to ask him about Jordan and Shaq. However, first, she would tell him about her visit with Dionne Davies.

"Speaking of which, this morning I went to Dionne Davies's studio to have a chat with her. Turns out, she wasn't honest with me when she said she didn't get into it with Margaux at the shoot. Glen had pictures of the two of them arguing."

The private investigator's eyebrows went up slightly.

"She said it was no big deal, but you'll never guess what I found in her studio."

"What?"

"The box of Château Margaux Mocktails bottles!"

"Are you sure?"

"I checked. Unless there were other bottles, they were the ones from the photo shoot."

"And why did Ms. Davies have them?"

"She said that Ronnie gave them to her, that she didn't need them anymore, because of the rebranding."

"But why give them to Ms. Davies?"

"She thought Dionne might want to use them as props."

"Hm."

"What are you thinking?"

"It's not important." But Guin sensed it was and wished she was able to read his mind.

"In any event, even though the two of them argued, I don't think Dionne killed Margaux."

"Why not?"

"She had a Lyft receipt, showing when she got home. So, did you speak with Jordan and Shaq?"

"I did."

"Separately this time?"

He nodded.

"And? Did you learn anything?"

"I did. It appears Mr. Abara lied to you."

CHAPTER 34

"Jordan lied to me?" Guin said. "What did he lie about? Did he have something to do with Margaux's death?"

"I don't think so."

"Then what did he lie about?"

"He and his friend saw Ms. Banerjee outside the studio building the night of the photo shoot."

"Jordan told you that?"

"No, Mr. Onyema did."

"And he's sure it was Ronnie?"

"He said he was pretty sure. However, he didn't recognize the man she was with. At least not at the time."

"So the man she was with wasn't someone from the shoot," Guin said more to herself than to Leong. "And you said Alex Morgan had an alibi."

The private investigator nodded.

"Wait. You said Shaq didn't recognize the man *at the time*. Does that mean he now knows who the man was?"

"Correct."

"Who was it?"

"Aleksei Smirnov."

Guin stared at the private investigator.

"Shaq saw Aleksei Smirnov, as in Margaux's partner, outside the studio building with Ronnie the night Margaux was murdered?"

"*Thought* he saw them. He wasn't sure."

"What made him think it was Smirnov?"

"Mr. Smirnov invited Mr. Onyema and Mr. Abara to a party he was DJing at the weekend after the shoot. Mr. Onyema thought he looked familiar and realized why."

"Because he had seen him with Ronnie outside the Studios at Hudson Yards." Leong nodded. "But you said he wasn't sure it was them."

Guin's mental wheels were turning.

"But Smirnov was supposedly DJing at some private party over at Chelsea Piers. You said you verified his alibi. So how could he have been outside the Studios at Hudson Yards? What time did Shaq think he saw them?"

"Between nine-thirty and ten."

"Had the party Smirnov was DJing at ended? Seems a bit early, even though it was a Tuesday."

"It had not."

"I'm confused. If the party hadn't ended, how could Smirnov have been outside the Studios at Hudson Yards between nine-thirty and ten?"

"The information I received was not completely accurate."

"What do you mean?"

"There was another DJ."

"Another DJ? So Smirnov could have left the boat while this other DJ played."

The investigator nodded.

"Do you know who this other DJ was?"

"Anatoly Petrov, the son of Mikhail Petrov, the man who owned the yacht. It was the younger Petrov's birthday. And as Anatoly is apparently an aspiring DJ, Mr. Smirnov kindly offered to let him play DJ for a while."

"And do you know when that was?"

"Between approximately eight-thirty and ten."

"Huh. So Smirnov could have been at the studio building between nine-thirty and ten. But why did he go there?

Unless…" Guin turned and looked at the private investigator. "Do you think he killed Margaux?"

"What motive did he have?"

"Well, there was Margaux's will for one. She was going to leave everything to him. Well, almost everything."

"But we don't know if that will is valid. And he claimed to not know about it."

"He could have been lying. But, okay, let's say he didn't know about the will. Maybe he'd had enough of Margaux's antics. Maybe Ronnie had told him how out of control Margaux was at the shoot and he decided to go have a chat with her.

"He gets Anatoly to take over DJ duties and goes to the studio. He confronts Margaux, and the two of them get into it. Next thing you know, he hits her over the head with a mocktail bottle, and boom! She falls down. Smirnov realizes he's killed her, panics, and flees."

"An interesting theory. There are just a few problems with it."

"Like what?"

"We have no proof Smirnov was there."

"But Shaq says he saw him."

"He said he thought he saw him. He wasn't sure."

Guin frowned.

"What about the security camera in front of the building?"

"It was knocked offline by the power outage."

"Right." She had forgotten. "What about other security cameras? Surely one of the neighboring buildings had one."

"I'm checking."

"Good."

"But there's another problem."

"What?"

"The bottle found next to Ms. Boucher's body contained your husband's fingerprints."

"But we don't know for sure if that was the bottle that killed Margaux!"

"The DA will say it was."

"There must be some way to prove Smirnov was there and could have killed her. I'll speak with him. Maybe I can get him to confess."

"I don't think that's a good idea."

"Why not? You saw how I handled the interview with Jordan and Shaq."

"This is different."

"How?"

"If, as you believe, Mr. Smirnov is a killer, what's to stop him from killing you?"

"You really think he'd kill me?"

"I think it would be better if I spoke with him."

"Could I at least come with you?"

"I don't think that's a good idea."

"Would you at least ask him about Margaux's shares, what happens to them?" Then something else occurred to Guin. "Did Mockingbird have a key person policy?"

"A key person policy?"

"It's an insurance policy companies get in case something happens to a key employee, like the president or CEO."

"I don't know."

"You should find out." Or she would. "And speaking of insurance, do we know if Margaux had a life insurance policy?"

"We're looking into it."

Guin saw that the private investigator's smartwatch was flashing. He looked down at it.

"I need to go," he said.

"Okay. But will you let me know what you find out?"

"Ms. Williams will let your husband know what we uncover." Then he got up and left.

Guin watched him go. Then she looked down at her

sandwich. She had barely touched it. She would take it home with her and have it later or tomorrow. She wrapped it up and tucked it into her bag.

Guin had planned on going home. But she turned around at Fifth Avenue and headed west instead. A half an hour later, she arrived at the building that housed Mockingbird Beverages. She paused before entering, wondering if she should have called or texted Ronnie. Well, too late now.

She entered the building and took the elevator up to the twelfth floor. Would Ronnie be there?

She peered through the glass door and saw a woman talking on her phone. From the back, she looked like Ronnie. Guin tried the door, but it was locked. She knocked, and the woman turned around. It wasn't Ronnie. But she looked to be Indian and was around the same age. Guin smiled and waved. The woman put down her phone and came over.

"Yes?" she said through the glass door.

"I'm looking for Ronnie," said Guin. "Is she in?"

"She's not here right now," said the woman.

"Do you know when she'll be back?"

"I don't."

"Could I leave her a note?"

"A note?"

"Is there a reason the door's locked?" Guin asked her.

"Ronnie said to lock it when she wasn't here."

"Do you work here?" Guin hadn't seen the woman before. Maybe she was new.

The woman nodded.

"Well, when you see Ronnie, could you let her know that Guin Jones stopped by and that I'd like to speak with her? Tell her it's important."

"You should send her a text or email her."

"I'll do that," said Guin. "But if you could just tell her I…"

Guin heard a phone ringing, as did the woman.

"I need to go," said the woman.

"Would you let me know if it's Ronnie?"

But the woman was already halfway across the office, and Guin doubted she'd be coming back.

CHAPTER 35

The cats were waiting by the front door when Guin got home and immediately began to meow. Guin leaned down and petted them, and they began to purr. She straightened up and headed to the kitchen to get a glass of water. The cats followed her, jumping onto the counter and meowing again.

Guin took out the container of cat treats and placed a few in front of each cat. As they chomped on the cat treats, Guin checked her phone. She had texted Ronnie on her way home, saying it was important that they talk. But Ronnie hadn't gotten back to her.

Guin was reading an email from her editor when Glen came in.

"How did your meeting with Adam go?" he asked her.

"Okay, I guess."

"Did he meet with Alex Morgan?"

"He did. Morgan has an alibi for the night of the murder."

"You didn't really think he killed Margaux, did you?"

"He had more of a reason to kill her than you did. She blamed him for their business failing and sued him. And then she refused to give him a piece of her new business. But I don't think he killed her."

"Did Adam have anything else to report?"

"Yes. It seems that Smirnov was at the studio that evening."

"He was? I don't recall seeing him."

"He was spotted outside the building after you left."

"I thought Smirnov was DJing at some private party and couldn't get away. Had the party ended early?"

"No, but he took a break between eight-thirty and ten."

"And he went to the studio?"

"He went to the studio building. We don't know for certain if he actually went inside."

"How does Adam know that Smirnov was at the studio building? I guess he found someone who spotted him there."

"He did: Shaq Onyema. Shaq told Adam he saw Smirnov there with Ronnie. Though he wasn't a hundred percent sure it was them. Still, it's suspicious."

"And you said this was after I left? What were they all doing there? Shaq and Ronnie left before I did."

"Shaq and Jordan had gone to check out the party up on the roof. As for Smirnov and Ronnie, Ronnie probably told Smirnov about Margaux, and he decided to go to the studio to have a chat with Margaux, but he couldn't get away until around eight-thirty."

"But how did he know Margaux would still be there?"

"I'm guessing he was the one who called her as you were leaving. And that he was the person who had called her earlier and pissed her off. Shaq said he overheard Margaux speaking to someone named Alex during the shoot. Maybe it was Aleksei. Aleks could be a nickname."

"Huh. But you said that Adam doesn't know if Smirnov or Ronnie actually went into the studio building."

"Correct. But he's working on that."

"So we don't know if one of them killed her. Though I can't imagine Ronnie hitting Margaux over the head with a mocktail bottle—or framing me. I know Margaux wasn't very nice to her, but Ronnie knew how to handle her. And I thought the two of us got along."

"Maybe Ronnie snapped. Or it could have been Smirnov who killed Margaux and framed you."

"There's another problem."

"What?"

"How did they get into the building? The door was locked."

"Actually, it wasn't. According to Adam, someone had propped open the door to the building. And anyway, people were coming and going because of the music video shoot. They could have easily slipped in undetected."

"Fine. Let's say that they were able to get into the building. How did they get into the studio? The door to Studio Three was locked, according to the night watchman and the cleaner."

"We don't know for sure that it was locked between the time you left and when the night watchman checked it. In any case, Ronnie knew the codes to both the front door and the studio, which were good until midnight. She could have locked the door after she or they left."

"I don't know, Guin. I still can't see them killing her."

"Okay, maybe not Ronnie, but I could totally see Smirnov. Imagine this: He hears that Margaux's out of control and tries to talk to her. But she doesn't want to listen. So he decides to go over there. However, he can't get away until around eight-thirty.

"He calls Margaux to make sure she's still there and immediately heads over from his gig, which isn't that far away. Maybe he calls Ronnie to let her know he's heading over to the studio to have a talk with Margaux.

"He gets to the studio, and Margaux is furious. They argue, and Margaux attacks him, just like she attacked you. Smirnov tries to stop her, but she's out of her mind. Maybe she tries to strangle him. Who knows? Smirnov, desperate, glances around and sees a mocktail bottle on the table. He grabs it and hits Margaux with it.

"Margaux collapses. He goes over to her and realizes she's dead. He panics, grabs the bottle, and flees the scene."

"What about the bottle with my fingerprints on it?"

"Either he put it there as a red herring or maybe it fell off the table."

"Has anyone ever told you that you have a vivid imagination?"

"Several people. But it doesn't mean it couldn't have happened like that."

"I don't know, Guin. It seems pretty out there."

"You have a better theory?"

"No but…"

"Also, Smirnov had the most to gain from Margaux's death. That is if no one could prove that he killed her."

"We don't know if the new will is valid."

"Even if it isn't, it's likely Margaux's share of the business would go to him upon her death. I asked Adam to look into it and see if Mockingbird had a key person policy for Margaux. Though I could ask Ronnie or Smirnov. I'm sure they would know."

"I don't think you speaking with Smirnov is such a good idea."

"Why not?"

"Why not? He could be a killer!"

"You sound just like Adam. And you just said you didn't think Smirnov killed her."

Glen frowned.

"If it makes you that unhappy, I'll ask Ronnie about the key person policy."

"I'd rather you leave any questioning that needs to be done to Adam."

Now it was Guin's turn to frown.

"What if he's too busy?"

"I'm sure he'll find the time."

"It's not like I'm going to accuse Ronnie or Smirnov of murder. I just want to ask them about Margaux's shares and if the business had a key person policy."

"Please, let Adam and Imani handle things. You've done enough."

"I can't just stand by and let you go to jail!"

"You were the one who said I should hire Imani. Have a little faith."

"And have a little faith in me. I promise, I won't do anything stupid. I just want to ask them a few questions."

Glen sighed. He loved his wife and saw how much this meant to her.

"Fine. I don't like the idea of you meeting with either of them, but I suppose I can't stop you."

"I promise to be careful."

"You better be. I'd be devastated if anything happened to you."

"And I'd be devastated if anything happened to you. That's why this case means so much to me."

Glen looked down at his watch.

"I have to get on a call. Just promise me you'll wait twenty-four hours before doing anything."

"Why twenty-four hours?"

"Maybe Adam or Imani will turn up something. You said Adam was going to look into the business."

"I doubt he'll be that quick. He seems so busy."

Glen gave Guin a look.

"Fine, I'll wait twenty-four hours."

"Thank you."

Guin was in her office the next morning, doing research for a new assignment, when she received a text from Adam Leong, letting her know he had news.

Guin was surprised to hear from him and immediately called him. She was even more surprised when he answered.

"What did you find out?" she asked him.

"Mockingbird Beverages did indeed purchase a key person policy for Margaux Boucher."

"Do you know when they purchased it?"

"The same time they registered the business, around a year ago."

"For how much?"

"A million dollars."

"That seems like a lot for a new business. And the company is the beneficiary, yes?" That was usually who the beneficiary was.

"Correct."

"And at this point, the company belongs to Aleksei Smirnov. So he can do pretty much whatever he wants with the money."

The private investigator didn't say anything.

"Do you know if Margaux also had a regular life insurance policy?"

"We're not aware of one."

"Could a million dollars be considered a motive for murder?" Guin thought so.

"Mr. Smirnov doesn't appear to be in need of money."

"But appearances can be deceiving. And a million dollars is a lot of money. What about Margaux's shares in the business? Do they go to Smirnov?"

"Based on the partnership agreement we found, it would seem so."

"Yet another reason to do away with Margaux. Now he can run the business however he likes."

"Though he said that he had no desire to run the mocktail business."

"You spoke with him?"

"I did."

"And he told you he had no interest in running Mockingbird Beverages?"

"He said that's why they hired Ronnie. That nothing had changed."

"So he's fine with Ronnie running things all by herself?"

"For now. He said they planned on hiring more people as soon as the insurance money came through."

"Hm." Guin wanted to have a chat with Mr. Smirnov and Ronnie. But she didn't tell Adam Leong that. "Anything else? Any luck getting security footage from the nearby buildings?"

"Still working on that."

"Okay. Thanks for letting me know about the key person policy. I appreciate it."

"You're welcome."

Guin sat back in her chair. She was pleased that Adam had shared information with her. But she still wanted to speak to Ronnie and Smirnov. She had told Glen that she just wanted to ask them about Margaux's shares, what happened to them, and the key person policy. But what she really wanted to know was what Ronnie and Smirnov had been doing at the studio building the night of the photo shoot, after everyone had supposedly left.

CHAPTER 36

Guin hadn't heard from Ronnie by late that afternoon. Was Ronnie ghosting her? Or was she just insanely busy? Guin sent her another text, asking for an appointment.

While she waited for Ronnie to get back to her, Guin checked out Ronnie's Instagram feed. Hm. She hadn't posted anything in a while. Was she too busy to post or had something happened to her?

Guin scrolled back through Ronnie's Instagram, not sure what she was looking for. Then she saw a photo of Ronnie with the Indian woman she had seen at Mockingbird. Ah. The woman was Ronnie's sister. Guin wondered if Ronnie had hired her. Or maybe she was just helping Ronnie out until the insurance money came through. Guin would ask her. That is if Ronnie ever got back to her.

Guin checked her texting app again. Still nothing from Ronnie. *Should I call her?* Guin entered Ronnie's number, but the call immediately went to voicemail. Now Guin was getting worried. Could something have happened to the young woman?

Over dinner that evening, Guin was going to say something to Glen about Ronnie, but she thought better of it. Glen would just say that Ronnie was probably busy.

The next morning, Guin checked her text messages again. Still nothing from Ronnie. She called Ronnie's cell phone. Again, the call went straight to voicemail. Guin looked to see if there was a number for Mockingbird Beverages, but she couldn't find one.

Although she had work, Guin didn't have any interviews to do that morning. So she decided to pay a visit to Mockingbird Beverages and make sure Ronnie was all right. She stopped outside Glen's office and peeked in. He was on a video call with Raj. Just as well. He probably wouldn't be happy with her going to see Ronnie.

As Guin rode the subway downtown, she wondered if she was overreacting. Probably. But she needed to see for herself that Ronnie was okay. She checked her phone before heading up to Mockingbird Beverages. It was a little before ten. And still no reply from Ronnie.

She got out on the twelfth floor and nervously approached the door marked Mockingbird Beverages. She breathed a sigh of relief upon seeing Ronnie pacing the floor with her phone to her ear. She looked annoyed.

Guin tried the door, but it was locked. She knocked to get Ronnie's attention. Ronnie turned, and Guin smiled and waved. Ronnie frowned and turned back to her caller.

Guin knocked again, louder this time.

"I need to talk to you," she shouted.

"Call and schedule an appointment," Ronnie yelled back. "I'm busy."

Ronnie turned her back on Guin, but Guin wasn't giving up.

"I've been trying to schedule an appointment!" she shouted through the door. "But you haven't been returning my calls or texts!"

Ronnie scowled at Guin.

"Please," said Guin. "I just need a few minutes."

"What is so important that you had to come here and harass me?"

"I'll tell you if you let me in."

Ronnie sighed and went to unlock the door.

"Thank you," said Guin, stepping inside. "So what's with the door being locked?"

"There have been some thefts in the building recently, and management advised everyone to lock their doors."

Guin noticed a large poster board with *Mockingbird Mocktails* printed on it, along with a new logo.

"I like the new logo," she said.

Ronnie looked over at the poster board.

"Thanks. I helped design it. So, what is so urgent?"

"Why did you return to the studio the night of the photo shoot?"

"I didn't return to the studio. I went home after the shoot."

"There's an eyewitness who saw you outside the studio building over an hour after you supposedly left."

Guin saw Ronnie thinking.

"Right. I forgot. I did go home. But when I got there, I realized I didn't have my phone, that I must have left it at the studio. So I went back to get it."

"You thought you left it at the studio, not in an Uber or a Lyft?" Guin assumed Ronnie would have taken a car service home. Though she knew it wasn't good to assume.

"I checked with the Lyft driver first, but he said it wasn't there."

Guin didn't believe her.

"Did you tell the police that you had left your phone at the studio and went back to retrieve it?"

"I didn't think it was important."

"You didn't think it was important? What time did you return to the studio?"

"I don't remember exactly."

"And was Margaux surprised to see you?"

"She was."

Guin grinned, and Ronnie immediately realized her mistake.

"So Margaux was alive when you returned to the studio."

It was a statement, not a question.

Ronnie didn't say anything.

"Which means Glen couldn't have killed her."

"Maybe he came back after I left. I thought I saw a camera there. Maybe he went back to the studio later to get it."

However, Guin knew for a fact that Glen hadn't left a camera there or returned to the studio.

"Was Aleksei Smirnov with you?"

"Aleksei? Why would he be at the studio? He was DJing at a private event."

Guin had to hand it to Ronnie, she was a pretty good actress.

"An eyewitness saw him there with you."

"He must be mistaken."

"I don't think so. There's security footage to prove it." Guin didn't know that, but she wanted to see Ronnie's reaction.

"So what if he was there? He was concerned about Margaux. We both were."

"Is that why you were meeting with him outside the studio building? Had you told him about Margaux's behavior during the shoot?"

"I was supposed to be his eyes and ears and keep Margaux in line. He was worried about her—and the shoot. Margaux had been experiencing some pretty serious mood swings and acting erratically."

"Yet Mr. Smirnov, her partner, was too busy to attend the photo shoot."

"He wanted to be there. But he'd booked that party months ago. He couldn't cancel. Besides, I told him I could handle her."

"But you weren't able to. In fact, things got so bad that two people walked off the shoot."

"I got them to come back."

"Did Smirnov call Margaux? She was overheard speaking to someone named Alex."

"It was probably Aleksei. She often called him Aleks when she was annoyed with him."

"So she was annoyed with him."

"She felt he was checking up on her, that he didn't trust her."

"Was he checking up on her?"

"What is your point, Ms. Jones?"

"My point is, Aleksei Smirnov had a lot to gain from Margaux's death."

"Excuse me? I don't like what you're implying."

"Did you know that he had taken out a million-dollar key person policy on Margaux?"

"I knew the business had a key person policy. It's standard practice. Though I didn't know how much it was for."

"And did you know Aleksei Smirnov was the primary beneficiary in Margaux's will?" Though Guin still didn't know if the new will was valid.

"You seriously think Aleksei killed Margaux for her money?" She laughed. "Aleksei has plenty of money. He doesn't need Margaux's. Now, I think you should go."

"Did he put you in charge of the business to keep you quiet?"

"He put me in charge of the business because I'm the most qualified person to run it. Now, I asked you to leave. Will you go or do I have to call security?"

"I'm going," said Guin.

As soon as she exited the building, Guin phoned Adam Leong, praying he'd answer.

"Leong."

"Adam, it's Guin. I just met with Ronnie Banerjee. She admitted that she went back to the studio later that evening and let slip that Margaux was alive when she got there."

Guin waited for him to say something.

"Did you hear what I just said? We have proof that Glen didn't kill Margaux!"

"Is Ms. Banerjee willing to swear in a court of law that Ms. Boucher was alive after your husband left? And if she knew Ms. Boucher was alive then, why didn't she tell the police?"

Guin frowned. He had a point. Still, she wasn't willing to give up.

"I think she's protecting Smirnov. When I asked her about him, she threatened to call security if I didn't leave."

The private investigator didn't say anything.

"Hello? Are you still there?"

"I am."

"No comment about Smirnov? He has to be the killer!"

"We don't know that."

Guin was ready to scream, but she forced herself to take a deep breath.

"Were you able to obtain security footage from any of the nearby buildings?"

"I was. I should be receiving it later today."

"Great! Hopefully, it will show Ronnie and Smirnov entering and/or leaving the studio building at the time of the murder."

"I wouldn't get your hopes up."

Guin frowned. Why did he have to be such a Debbie Downer?

"What about Ronnie's phone? She said she left it in the studio. Though I'm sure she's lying and had it with her. Still, either way, it would show if she was there."

"Unless she left it at home."

Guin was growing frustrated.

"Shouldn't someone at least check it?"

"That would require a search warrant."

"Even to just access her location data? You can't check with her wireless network provider?"

"It still requires a warrant."

"So how do we prove Margaux was alive after Glen left?"

"Let me take a look at the security footage, see if Ms. Banerjee and Mr. Smirnov were even there."

"We know that they were there! Shaq saw them!"

Guin heard beeping on the line.

"I have to go," said Leong.

Guin was about to say something, but the private investigator had already ended the call.

Guin was working on an article when she heard Glen knocking on her door.

"Yes?" she called.

"May I come in?"

"Go ahead."

"Where were you this morning?"

"Why do you ask?"

"I came to see you, and you were gone. And I don't remember you saying you had an interview."

Guin thought about lying to Glen, but they had made a promise not to lie to each other.

"I went to see Ronnie Banerjee."

"I thought we agreed that you were going to leave any questioning to Adam."

"We agreed that I would wait twenty-four hours before doing anything, which I did."

"And you had to go see Ronnie? You couldn't just talk to her over the phone?"

"I tried calling her—and texting her. But my calls

went straight to voicemail. And she wasn't getting back to me."

"Maybe she was busy."

"Or maybe something happened to her."

"So you went to Chelsea."

"I did."

"And did you speak with her?"

"I did, briefly."

"And?"

"She admitted to going back to the studio."

"She did?"

"After I convinced her that someone had seen her there."

"Did she say what she was doing there?"

"She claimed she had left her phone there."

"I don't recall seeing a phone, but I guess I could have missed it."

"She probably lied about the phone. The important thing is that Margaux was alive when she went back there."

"She was? Ronnie spoke with her?"

"She did. Or she intimated as much."

"What do you mean?"

"I asked Ronnie if Margaux was surprised to see her, and Ronnie said that she was. Then she realized what she had said and clammed up."

"Why didn't Ronnie tell the police?"

"That's a good question. I think she's covering for Smirnov."

"You really believe Smirnov killed Margaux?"

"He had a motive. And if we can prove he was there… Adam's supposed to receive security footage from some nearby buildings today. Hopefully, it will show Smirnov and Ronnie entering and/or leaving the studio building."

"Even if it shows them entering and leaving, we don't know that Smirnov killed Margaux."

"True, but it could be enough to make a jury think twice about convicting you."

It was nearly five o'clock, and Guin hadn't heard from Adam. Had he received the security footage? Guin wanted to ask him. But surely he would have let her know if he had found something. Guin couldn't help herself and texted him, asking if he had received the footage.

He wrote her back half an hour later, saying that he had.

"And?!" wrote Guin. "Did it show Ronnie and Smirnov at the studio building?"

"I sent the footage to a colleague," he replied.

"Why?"

"The quality wasn't very good. So I'm having a colleague see if she can make it more legible."

"Do you know when you'll get it back?"

"I do not. But I told her it was important."

"Okay. Just let me know when you get the edited footage. Better yet, have her copy me."

The private investigator didn't reply. However, the next evening, Guin received an email from Adam with a link to the edited security footage. There was no note, just the link. And Guin feared that meant that there was nothing to see.

She clicked on the link and began to watch. She saw Glen leaving the studio building at 8:48. But there was no sign of Ronnie or Smirnov. Guin waited a few minutes and then hit fast-forward. She stopped it at nine and started watching again. There! She paused the video. The man and the woman in front of the building sure looked like Smirnov and Ronnie, but Guin couldn't be a hundred percent sure.

She pressed play and watched the couple enter the building. Then she waited to see when they came out. It was around nine-thirty. They appeared to be arguing. She watched as the man, who Guin was pretty sure was Smirnov, grabbed the woman's bag and went over to a trash can. The woman—Ronnie?—followed him.

Guin wished there was audio to go with the video as she could swear the two people were arguing.

And what was Smirnov removing from the bag and shoving into that trash can? Was it a bottle? It was hard to tell.

She continued to watch. A couple of minutes later, she saw Shaq and Jordan leaving the studio building. They stopped to watch the couple who Guin believed to be Smirnov and Ronnie. Then Jordan pulled Shaq away.

A few seconds later, Ronnie headed east while Smirnov headed west. Guin watched for a few more minutes. Then the screen faded to black.

She stared at her screen. Had that been a mocktail bottle in Ronnie's bag that Smirnov threw into the trash can?

Guin watched the footage again. She was convinced that the two people entering and leaving the studio building were Ronnie and Smirnov and that Smirnov had shoved a bottle into the trash can right after they left.

Had the police searched the trash cans? Guin doubted it. Why would they? They thought they had the murder weapon. And while the footage didn't show Ronnie and Smirnov going to Studio 3 or killing Margaux, Guin felt that Imani Williams could use it to create a reasonable doubt in the minds of the jury that Glen was the only one who could have killed Margaux.

CHAPTER 37

Guin texted Adam after she had viewed the security footage, asking him to call her, but he hadn't as yet. She texted him again the next morning. A half-hour later, she saw his number flash up on her phone. She immediately swiped to answer.

"Finally! Did you view the footage?"

"I did."

"So you saw Ronnie and Smirnov entering the building around nine—and then leaving around nine-thirty."

"We don't know for sure it was them."

"It sure looked like them to me."

"Did you see their faces?"

"No, but… It had to be them. And did you see Smirnov grab Ronnie's bag and remove what looked like a Château Margaux mocktail bottle—and then stuff it into a trash can?"

"We don't know for sure that the man and the woman were Aleksei Smirnov and Ronnie Banerjee or that it was a Château Margaux mocktail bottle."

"Seriously? You think it was just some random bottle?"

"You could tell it was a Château Margaux mocktail bottle? If so, you must have extraordinary vision."

Guin made a face.

"You're impossible."

"I'm only telling you what the DA will say if Imani presents the footage as evidence."

"*If* she presents it?"

"It's up to her to decide if it's in her client's best interest."

"But it shows Ronnie and Smirnov going into the building after Glen left!"

"We don't know if they went to the studio—or that it was them."

"Let's assume it was them. Where else could they have gone?"

"Maybe they went up to the roof. Mr. Smirnov is a DJ. Maybe he wanted to hear the band."

Unbelievable, thought Guin.

"You seriously believe that?"

"Again, I'm only telling you what the district attorney might say."

"What about Ronnie's phone? Did you tell Imani about that?"

"I did."

"And is she going to ask a judge for a search warrant?"

"On what grounds?"

"On the grounds that it could prove Ronnie was involved in Margaux's death!"

"I doubt a judge would agree to it."

Guin was feeling increasingly frustrated.

"Would you at least talk to Smirnov again, see if you can get him to confess to seeing Margaux that evening?"

"I'll speak to him. However, I have to go out of town for a few days."

"You chasing another suspect?"

"No. It's a personal matter."

Guin wondered what was up. She wanted to ask him if he was okay, but he'd probably say everything was fine. So she didn't. Instead, she asked him to let her know what Smirnov said.

Guin was antsy the rest of the day. She had promised Glen and Adam that she wouldn't confront Smirnov, but she didn't want to wait several days, or longer, to confirm that he had gone to the studio and seen Margaux. She needed to know now. (As Guin's mother used to say about Guin, patience was not one of her virtues.)

Guin reached into her desk drawer, where she kept business cards, and found the one Smirnov had given her. It had his private number on it. She thought about texting him but decided to call instead.

He picked up after three rings.

"Smirnov."

"Mr. Smirnov, this is Guin Jones, the reporter with the *New York Times*."

"Ah yes, Ms. Jones. How can I help you?"

"I was just assigned a piece on the hottest DJs in New York, and I immediately thought of you."

"I'm flattered. How can I help you?"

"I'd love to get a tour of your studio and learn more about how you work."

"I'd be happy to give you a tour and talk to you. When were you thinking?"

"Are you available this weekend?"

"I'm booked solid this weekend. But I could meet with you Monday morning. Say ten o'clock?"

"Monday at ten works. Where's your studio again?"

"I'll text you the address."

Guin felt slightly guilty as she rode the subway downtown Monday morning. She hadn't told Glen where she was going. Nor had she told Adam that she had arranged to meet Smirnov. No doubt, both of them would have tried to stop her if they knew. Though Adam was still away.

Guin told herself she wouldn't do anything stupid, like accusing Smirnov of killing Margaux. She just wanted him to confess to being at the studio that evening.

She arrived at Smirnov's building a few minutes after ten and pressed the buzzer to be let in. Then she took the elevator to the top floor. She rang the video doorbell, and a minute later Smirnov opened the door. He looked relaxed, wearing a T-shirt and jeans. And Guin noticed he was barefoot.

"Do you want me to take off my shoes?" Guin asked him, seeing a rack of shoes by the front door.

"If you don't mind."

Guin stepped inside and removed her shoes.

"Could I get you something to drink?"

"I'm good," said Guin. Though her mouth felt suddenly dry. Maybe being alone with Smirnov wasn't such a good idea. But too late now.

Guin glanced around. Was this where Smirnov lived? The place looked more like an apartment than a music studio.

"Do you live here?" she asked him.

"I do."

"Where's your studio?"

"I'll show you."

Guin followed him down a hall.

"Voila!" he said, opening a door.

Guin peered inside. The room had acoustic tiles everywhere and contained a large mixing board with two turntables, a microphone, speakers, and a computer with a large monitor. There was also a keyboard, a guitar, and a bass.

"Wow," said Guin. "Do you record music in here as well as DJ?"

"I've been experimenting with combining live tracks with prerecorded music. Shall I play you a sample?"

"Uh, sure."

Smirnov put on some trance music and then picked up the bass and began to play. Guin politely listened, though the music was giving her a headache. Finally, he stopped.

"What do you think? Pretty dope, right?"

"Absolutely," said Guin. "Shall we go someplace quiet and talk?"

Smirnov put down the bass and switched off the equipment. Then he led Guin back down the hall to the living area.

"Are you sure I can't get you something? Maybe an herbal tea or some kombucha or an energy drink?"

"Could I get a glass of water?"

"Sparkling or still?"

"Still is fine. Thank you."

He returned a minute later with two bottles of water, handing one to Guin. Then he took a seat in an oversized armchair.

"So, what can I tell you?"

Guin asked him if it was okay to record their conversation. He gave his permission, and she started by asking him about his background, how he got into DJing.

"And that's when I decided to do it full-time," he said in conclusion several minutes later.

"And do you DJ mostly at clubs or private events these days?"

"It's split pretty evenly. Private events tend to pay better, but I get more exposure from playing at clubs."

"And these private events, are we talking bar mitzvahs? Weddings? Corporate events? Parties for Russian oligarchs and their children on their mega yachts?"

Smirnov smiled.

"All of the above."

"Speaking of parties on mega yachts, I understand you DJed at Anatoly Petrov's recent birthday party."

"How do you know about that?"

"It was on his Instagram feed."

"Right."

"It looked like you were showing Anatoly the ropes, even letting him be DJ for a while. Very generous of you."

Guin had found Anatoly's Instagram feed over the weekend, where he had shared over a dozen photos and videos from his birthday party.

Smirnov smiled.

"Anatoly wants to be a DJ. I didn't see the harm in letting him take over for a while."

"So what did you do while he played DJ? Did you go for a walk?"

"I don't remember."

"You don't remember meeting up with Ronnie Banerjee over at the Studios at Hudson Yards?"

Smirnov frowned.

"I'd like to show you a video."

Guin had made a clip of Ronnie and Smirnov entering the building and another of them leaving. She played the first clip for Smirnov, holding up her phone so he could see.

"Why are you showing me this?" he asked.

"That's you, isn't it?"

Guin replayed the video.

"I admit, it looks a bit like me but…"

"And that's Ronnie Banerjee with you." Guin opened the next clip and turned her phone around. "And here are the two of you leaving the studio building."

"Why are you showing me these videos?"

"An eyewitness said he saw you outside the Studios at Hudson Yards the evening of Anatoly Petrov's birthday party."

"And he's sure it's me?"

Guin nodded.

"So I was just wondering what you were doing there."

Smirnov let out a dramatic sigh.

"Fine. You caught me." *Was he about to confess?* "Ronnie

was concerned about Margaux, as was I. Margaux had been behaving erratically at the photo shoot, screaming at everyone. She even attacked the photographer. Ronnie begged me to come to the shoot and talk to Margaux. But I couldn't get away."

"Yet you did go over there."

"Yes, but by then it was too late."

"What do you mean, too late? You mean she was dead when you got there?"

"She must have been. She didn't answer when we knocked on the door to the studio."

"How did you even know she was still at the studio?"

"I phoned her when I was leaving the pier."

"And she answered and told you she was still at the studio?"

"She did. And told me to go to hell," he added with a smile.

"What time was that?"

"I don't remember."

"You could always check your phone."

"I'm sure I deleted the call log."

"Do you regularly delete your call log?"

"Why do you care?"

"Just humor me and check your phone."

He sighed dramatically again.

"If it will make you happy."

He retrieved his phone and started scrolling.

"Did you find it?"

"Give me a minute."

Guin waited, but she was impatient.

"Here it is."

"What time did you call her?"

"At eight-forty-four. Are you happy now?"

"And how long did the two of you talk?"

"Seriously? How does any of this relate to your article?"

"Just tell me how long the call lasted. Or do you have something to hide?"

"Of course not." He looked down at his phone. "We spoke for seven minutes and thirty-six seconds. Now can we get back to my career? I'm sure your readers would be interested to know who I DJed for this weekend."

He mentioned some B-list celebrity, but Guin wasn't really listening. That was because she now had proof that Glen hadn't killed Margaux. Smirnov had been chatting with her after Glen had left the building.

"Wow!" said Guin when Smirnov had finished. "That's very impressive. As is your whole career. I'm sure my readers will be fascinated."

Smirnov grinned.

"Well, that does it for me," she said. "Unless there's something you wanted to add?"

"I could go on for hours," he began, and Guin started to feel nervous. "But I understand I'm not the only DJ you'll be featuring. Who else will you be including?"

Guin had been prepared for that and rattled off the names of a couple of other DJs she had found. Then she said she needed to go.

As soon as she got outside, Guin took a deep breath and exhaled. She couldn't believe she had done it. She immediately phoned Adam, but the call went straight to voicemail. Of course. She left him a message, saying to call her. Then she headed home.

As soon as she got home, she went to Glen's office. She knocked and then entered, not caring if he was on a call. Fortunately, he wasn't.

"Is everything okay?" he said. "You look like you're about to burst."

"That's because I just proved you didn't kill Margaux!"

CHAPTER 38

Glen wasn't happy about Guin going to see Smirnov.

"But if I hadn't gone to see him, we wouldn't have proof that you didn't kill Margaux!" she said.

"You should have let Adam speak with him."

Guin huffed.

"Well, I didn't. Now, shall we call Imani and tell her the good news?"

"You call her. It's your scoop."

Was Glen angry with her?

"Fine. I'll call."

Guin took out her phone and entered the attorney's number, but she was told that Ms. Williams was unavailable. So she left a message.

A couple of days later, thanks to Guin's sleuthing, the attorney obtained a search warrant for Aleksei Smirnov's and Ronnie Banerjee's phones—and got the phone records for Margaux'sphone from her carrier. As Guin had hoped, between Smirnov's confession and his and Ronnie's phones, Imani Williams had enough evidence to show that Margaux was alive after Glen had left the studio—and that he wasn't the only one who could have killed her.

Guin had hoped that the charges against Glen would be dismissed before the trial, which was set for the end of January. But that hadn't happened. Still, everyone was feeling confident that Glen would go free.

Guin was surprised to hear that December that the Mockingbird Beverages New Year's Eve party was still on. She hadn't received an invitation, but she hadn't really been expecting one. Besides, she and Glen would be in Florida. They were to fly to Fort Myers Christmas afternoon and would be spending a little over a week there, staying at Guin's house on Sanibel.

Guin and Glen spent Christmas eve with her family. Then they had Christmas dinner with Glen's in Fort Myers. They spent the rest of the time catching up with friends, Guin spending time with her best friend Shelly, as well as with her friend Craig, who covered fishing and crime for the *Sanibel-Captiva Sun-Times*, Guin's former employer, and his wife Betty.

Guin had told Shelly and Craig about Glen's arrest, swearing them to secrecy. But she hadn't told anyone else. And even though it looked as though Glen would be a free man soon, she didn't want to jinx things by discussing the case.

Being back on Sanibel had made Guin wistful. She loved her house and the friends she'd made there—and the beach, where she had gone shelling practically every morning. But she had been enjoying living in New York and working for the *New York Times*. And now it looked like the *Times* might hire her full-time.

Just before Christmas, her editor had told Guin that there should be an opening for a full-time business reporter after the new year. Was Guin interested? She was. But being back on Sanibel made her reconsider. Did she want to live in New York City full-time?

If she remained a stringer for the paper, she'd have some flexibility. And Raj, Glen's boss, had told Glen he didn't care where he worked as long he would remain president of Photog US, which had just opened a second office in Los Angeles and was planning new outposts in Chicago and Miami.

Miami wasn't that far from Sanibel, just a couple of hours. And flying to New York or Chicago was easy to do from there or Fort Myers. Yes, she and Glen had a lot to think about. But for right now, they were enjoying being back on Sanibel and ringing in the new year with old friends.

It was unseasonably cold the day of Glen's trial, and Guin was feeling nervous. They had met with Imani Williams and Adam Leong the day before, to go over everything one last time. So they knew what to expect. Still, it had been a long time since Guin had been in a courtroom. Or one in New York City. Probably not since she had jury duty in her twenties.

And being in court to support your husband, who was being tried for manslaughter—or womanslaughter in this case—was quite different than serving on a jury where the defendant was accused of robbing a jewelry store.

The trial lasted four days, and Guin knew they had chosen the right attorney watching Imani Williams work. It reminded Guin a bit of those Perry Mason movies she used to watch with her grandmother.

The biggest surprise of the trial was Ronnie Banerjee. Imani Williams had relentlessly questioned her about her relationship with Margaux and what she had been doing at the Studios at Hudson Yards between nine and nine-thirty the night of the murder when she had told the police she had gone home.

Why had she lied? the attorney asked her.

It was too much for Ronnie. She broke down, claiming

Margaux's death had been an accident. She told Ms. Williams that she and Aleksei had gone to see Margaux, just to talk to her, but Margaux had gone berserk and accused them of trying to steal the company from her.

Ronnie claimed that Margaux had lunged at her, placing her hands around her neck and strangling her. That was when, she said, Aleksei had grabbed a mocktail bottle and hit Margaux with it, saving her (Ronnie's) life.

Ronnie claimed they never meant to hurt Margaux. That they panicked when they realized Margaux was dead. She said Aleksei grabbed the bottle and Margaux's phone and shoved them into her bag. Then they got the hell out of there.

Guin found Ronnie's testimony convincing. She just hoped that the jury did too. Of course, she wasn't surprised when Smirnov denied being involved. However, there was now more than enough evidence to prove that Glen hadn't killed his ex-wife, and the jury delivered a verdict of not guilty.

Guin never felt so relieved in her life.

"You're crying," said Glen.

"They're tears of joy."

He wiped them away and kissed her.

Guin looked over at Ronnie Banerjee. Would she be arrested? If she was, Guin hoped she'd get off. Or that a judge would go easy on her. However, she didn't feel the same way about Smirnov.*

"Come. Let's get out of here," said Glen.

---

* Many months later, Guin learned that a jury had found Ronnie Banerjee not guilty. However, things didn't go so well for Aleksei Smirnov. Before he was tried for Margaux's murder, he was convicted of tax evasion and sentenced to three years in jail.

They celebrated the verdict that evening with Guin's family. Then, a couple of weeks later, they flew to Florida to celebrate with Glen's parents and their friends there. Guin had surprised herself by turning down the full-time position at the *Times*, remaining a stringer. She liked the freedom of being a freelancer. And Glen made enough money running Photog US, especially after Raj gave him a raise, to support them living in Manhattan. Plus, he had good benefits, including unlimited paid time off (at least in theory).

Guin and Glen had gone to the beach along West Gulf Drive on Sanibel to watch the sunset when Guin received an email from her cousin Toby, who lived in Hawaii, on the Big Island. It was a wedding invitation. Guin followed Toby on Instagram, and they were Facebook friends. But she hadn't seen Toby in years, not since she and Art, her ex-husband, had visited Toby on her farm.

The wedding was on April 1st, a Saturday. Guin turned to her husband.

"How would you like to spend April Fool's Day in Hawaii?"

"Is that a joke?" he asked her.

Guin smiled.

"It isn't. At least I don't think it is. My cousin Toby's getting married. And she's invited us to the wedding."

"Is Toby the one with the coffee farm?"

"That's her."

"Let's go!"

"Are you sure? What about work?"

"I'll bring my computer. But I'll tell Raj I'm on vacation. I can have my new assistant handle things while we're gone."

Glen had recently hired Eric to work full-time for Photog, a smart move, Guin thought.

"What about you?"

"Maybe I can get the *Times* to assign me a story about small coffee producers on the Big Island."

Glen smiled.

"Always thinking of an angle."

"So, shall I tell Toby we'll be there?"

"Go ahead."

Then they watched the sun sink into the Gulf of Mexico.

ACKNOWLEDGMENTS

First, thank you for reading this book. If you enjoyed it, and I hope you did, please consider leaving a review or rating it on Amazon and/or Goodreads.

In addition, a big THANK YOU to my first readers: Nanci Gage, Robin Muth, C. L. Quillen, Kenny Schiff, and Amanda Walter. Your feedback and error spotting have made *A Mocktail for Murder* a better book.

For the great cover, my thanks go to super designer Vesna Tisma. And for making all of my books look as good on the inside as they do on the outside, my thanks to Jason Anderson at Polgarus Studio.

ABOUT THE AUTHOR

Jennifer Lonoff Schiff is the author of the popular Sanibel Island Mystery series and the novels *Tinder Fella*, a rom-com, *Something's Cooking in Chianti*, a mystery set in Italy, and *Finding Gemma Lovegood*, a contemporary romance set in England. Before becoming a full-time author, Jennifer worked as a writer and/or editor for several magazines and book publishers and founded a boutique marketing communications agency that helped companies tell their stories, for which she won several awards. When not plotting how to kill people (fictionally, of course), Jennifer can be found reading, planning her next vacation, taking long walks, or playing with her two cats.

For more information about Jennifer and her books, visit https://www.shovelandpailpress.com.